~~PRACTICE GIRL~~

PRACTICE GIRL

Estelle Laure

VIKING

VIKING
An imprint of Penguin Random House LLC, New York

First published in the United States of America by Viking,
an imprint of Penguin Random House LLC, 2022

Visit us online at penguinrandomhouse.com.

Library of Congress Cataloging-in-Publication Data is available.

Book manufactured in Canada

ISBN 9780593350911 (Hardcover)

1 3 5 7 9 10 8 6 4 2

ISBN 9780593527399 (International Edition)

1 3 5 7 9 10 8 6 4 2

FRI

Design by Opal Roengchai
Text set in Garamond MT Std

To my mother, Dhyana Eagleton, and my daughter, Lilu Marchasin.

Miracles, both.

~~PRACTICE GIRL~~

practice girl *n.* **1** the girl in your school that everybody uses to fulfill sexual needs and nothing else. This girl is not good for a relationship.

—Urban Dictionary

CHAPTER ONE

"Frosted Flakes or Cocoa Puffs?" Ty asks, opening an extremely organized cupboard in his massive kitchen.

"Uh," I say. I'm not hungry, but Ty seems to assume our appetites match. I am used to this type of assumption. It's the price of having a bunch of guy friends.

"We also have some muesli. My mom says it's healthy, but I think it tastes like ass. I don't need pumpkin seeds in my breakfast, you know?"

I giggle. To my horror, it echoes off the quartz countertops.

This is the third afternoon in two weeks I've spent at Tyler's house after school, gradually removing more and more articles of clothing until today, when it was all of them. We had naked actual sex with each other. It was pretty sweet until about thirty-seven seconds after Tyler's completion, which is when he bounced out of the bed, claiming to be starving to death.

Now I'm sitting across the kitchen island from him while he pours us each a bowl of Frosted Flakes (note to self: I never answered him about the kind of cereal I wanted or if I even wanted any at all). He douses them in milk and I repress the desire to lecture him. Coach and I have tried so hard to get the guys on the wrestling team to care about their nutrition, even got a doctor to come in and talk to them after a kid in Denver gave himself a heart attack from dehydration and mass quantities of bodybuilding supplements. He had been using them to gain muscle, but they were not supposed to be taken by people under eighteen, especially with too much caffeine, no water, and no supervision. It doesn't matter what we do though. I've seen Ty weigh a Snickers to see how it would move the needle on the scale. The guys obsess over calories and density but that's about it. That's how much of an impact the doc made, all told.

I try to make myself more comfortable, less self-conscious about everything that just happened between us. I definitely need to keep myself from leaping onto the countertop and yelling, "WE JUST HAD SEX. WHAT DOES IT MEAN, TYLER? ARE WE DATING NOW?"

I take a bite of cereal. It crunches loudly throughout the room and I let the spoon drop to the side of the bowl, too nervous to eat. My thighs are still warm. I can still feel him pressed against my chest.

Ty slides the box of cereal over and considers me. I'm hoping he's thinking about how we just crossed over a new relationship threshold, maybe doing a little obsessing of his own. What I really want is to believe that the tenderness he showed me as we climbed the stairs to his room, as he held my hand, took his time removing my clothes, made appreciative noises at the sight of my nude body, is still there now that we've done it. I cross my arm over my chest and grip my own shoulder even though I'm not naked anymore.

He leans over and pats my free hand. My stomach plummets into my feet. This friendly patting of the hand does not bode well.

"Beckett?" he says, his eyes deep, the color of mountain earth.

"Yeah?"

"Can I ask you something?" I recognize the look he gets when he's trying a new wrestling move—total concentration.

"Of course." I arrange my face into its best approximation of attentive and extremely attractive.

He doesn't meet my eyes. "Was that . . . okay?" he asks.

"Okay?"

"Yeah. I mean, am I okay? Was it . . . satisfying for you? When we . . ." He tilts his head toward mine. "I just want to make sure I didn't suck. That you weren't like, 'I wish he would hurry up and stop touching me like that' or counting down the seconds until you could get away from me or something. I mean . . . when I put my finger on your—"

"No!" I cut him off.

"No? No, that was not good?" He leans forward, spoon in hand. Little droplets of milk hang at its edges. I would not be surprised if he produced a notebook from his pocket and started taking notes.

I put my hand over his to reassure him. "Yeah, Ty. It's good. You're good. Great."

Ty's face relaxes. "Okay, cool," he says. "It's hard to know, you know?" He resumes eating. Vigorously.

I want to tell him that it's actually not hard to know, but I decide there'll be time for that later.

Looking at him now with his pinked-up cheeks and shifty eyes, I'm pretty sure Tyler Martinez is actually into me, and what I had mistaken for ambivalence has been insecurity all along. It can't be easy to be a guy. They've had to put themselves out there and risk rejection for as long as our social norms have been in place.

Now his face transforms from grave concern to his usual confidence. "I mean, I thought you liked it." Ty chews on a huge, happy bite of cereal. "But you could have been faking or something."

"Faking?" I mean, I was faking a little, adding some extra drama.

"I heard girls do that. I don't know! I've only ever been with one other person and it was a couple years ago." He points to my bowl. "You're not eating."

"You're great, really." I take a soggy bite. I hope more reassurance will take us out of the sex-talk zone, which is all full of skin and bodily fluids, and into the other one, where I find out where we actually stand. I know these are conversations that should happen *before*, but it's like I forget or something.

"I'm so glad we're friends," he says after gulping down his sugar milk. "I want you to know that. Sincerely. You're the coolest girl I know."

I'm almost positive all the blood drains out of my face.

Friends?

"But I've been thinking . . ." he says as he goes to the sink and rinses his bowl. "Maybe we should stop this before it gets awkward. It's been amazing, but it feels like the right time, don't you think?"

Wait, *what?*

Less than ten minutes ago we were breathing hard, the closest two people can be to each other. The world wobbles itself upright again as I realize what's happening here.

"Wait. Did you say, 'before it gets awkward'?" Because on the topic of awkwardness, literally everything is already awkward. This couldn't get any more awkward if this entire afternoon went viral in the form of a dubstep remix. That is how awkward everything *already is*.

"I mean, you're one of the team managers and everything." He's still talking, but now has come around the island and is close enough I can smell his milky breath. He lays a hand on my shoulder. "We're together so much of the time, and I don't think Coach would be into it. And we're friends. I mean, our friendship is important to me, and it's, like, if we do this again—"

"No, totally," I say with a high-pitched laugh that makes me want to choke myself. I edge myself off the stool, which makes an ugly squeak as it rakes the floor. "If we keep on doing this . . ." I can't finish the sentence. I can't make any more words come out. He definitely didn't seem to give a crap what Coach thought when we were in his room, or any of the other times we've hooked up. My brain needs a disinfectant shower. So does my body. Did I override all the red flags and unstable feelings I had about all of it? Did I just tell myself lies so I could justify doing what Ty wanted me to do, what I wanted to do? Or what my body wanted, anyway.

"Hey, are you okay?" Tyler seems to have finally noticed I'm not exactly in the same mood I was in two minutes ago.

"Of course I'm okay, Tyler," I snap.

"Okay. I didn't mean—"

"What?"

"Um. Nothing."

Two minutes ago I was completely detached from reality and the flood of truth, and now I'm not and it's making me dizzy. I'm not going to be Tyler's girlfriend. We have just done the most physically intimate thing two human beings can do, and Tyler Martinez is already ensuring he won't ever have to deal with me again. And maybe, maybe if this were the first time this has happened, I wouldn't feel like I'm losing my mind.

But it isn't the first time.

Bowling? Movies? All those fantasies about meeting his parents and going to parties together. *Oh my gosh, Jo. You are a complete idiot.*

I get to his mudroom at just short of a run, before the dam at the edge of my eyelids breaks. I grab my backpack, trying not to remember how I dropped it when he slid his hand under my jacket and kissed me against this very doorway, how he could barely wait because of how much he wanted me. Ty stumbles along behind me with panic splayed over his blessed good looks, his eyes wide and wondering.

"Beck, are you mad?" He sounds flummoxed. "Please don't be. It's for the best, really."

"I understand, okay?" I grab my big red overcoat from his arms and fling open the back door. "Can we please not talk about it ever again? Literally forget this ever happened." I'm talking to myself as much as to him.

Forget this ever happened, Jo. Forget this ever happened.

He nods, squints. The wind is blowing its October Colorado self right into his nice warm house and all over him. For me, it's a welcome relief from my own stinging red cheeks, the curse of white English skin. I can never really hide distress.

I flee into Charly, the old Ford Bronco I inherited from my dad, and as I start it up the Patsy Cline I was listening to on the way here, following behind Ty's BMW, blasts out of the speakers. I slam the stereo knob to silence her wail.

Ty, who is still watching me from the doorway, raises his hand in a wave. It takes all my willpower not to flip him off. I reverse, trying not to screech out of the cul-de-sac.

I don't know how I could have been stupid enough to think Ty would be different. It's not going to be different, because the problem isn't him. It's me. It's always me. Because I want to know what it's like to fall into someone and have them fall back with equal intensity, I fall absolutely everywhere.

When I fantasize, it's not about steamy sex, close breaths, skin on skin—it's about lying side by side in a field of wildflowers, holding hands, and looking at the sky; or petting puppies together; or leaning on a shoulder in a movie theater. I have never understood what I'm supposed to do to get there, but so far everything I've tried has been a serious failure. I'm not the kind of girl guys want to introduce to their parents. I'm the kind of girl they want to introduce to the back seats of their cars.

I pull out onto the highway and attempt to gather myself, let the slate mountains, sherbet sunset, and snow guide me away from Ty, but I'm caught in Josephine Beckett's House of Romantic Horrors.

First there was Joost, a white Dutch exchange student who sent me texts during wrestling practice when I was a sophomore about how it was hard to focus with me around, about how he couldn't take his eyes off my elf ears and cute, small feet.

No one had ever told me I had elf ears or cute feet, especially with an accent.

I was practically planning our wedding. We would run away together, eat Dutch pancakes and broodje kroket, and vacation in Aruba. Everyone would think we were foolish, but we would finish high school and go on to do great things . . . together, always together. Joost and I had sex everywhere: under the stars by the river, in an actual closet at a party, even once below the stage in the orchestra pit at school. It felt like love.

It took me a few weeks to realize he only came near me in the dark, away from everyone else, and that everything he liked about me had to do with my body. It wasn't that he didn't want anyone to know because of me managing the wrestling team, which is what I thought at first. He had never asked me about myself, about who I hoped to be or who I had been up until then. My little sister, Tiffany, had been having all these tantrums, and when I said something about having a toddler in the house, he yawned. *Yawned.*

When I stopped texting him to see if he would notice or text me first, he never asked me about it. Within two weeks he was on to Delilah Vargas. In the daylight. I was so relieved when he graduated and went back to Holland. It was like I had another chance.

But then there was Lucas. Another guy from the team. A lot happens when you're a wrestling manager and you spend twenty-hour weeks with a bunch of sweaty dudes. Also, Lucas, who is half Japanese, has black hair and cheekbones that could cut a diamond. He looks like a character from an epic fantasy novel. I love epic fantasy novels and so I can't be held responsible for my actions.

Mrs. Luke Fender.

Mrs. Josephine Beckett Fender.

He spent weeks asking me out before I said yes, because this time was going to be different. I was going to do it right, and isn't there some rule about how much time you should play hard to get, at what rate kisses should occur, and when those kisses should naturally progress to the next step?

After a few dates, and prompted by various hinting gestures on his part, I gave him a blow job in the movie theater and then told him I had real feelings for him, which in hindsight was not the most brilliant sequence of events.

He spoke earnestly, face cloudy with concern when he said, "I think there may have been a misunderstanding. I'm sorry."

I don't know why they apologize. Like it's going to make anything better. It makes me feel damaged, like I've taken another hit and have to get back up again in spite of the fact that I am already so, so tired.

Because in the midst of all the rest of it, I am also the girl whose father died. The wrestling coach, the school's favorite person, my most beloved guy, the legend who brought everything good and warm and understanding into my life.

Without him, there are no more pizza nights watching bad TV, there's no more throwing on loud music and raging against the machine in the living room, no more random road trips to odd corners of the United States for dinners in hole-in-the-wall restaurants. Without him, I am unseen.

There's that, always that.

Also, I may have cursed myself when I lost my virginity. I don't like to think of such things, but I have to consider the possibility that that may be true.

Because before Joost and before Lucas, there was Sam.

I groan out loud even though it's just Charly and me. I like to keep these thoughts nice and repressed and I hate when one makes it past my inner gate.

Sam and I have been best friends forever. We'd gone to the same school for years, but it wasn't until he joined my dad's Little Wrestlers program in fifth grade that I realized he was as self-conscious and nerdy as me. He was this compact white kid who was more outgoing than me, but also liked watching cartoons. We both obsessed over Marvel, loved graphic novels, and had seen every Star Wars there was (including all of *The Clone Wars*, twice), so we were a perfect match.

Since then, Sam and I have been together every day. One post-season spring afternoon, we were watching *Wolverine* and he laughed at something random and the whole world lit up and I saw him like he was a different person. He was the only one who had been by my side through everything. He was . . . beautiful. Magical. I remember taking him by the hand and leading him to his bedroom, him looking at me so surprised, so *pleased*. I said we should practice with each other so someday when we did it with other people we would be ready.

So that's what we did. He was so careful, he held on to me until I was ready to let go. It was gawky and fumbly, but we got through it and I guess it was sweet in its own cringy way.

A couple of weeks later Jennifer Evans got moved into our English class and Sam opened up like a flower, turned to face her like she was the sun every time she walked by. I didn't really care, thought it was kind of cute.

I can't say I regret losing my virginity to Sam. I can't say I would take it back even if I could. Joost and Lucas—that was my bad, making assumptions that sex meant we would be in relationships. But with Sam it was different. An innocent little pocket. And I get to keep him for life.

But I still think I might have cursed myself. What happened with Sam was a planned, one-time thing, and I've been having unplanned endings ever since.

Any therapist would tell me my search for romance is all about my daddy issues, about having a dad one day and having him gone the next, about hearing a thud and running into the living room to find him facedown on the striped rug he'd bought from Target to decorate the apartment he'd just rented a couple weeks earlier over Bailey's Furniture in the town center. Any therapist would tell me it's perfectly natural to go looking for unconditional love in the arms of boys. I mean, they *have* . . . Therapists have told me that.

But even though I know all those things and accept they may be true, I also know it would be so nice to hold someone's hand, to have someone walk down the hall with me, out where everyone could see it. I want a giant teddy bear and cheap chocolates for Valentine's Day. I want dinners with the family and to plan our weekends together and to get mad when he's tapping his toes and I'm trying to get ready to go out. I know it's basic or whatever but I want . . . *everything,* and I don't think wanting that should equal being pathetic. I always thought that's what high school was supposed to be: romance good enough to make me forget everything else. Turns out high school is mostly about homework and stress.

It takes me ten minutes to get from Ty's gated community, Willow-shade Heights, to my own subdivision in the Liberty Township, Coyote Valley. I'm supposed to go meet Sam for dinner at 66, the restaurant where I work a few nights a week, but I don't think I can face him right now. He would know there was something wrong and he would ask questions. So many questions. So I drive past his house and pull around my cul-de-sac and into my driveway just as I'm actually about to consume myself. I pause to make sure my hair isn't too messed up and that my clothes are all on straight, and mostly that utter misery can't be read in my eyes, then I take a deep breath and go inside.

Kevin Keller's house has been my house for the last five years, ever since he married my mother and then impregnated her in unreasonably rapid succession. I still call it exactly what it is: "Kevin's House." It is essentially a two-story rectangle with an entryway, living room, kitchen, dining room, laundry room, and pantry, and upstairs is my room with its own bathroom and door leading outside to a little balcony, down a long hall from the three of them. It's impeccably clean at all times and always feels empty to me. Home with my dad looked really different, filled with color and personality. Kevin said it was lucky this house came with a room separate from the rest of them, so I could have some privacy. I think he meant well when he said that.

The house is decorated with prints of famous paintings and coffee mug inspo. LIVE LAUGH LOVE. That sort of thing. It's entirely taupe, because Mom says taupe is soothing, neutral in a chaotic world. Sometimes I can't believe she was ever with Dad. Dad made messes and didn't tidy up. He had Iron Maiden and Guns N' Roses posters on his wall, even in his new apartment, and a row of shot glasses on his counter. He played pranks, like when he put plastic wrap on the toilet bowl.

Mom did not think he was hilarious or fun or charming.

She left him a year before he died, when I was twelve. I don't know whether he would still be alive if she hadn't done that. Sometimes I think so.

The timing of Kevin's entrance into our life is something I've never quite been able to figure out, but let's just say by the time Dad died, Mom was remarried and six months pregnant with Tiffany. They'd sold the house and Dad moved into a motel for a while, then his own apartment, a one-bedroom with a pullout couch in the living room for me. Teacher's salary and all that. Kevy Kev was right around the corner. She met him at her favorite Denver restaurant, Berlin, of which he is both the owner and head chef. That used to mean he was there all the time, but lately he's home most nights. By the time Dad died I was forced to inhabit Kevin's House part of the time, but at least if he'd lived I would have been able to spend weekends away, plus all of wrestling season, I'm sure. I'd take a pullout couch over this place any day.

The kitchen hums with the sounds of the mixer, some kind of horrible kid music piping out of Alexa, and my four-year-old half-sister, Tiff, singing along. Tiffany is upside down. She is always upside down, unless she is in the process of *getting* upside down. It's amazing how hard it is to have a conversation when it's always with a person's feet.

"Jojo!" she says brightly, spinning herself upright. She comes to hug me and I pat her shoulder. Tiffany is the picture of 1950s white America, with her blond hair and blue eyes and her little apple cheeks. Even I am charmed by her innocence, her simple acceptance that the universe has nothing in store for her but pure, blessed goodwill.

Mom peers at me from behind the refrigerator door. She looks like she's spent too much time studying black-and-white sitcom moms, taking notes on their dialogue and behavior, then regurgitating them at me. "Well, hello, stranger!" She shuts the door, bringing some butter and whipping cream along with her. "How was your . . . uh . . . thing?"

My mother never has any idea what I'm doing and always looks surprised when I walk through the door, like I'm an unexpected guest.

Before I can make up a lie, she says, "Wait, wait, wait!" to Tiffany who has gone over to the counter. "Don't touch the sprinkles without Mommy."

Kevin comes from the pantry holding a couple of plastic jars. "Rainbow sugar crystals! Is this what you were looking for, Lou?" That's my mom. Louise Keller.

"Yep." Mom leans over to kiss him and he grabs her by the waist and dips her backward. Kevin is tall and blond and nice, derived from Germanic peoples. I hate when they publicly display their affection. This is shared living space, not some hotel room somewhere.

"We're in the middle of a project." Mom rights herself, glowing with blissy love, and lays the food on the counter. "Tiffany's ballet class is having a bake sale."

No one has ever offered to do anything for my team. No one has ever even gone to a match. That was all Dad. *My* dad.

The music squeaks out something rhythmic and nasal.

"If you let Tiffany listen to this for much longer, she's going to grow up to be a pod person," I say. "You're just contributing to Generica and its determination to commodify everything, even childhood."

Kevin laughs uncomfortably.

Mom sighs. "Don't you have some social media to obsess over?"

No one asks if I want to join in the cupcake-making process.

Tiffany says, "Mixer?"

"Yes, we're going to make the frosting. Just one minute." Mom pulls Tiff off the stool she's on and plops her onto the one closest to the bright red KitchenAid.

"This has been amazing, really," I announce, "but I'm going to have to catch you all later."

I wait a second or two for Mom to turn around, but she's busy making sure Tiff doesn't destroy her newly remodeled kitchen (thanks again, Kev), while Kevin checks inside the fridge for something.

I head down the hall.

Not that anyone cares.

CHAPTER TWO

In wrestling, sometimes an entire match comes down to two seconds. Two seconds to keep your opponent's back on the ground. Two seconds until the bell rings.

Two seconds and a life can be over too.

Two seconds for a heart to explode.

Two seconds to glory.

Wrestling is poetry, nothing wasted. My dad knew that. Every second counts in life and it especially counts on the mat.

Before he dropped dead of a catastrophic heart attack one sunny Sunday morning just before the start of eighth grade, my dad called me his mini-manager. Little did he know he was being prophetic. He was a World History teacher who had been the wrestling coach at the high school for fifteen years. He told me Mom had always hoped he would move on from teaching to something that paid more for his time, because as she pointed out on a regular basis, she was tired of sacrificing her entire life to his wrestling obsession. But that was his world.

After my parents got divorced, Dad and I became two peas in a pod. That's what he used to say. "You and me, kid, we're the same. Two peas in a pod." He loved it, and I loved it too. I was also one of the only girls in his Little Wrestlers after-school program. Every Monday, Wednesday, and Friday during wrestling season, after Dad was done coaching the high school team, he would give lessons to kids through eighth grade, including Sam and a lot of the guys that are on the team now, and we would all wrestle together. That is, until Dad died. After that, I stuck with wrestling for a while . . . but without Dad's encouragement, without having him by my side, it just wasn't the same, so I quit.

I don't know if Coach Garcia felt sorry for me or what, but one afternoon during freshman year he stopped me in the hallway saying he didn't have enough help and offered me the statistician/manager position. It wasn't wrestling, but it was something in school that helped me connect to my dad, one step beyond wearing the big hoodies I rescued from the boxes of his stuff Mom had pulled together to donate. This related to the essence of who my dad was.

When I ventured back into the gym after a year away, my dad wasn't there, but even with newly painted blue-and-yellow lockers and shiny benches, the sweat and blood of his years in this gym wiped away and refurbished, I felt him everywhere. Ever since, for two hours a day, Monday through Thursday plus meets, the guys and I belong to each other and it's like I can leave everything that happened in Algebra II or English behind. Better than that, I can almost feel my dad behind me dispensing advice; I can relax and let him guide me, like he's more than a figment of someone so long gone he couldn't possibly ever reach me. I always wanted to believe he was watching over me, but in the gym I can feel it.

At those times, I can forget that this morning when I walked into the kitchen, stepfather Kevin Keller was in the middle of making pancakes in the shape of a T, fussing over maple syrup, while Tiff sat at the table on her iPad humming to herself.

There's an art to wrestling.

It's beautiful.

It's *honorable.*

Still, I have to admit I'm a little prickly today, not exactly totally in my skin. I have to see Tyler and interact with him, and every time I think about our last moments hanging out, I'm mortified. I embarrassed myself and overreacted. I made a mistake assuming he had real feelings for me.

That's the thing about sleeping with guys on the team while thinking I'm in relationships with them when they *actually* just want to see what's under my clothes: There's nowhere to hide when things go awry. I can't calmly avoid Tyler until my humiliation has worn off. I have to see him every day until the season's over and find a way to be okay with the fact that Ty has seen me naked and emotional and has rejected me because he doesn't want things to get "awkward."

Ha.

Every time I think about that, which is approximately nineteen hundred times per minute right now, I want to find him and shove his nose into a dictionary.

Awkward (adj.): *causing or feeling embarrassment.*

I spot Ty in the corner of the locker room, talking to Sam while they get ready to spar. I'm not usually in here before practice, but Coach wanted us all to meet for a minute before warm-ups. Buzz and Santiago are wrangling the guys into sort of a circle. Everyone's in regular practice clothes, sweats and T-shirts, waiting for instructions.

Ty glances up at me like he can read my mind and for just a beat I see something there. Regret, sorrow, happiness to see me. But it's only a flicker.

I hate that my limbs go all floppy at the sight of him.

"Catch, Beckett!" Mason, a noodly white boy, throws me his water bottle. "Fill it up for me?"

I throw the bottle back. "Get your own water," I say.

Lucas of the movie theater blow job and the misunderstandings makes a honking/laughing noise at him and points. You know, when the buzz wears off and you see a guy for the fuckboy he is, it's a very liberating moment.

"But you're the water girl . . . I mean, in addition to being a highly respected member of our team." Mason puts his hands together in prayer and bats his eyelashes.

"There's a giant fountain right across from your dumb ass," I say.

"Ooooo, you made her maaaaad!" Lucas sings.

"What? She could never be mad at me."

It's kind of true. Mason is a complete jackass, but I love him anyway, even if Tiffany has a more advanced sense of humor than he does. It's just sometimes I do get irked. It's like they forget that before I was manager I was one of them for real, like I got boobs and they all totally swept their minds clean of the memory of me pinning them three nights a week.

"What are you doing this weekend, Beck?" Mason says to me. "Other than coming to Ty's."

Oh, right. Ty is throwing a party before his parents come back. Of course.

"Who says I'm going to Ty's?" I say, checking for signs they know what happened. "My whole life is not you guys."

"What's more important than us?"

I tousle Mason's hair. "Not a thing, Masc."

"Don't let her fool you," Lucas says. "She only cares about Sam."

"Don't give me shit."

"But I live to give you shit," he says.

"Hey, did I see you making out with Dana Delaney before lunch today?" Mason says to Lucas.

Lucas colors. "So what? I like her. She's a fox."

"She's pwetty," Mason mocks in a baby voice. "She smells good and she has pwetty hair."

I'd like to say I've evolved beyond the point of caring about what Lucas does, and in many ways I have. I don't actually want to be with him or anything, but this news does make me wonder if maybe I grew my hair out long and wore body spray, things might be different for me.

"You are a giant loser," Lucas says. "Like, this big!" His forearm slaps against my chest as he spreads his arms out wide.

"Ow!" I fold my arms around myself.

"I'm the loser?" Mason says. "I'm not the one forgetting Beckett has lady parts."

"Oh, I haven't forgotten." Lucas grins, then leans against the locker. I should probably be annoyed that he ever makes reference to our moment together, but I'm not because it's never actually that far out of memory. It's a relief in a way—we are friends who once shared a brief crush and an even briefer blow job. No big deal. Anymore.

Everyone goes quiet as Coach stalks in with his clipboard, compact and muscular, and Sam comes from across the room to sit next to me, Mason on my other side. Squeezed between them, I wait.

Coach Garcia is one of those semi-uptight guys in his early thirties who always looks like he just stepped out of a shower. Mrs. G, who teaches algebra, comes to all the meets with their adorable baby, Camille, and I sometimes want to ask him how he's here all the time with a family at home. I sometimes want to ask him if everything is okay.

Now he hikes one knee up so he looks like the statue of *The Thinker*, and then he begins. "As we really start in on this season, I'd like you all to keep in mind that we've built this team on the legacy of the greatest coach this school has ever seen, my personal mentor and hero, Coach Beckett."

There's the kind of silence that makes it hard to breathe, like even the dripping showers feel bad for stealing focus. It's that way whenever anyone mentions my dad, almost like they're waiting for him to reappear. A few of the guys cast mournful, empathetic glances my way. Even though some of them didn't know him, everyone knows what happened and how sad it was.

Sam wraps his arm through mine.

"I bring him up because I want to remind you that our reputation and ethics are not things we can take for granted, nor are they things I'm willing to sacrifice," Coach Garcia says. "We stand on the shoulders of our heroes. We need to remember to have one another's backs, to support one another, not just as people, but as teammates. Together, we are the Sentinels, state champions." He looks around, meeting each person's gaze. No one dares look away. "We have been able to achieve that not only because of our tremendous skill and discipline, but because of the way we treat each other. Now I'm only going to say this once, and the next time I have to open my mouth on this topic will be the last time you wear the Sentinel singlet, I don't care how important you think you are. We are leaders in this school and what we do as individuals matters. That means we take in nutritious food, we drink our water, we get sleep, we study hard, we serve our families and our community, and we do our best in every moment of our lives." He pauses. "And most important, there is no room for hazing or harassment of our teammates, regardless of weight class or skill level. A rising tide lifts all ships. Am I being understood?"

Everyone nods.

"Am I being heard?"

Again, yeses all around, louder.

"Good. I have an announcement. Barney Flickstein has requested a wrestle-off with Tyler Martinez."

He didn't tell me anything about this. I feel a ripple of consternation flutter through the room and there's quite a bit of laughter. Ty's pretty good and Barney's . . . well . . . not. He's a ninth grader, new to the team. He's not even on the radar yet and Ty's varsity.

"You can't do that." Ty points at Barney, who sits pale in the corner, slumped into himself like he's trying to disappear.

Coach puts his hand up before Ty can say anything else. "It's his right to make the request. He wants to wrestle at the meet, he wants to be varsity, and he can absolutely challenge you."

Knowing Ty, I bet he isn't worried about losing to Barney. I think Ty's embarrassed to have to wrestle a ninth grader, especially one who's never even been off the bench. Barney looks petrified, but he told me a few weeks ago that his therapist made him join the team so he's been facing his fears ever since.

"No more discussion. Go warm up right now. Wrestle-off in five minutes," Coach says. He looks from me to Sam. "Bring the timer and the chart."

"Aye, aye," I say.

"And remember, everyone—"

"Heart wins!" we all respond. This is something my dad used to say all the time. I think he actually believed it.

"Damn, that was intense." Sam waits for me as he always does, while I get the towels ready and pull up the roster of who is going to be working with whom today. "Now I feel triple guilty for drinking beer last night."

"You think Coach's speech was about *beer*?"

Sam stares at me, clueless. He always thinks everything is about him and about things he's done wrong. Some might say he has a dribble of narcissism running through his veins, but I think he's so self-conscious he's analyzing himself all the time. "What, then?" he asks.

"Think, Sam."

He follows me into the closet and grabs some towels. "I'm thinking. It's what he was saying about nutrition and water. I barely drank any today and I missed my workout. It made me feel like I'm not taking this seriously."

Sam takes everything seriously lately. The guy who used to watch six hours of cartoons after school every day disappeared this year. It's like he can't get comfortable staring down the barrel of real life.

"You should be more like me," I tell him.

"Yeah? How's that?"

"Less ambition. Acceptance of a totally mediocre life filled with loss and regret. It's extremely liberating."

"Beck—"

"And anyway, that was just him saying the things we all know so he could say the really important thing."

Sam's mouth hangs open in a question.

"About the hazing," I say. "It wasn't about you or your scholarship. I promise."

"Oh," he says, finally getting it. "Barney. Yeah, that was not cool what they did to his shorts. A guy needs to be able to leave the locker room fully clothed."

"You could make the rest of the team behave," I suggest. "You have the pull."

"I could try, but I don't think I'm all-powerful or anything."

Sam's a state wrestling champion in the 152 class twice over, although we don't talk about last year. He almost lost his title to a showboating guy from Denver, and losing his title is not something he can afford if he wants to live the life he hopes to. The fact that Sam has no idea how his championship and kindness and physical attractiveness translate into social currency for him is but one of the things that makes him beautiful.

"Why are you looking at me like that?" he says.

I shake off my momentary best friend adoration, load the towels on the cart, and let my hand fall across the picture of my dad that hangs on the wall. It's tradition or superstition or something. Everyone on the team touches that picture when they leave the locker room, so the glass has to be cleaned daily or it starts to grow a variety of viruses.

"Don't worry, Sam, Coach won't find out about your torrid affair with Domino's." I pat him on his six-pack.

Sam looks at me. "Speaking of, where were you yesterday? You just totally disappeared after school. I thought we were going to meet at my house and go get dinner."

"I texted you."

"Yeah, but 'not coming' isn't really an explanation now, is it?"

I hesitate. I want to tell him everything, but then again I don't really want to hear about his sex life with Jen, so the boundaries are sometimes unclear.

"Tyler?" he says, studying my expression. "I figured you were with him."

I glance through the doors into the gym, see Ty stretching in the corner. He looks so good stretching. I sigh louder than I mean to. "Yeah. I thought . . . I guess I was starting to like him or something ridiculous like that, but apparently he's not into me."

"Yeah?"

"Yeah." I hate so much to admit it. "I thought maybe we were going to start dating. For real, I mean."

Sam snorts derisively. "I know Coach just told us to be nice to each other, but Ty is a loser. Look at the way he's been picking on Barney, how he treats the freshmen. You're too smart and interesting to be with someone like him. After he showed you his eighty-fifth workout video, you would have gotten so bored you would have dumped him anyway."

It's true. Ty's hobby is making demos called Tummy Time with Tyler, occasionally accompanied by rap he writes and produces himself. Both are objectively bad, although I admire his entrepreneurial spirit.

Sam makes everything better.

"You laugh," he says, "but I'm totally serious."

"Let's not talk about me and my tragic love life anymore. Let's talk about yours."

"Leave Jen alone."

"If only, Sam, if only."

"Beck."

"Sam." He looks genuinely sad, so I say, "Oh my gosh, okay, fine. I will not give you a hard time about your girlfriend. I just think she's kind of a tight-ass and not that interesting."

"Beckett!"

Barney is on the mat right now, and he is actually shaking as he jogs in place. He weighed in at 117 today and I bet he's lost a pound in sweat since then.

Sam and I grin at each other. It's been hard for some of the guys to accept another ninth grader, especially one who is clearly on some kind of self-help mission rather than being here because he's actually good at wrestling or even interested in it. Ty's been an asshole to him, but I don't know if it's worth Barney actually putting his life on the line.

Coach Garcia nods at me. "You ready, Beckett?"

"Sure am." This will definitely not be completely intense or anything.

Coach huddles up with Santi and Buzz for a minute.

Ty steps toward me. "Can I talk to you?" he asks. He seems shifty and nervous, unsure of himself.

"I guess," I say.

We move off to the side while Barney does some high kicks and runs in place next to the mat.

"Are you okay? Today, I mean?" he says.

"I'm great," I say, forcing myself to sound chipper.

"Because you seemed . . . mad when you left my house yesterday."

"Not mad, exactly. Confused, maybe."

"Yeah." He nods. "I think I should explain myself. I had a great time, really."

Barney punches the air and Coach looks over, then shakes his head. The kid can't even warm up right.

Some of the roiling in me has settled at Ty's words. Maybe I'm not as foolish as I thought. "We can talk at your party, okay?" I say.

"Yeah?"

"Yeah."

He seems relieved. "Okay, because I think I might have been kind of a—"

"You *were* kind of a . . ." I say, but I'm smiling. "Let's just focus on not killing Barney right now."

Ty nods and gets into place.

"Get him, Big Daddy," Mason says. "You show him who's boss."

"Shut up, Mase," Ty snaps.

"I wasn't talking to you. I was talking to Big Daddy Barney."

"Mason!" Coach warns.

"Ty, you ready?" I say.

Ty returns his focus to Barney, who looks like he's going to stroke out.

"Let's get started then. Barney? You need another minute?" I hold the stopwatch at the ready.

He shakes his head no. With his fine brown hair, skinny limbs, and terrified eyes, he's all Chihuahua.

"Let's do it," he says bravely.

"Shake," I say.

They do, and then in a flash, Barney drops to his knee, lunges between Ty's legs, and pulls him down in a tackle, driving him straight to his back for a five count, almost pinning him until Ty realizes what's happening, fights aggressively off his back, and springs to his feet.

"Escape!" I shout. But barely.

"That was a double leg takedown and three near-fall!" Coach yells, like I don't know.

"What the fuck?" Ty says. "How did you do that?"

Everyone around the mat is either laughing or clapping or has a hand over his mouth.

Barney adjusts his goggles. "Not wanting to die is highly motivating."

I smile so hard my face hurts.

They stand again. Barney is shaking a little less.

"Beckett?" Coach says.

"Ready."

In spite of Tyler's high level of concentration, Barney is so fast Ty is on the ground in less than a second, and this time he doesn't get away. He squirms but he can't recover from the drop to his back.

"That's the match!" I yell.

"What the hell just happened?" Ty has his hands over his face so his voice comes out muffled.

Coach puts his hands on his hips and leans back on his heels, glowing with joy. "Barney, you can come to my office and Beckett will give you your new varsity gear. You compete this weekend."

"Coach—" Ty begins.

"No. No, Tyler. You can still come with us and be the alternate at the meet. Barney wrestles. That's how a wrestle-off works. You know this."

"Harsh," Mason whispers.

Ty, still seated on the mat, looks like he's about to cry.

The gym is silent. The guys can screw around a lot, but not when it comes to wrestling.

Coach folds his arms across his chest and walks over to stand next to me, never taking his eyes off Barney. "Time for drills!" he announces.

As our shocked team separates into partners, Coach is so ecstatic he's near levitation. "I think that kid might be one hundred seventeen pounds of wonderful." He slaps me on the shoulder. "Yup, I do."

"Are you okay?" Barney says to Ty, offering him a hand up.

Ty shakes him off. "I'm fine!"

"This is going to be our year, Beck," Coach says. "I can feel it. Forget one state championship. We're going to take every single one!"

I smile. Heart wins. Maybe that's true after all.

CHAPTER THREE

Ty's party is tonight, which is both good and bad. I keep turning the conversation Ty and I had in the gym over and over in my mind, looking at it from every angle. Did I imagine his regret? He pulled me aside in front of everyone, like he wasn't even hiding that there was something between us. Maybe he thinks he was hasty in breaking it off with me and has changed his mind.

Either way, I'm definitely not going to this shindig alone.

Sam would usually go to something like this with Jen, but I've harassed him into letting me pick them both up, so I can avoid walking into Ty's house solo. I could have gone with one of the other guys, but I don't want Ty thinking I'm into anyone else. So Sam and his very, very annoying girlfriend it is. Sigh. Sometimes, occasionally, I wish I had other friends.

Sam's house is a few cul-de-sacs away from mine, on the outskirts of Coyote Valley, which is laid out so it looks like it's resting against the bottom of one of the Rocky Mountains. It's glorious from a distance: the reddish rocks, huge green-and-gold trees, and then the sky that is almost always a cloudless blue, the houses tucked into a protective valley. There's a gas station, a Starbucks, an ice-cream shop, a breakfast place called the Happy Tortilla, 66, and a health food store. Other than that, you have to drive ten minutes in either direction past a whole bunch of cows and horses for anything.

I guess I should be glad that Mom met Kevin and we all moved into this adorable manifestation of the American Dream because it put me closer to Sam, geographically speaking. Now I can just walk a few well-planned blocks and there he is.

Sam's parents bought the very first model house in Coyote Valley fifteen years ago when Sam was two. They both work for Game and Fish and are basically poster children for the great outdoors. It's Cabela's and Carhartt all the way.

"Hello?" I call, opening the door.

The floor plan is identical to Kevin's, but the house is decorated so differently you almost wouldn't know it. Fishing trophies and cowboy hats are everywhere. Where at my house the sliding glass doors lead out to a large green lawn and a basketball hoop where Kevin sometimes practices for his weekend pickup games, here there's a huge garden, xeriscaped and brimming with red volcanic rock and giant aloes.

Sam's parents are home today, both sitting at the kitchen table with open laptops and a bunch of maps, their giant Great Dane, Ollie, lounging beside them on the floor like an enormous pillow. He opens one eye and makes a whining noise. He's either used to me by now or he's the worst guard dog ever.

"Good boy," Sam's dad says.

They just got back from a trip they had to make to the San Juan River, so there are fly rods and waders slung across the chairs and it smells a little like mossy feet. For years they couldn't go into the field as much as they wanted to because Sam was too little and it wasn't safe. But now that he's a senior, they've been leaving more and you can tell how much they love it.

Sam's dad is enjoying a Fat Tire beer and looks up from his paper-work, but only for a second. "Sam's in his room."

Sam's mom smiles. "Jo, hi! Nice to see you. Don't you look adorbs." She likes to say things like "adorbs." Sam says it makes her feel more connected.

"Thank you, Mrs. Sloane. Nice to see you too."

"Sam seems kind of off. You know of anything?"

"No."

"Maybe he's fighting with Jenny. I tried to lure him out here with some pineapple upside-down cake we got from 66, but not even that would do the job. Whatever it is, he won't say a word to me about it."

"Party will do him some good," his dad says.

"May I? Go find Sam?" I say.

"Of course, sweetheart," Mrs. Sloane says.

Sam is lying on his bed with the headphones I gave him for his birthday beside him. Sam's room is the opposite of his house, just like mine is the opposite of my house. It's almost austere in here. No posters, a small bookshelf, a neat desk with a computer on it, and a full-sized bed. If you went in his closet, you would find his clothes hung with a two-finger distance between each hanger. He's kind of a monk. For just a second before he knows I'm there, I see him staring at the ceiling with a worried expression. There is definitely something going on. He scoots over as soon as he sees me in his doorway and puts his arm up, folds it under his own head. I slide into it, fitting myself in the crook. I put my feet over his. Otherwise our bodies don't touch.

"How's it going?" he says, glancing to the side. Then he stops and really looks at me. "Hey, you look kind of hot, Beck."

"Shut up."

"No, really. Take a compliment. You look utterly decent."

I'm in a black bodycon dress with tights and combat boots. I even painted my nails and have butterfly earrings resting on my lobes. I want to be ready for anything. I want to be ready to be kissed, if it comes to that.

"You look all right too," I say.

Sam's traded his T-shirt for a button-down and his hair is semi-styled.

"How are Tiff and the gang?"

"Okay," I say.

"Peachy as ever, eh?"

"You know it." I'm fine, actually. Home is the same old thing, and to be honest, the whole Barney revelation and the fact that Coach is now grooming him to be our secret dark horse has left me feeling downright chipper. As long as I can avoid my family, I'm good. But Sam. I can read him so well. He's hiding. The thing about him is he'll never just come out with it.

"What's going on with you?" I ask. "And don't tell me nothing because I won't believe you and then we'll have to go in circles until you tell me the truth."

His breathing accelerates but he doesn't say anything.

"Samuel Sloane," I say. "I am your best friend."

"Fine. If I tell you something, do you fire-promise not to say anything?"

"Oh, dang. Fire-promise? That serious?" In eighth grade, we decided if either of us broke a fire promise, we would have to pay by being burned at the stake. I nudge him. "Go on. I'm a vault. Spill."

"Well . . ."

While he hems and haws, my brain fills with all my worst nightmares. I can't imagine what could be so bad he wouldn't be able to say it out loud. Then it hits me.

"Oh my gosh." I sit up and poke him in the chest. "Jennifer's pregnant. You impregnated Jennifer Evans and now I'm going to have to take care of your devil spawn during meets. I'm going to have to pretend to like her for the literal rest of my life! This is a monumental disaster."

He laughs and sits up too. "No, doofus, although if I did actually impregnate her I would expect you to have the decency to not call the fruit of my loins devil spawn."

I am truly relieved to hear there has not been Jen impregnation yet, so I lean back against his headboard. "What is it, then? Don't leave out any good parts. I want all the blood and guts you got."

"Jo," he says, "have you ever thought about being less edgy?"

"I don't know what you're talking about. I don't do drugs. I get good grades. I'm a perfect angel."

He rolls his eyes but keeps going. "Okay, I'm telling you, but I'm serious about not telling anyone else."

"Okay, okay!"

"One of the scouts contacted me from Duke. They offered me a scholarship." Scouts were around so much of last season we got used to seeing them typing out notes on iPads and talking on their phones. By the end of last season Sam had gotten paid vacations to three different schools. He came back silent and pale every time, like it wasn't a total thrill. I would have been ordering up lobster and geeking out on college life, but he just seemed worried. And now he's acting like getting a full ride is a curse or something. I'll have to be enthusiastic for both of us.

"What?" I stand on the bed and jump on either side of him, then finish with a happy dance. "That is *amazing*! Why aren't you dancing? Why are you looking so grim, for God's sake? This is incredible news. *I am freaking out!"*

"Shut up," he hisses, but he's smiling a little. "My parents are going to hear you and then they'll want to know what's going on."

"They already want to know what's going on. If you want them to stay out of your business, you should be subtler about your low-grade depression."

"I'm just not ready to have them know yet, you know? Not until I know how I feel about it myself."

I jump down and sit next to him, look at him closely. I determine it's not a great time to explain to him how I'm applying to five schools and have no idea if I'll get into *any* of them. I'll have to wait until December to know anything at all. I keep my mouth shut because he's an odd shade of green, like he might actually spew.

"Explain." I gently pull back his hand and he relaxes, leaving it in mine.

"It's just . . ." He forces the words. "I'm not actually that smart, you know."

"Oh, I know. I've been keeping you afloat for years," I say seriously.

"Fuck you," he says.

"Exactly." I nudge him. "That's not true and you've been doing fine."

"I know, but Duke is, like, a really good school."

"Sam."

"And I keep having these dreams where they tell me it was all a mistake or something goes horribly wrong and I flail this season—"

"Sam, Sammy boy, Sammela, come *on*." I squeeze his hands. "Listen to me, for I am wise."

He looks at me openly.

"You are smart. You got into Duke for a reason. You are in the top of the top, the cream of the cream, and they want you to be a Blue Devil like you've always wanted to be. And how much do you have to pay?"

"Nothing."

"Not even room and board?"

"Nope." He cracks a grin, finally.

"Well, then, you just saved your parents literally tens of thousands of dollars. Maybe *hundreds* of thousands."

"If." He sits up next to me.

"Yeah, if. Of course there's always an 'if,' but it's going to be great! And if you aren't ready to tell anyone about it, then don't. In the meantime you can know inside your heart that you have already mostly conquered the world!"

"Yeah?"

"Yes, and I'd say that calls for a major party. Epic, even."

He wraps an arm around me and tugs in. "Oh man, if you would just get along with Jen, you'd be the perfect woman."

I'm not going to point out the various issues with what he's just said, because pulling Sam out of a funk isn't especially easy, and I have to get him out of the house before he sinks into his stagnant self-destructive brew again.

"Let's go!" I say.

He eyes me cautiously. "I'm not ready for anyone else to know, still. Fire-promise."

"I already told you."

"I know, but you have to promise. Fire."

"Oh, fine. Fire."

We do our super-ridiculous, burning-in-flames faces, and then shake and I pull him up.

I pick up my bag from where it's lying in the corner.

"Hey," Sam says. "You sure you want to go to this thing tonight? I could call Jen. We could order pizza, eat pineapple upside-down cake, watch something?"

I get a brief but powerful image of myself spending the rest of the evening on the couch with Sam, Sam's parents, and Jen. "Hard pass."

It's not just that though. I know I'm supposed to have given up on Ty and that his workout videos are stupid, but I feel like this party will be the true determining factor of what happens with our relationship. I don't trust myself to read other people correctly, especially not after my most recent assumptions about him, but I know I'm not imagining that Tyler cares. Maybe he was scared because his feelings are too strong for him to handle. He seemed so relieved to hear I'd be over there tonight.

"I'm wearing *mascara*," I say. "I refuse to waste my efforts on trash TV. Anyway, you need to get over it and have a good time tonight. We are young!"

"I do love you, Beck." Sam looks at me like I'm something breakable. "I don't know what I would do without you."

"Love you too, " I say, trying to shake off Sam's strangeness, because it's making me feel even more nervous than I already do. "Now let's go party."

Of course we have to pick up Jen on the way. Sam gets in the back with her so I play chauffeur and we take most of the trip in silence. I *might* hit a speed bump a little too hard while Jen's reapplying her gloss and fixing her perfectly wavy chestnut hair, and Sam *might* give me a little bit of a knowing dirty look, but otherwise the ride is okay. It's not that Jen isn't a decent person. The fact that she and Sam are so sickeningly in love combined with the fact that Sam actually can't function without me creates this vortex where it's like we speak two completely different languages. As soon as we get to Ty's she basically leaps into Leah Herrera's arms and they run off to reapply their makeup (again) or whatever.

Ty's place looks like a different house from the other afternoon. There's music bumping and people are dancing in the living room, and girls are strewn across the counter in the kitchen while others jump in the heated pool outside. I'm sure Ty has an emergency cleaning scheduled for the morning, but this house is getting wrecked.

I search for him, hoping to run into him somewhere private, eventually making my way down the stairs to his refinished basement, which has a huge TV, sound system, and ping-pong and pool tables. It's filled with people, and as a cluster moves off to the side to start up a new game of beer pong, I spot Ty wedged into a love seat across from a full couch.

My stomach lurches like I'm going down a hill at high speed when I see what Ty is doing, smiling widely, listening with full attention to what the person next to him is saying. Amber. Amber who is the only Black girl in our school, whose high-waisted jeans and cropped shirt presently look painted on to total advantage.

I should leave. Everything about their body language says they're having a conversation they don't need anyone joining, but I go over to them anyway, pulled as though by an invisible string.

Mason emerges from the pile on the couch. "Hey, Jo!" He extends his arms, knocking Kailey Lee off of him and sloshing some red liquid over the edge of his cup. "Come sit down with us!" He's slurring fuzzily.

I pat Mason's hat, which seems to satisfy him, and he takes another swig of the red drink he's holding.

"Hi, Tyler," I say, trying to keep all emotion from my voice. It still comes out accusatorily.

"Oh, hey, Beckett!" He doesn't seem fuzzy, or upset to see me, and he doesn't look guilty either. He just looks up.

"Hi, Jo." Amber moves an inch away from him.

Tyler doesn't make a move to get up and hug me or to invite me to sit with them. He pauses, then looks at Amber and back at me, a question on his face.

The question is *Why are you standing there, Beckett?* Followed by, *Please go away, Beckett.*

I can hear it like he's said it out loud.

"Right here, Beck." Mason pats the spot next to him again. "Come join our love-in!"

"You're literally so dumb," Kailey says, but she doesn't push him away when he pulls her back to him. Instead, she boops him on the nose and then leans forward for a quick kiss.

Mason pulls back, goofily surprised.

"Did you need something?" Ty says. "The keg's outside."

"Oh, it is?" I say. "Thanks."

"Sure," Ty says. "Help yourself!" And with that, I'm dismissed.

I climb back out of the basement, push my way through the upstairs crowd and out the back door. I'm sweaty and jittery, so the cold air feels great. It's surreal. All the people around me, shrieking and having fun while I can only contemplate that reality feels like a moving target.

With Sam playing pool and the rest of my friends mating, I have nothing to do but wander over to the keg, which is currently being supervised by Jen and Leah under one of the outdoor heaters Ty has peppered all over his yard. It's a relatively nice night anyway, but the heaters mean people aren't out here in winter coats shivering at each other.

Much as I don't want to talk to either of these girls, I don't know what to do with my hands other than wrap them around a plastic cup full of flat beer. I am so, so deeply regretting not having taken Sam up on his offer of pizza and pineapple upside-down cake. Although I guess Jen would have been there too.

"Jo!" Jen says in a surprised voice, like we weren't recently in the car together and she's shocked to see me materialized in front of her.

"Hey," I say.

She hands me a cup.

"Hi, Jo," Leah says. She's in a super-cute, navy-blue midi dress with a princess cut and has traded her cowboy boots for flats, a silver horse hanging daintily from her neck. There's not a hair out of place, her nails are done, and she somehow looks chic and clean and innocent all at once, right down to her delicately placed freckles and single dimple.

I glance down. My outfit suddenly seems cheap and ridiculous.

I wore too much eyeliner.

"Hi, Leah," I mutter.

We all three look at each other for a minute and I have to stop myself from being like, *helluva party, right?* and then Jen and Leah gaze off into the distance like maybe their clear disinterest will make it easier for me to take the hint and skulk away.

I know we're almost done with the torture that is high school, but we have history that's hard to forget, even now. Leah was once my best friend, the kind where you braid each other's hair and let each other read secret journals. But as I got more into wrestling and boys, she got more into horses and girls, and one day it was like she developed an allergic reaction to everything that was me.

In seventh grade, Amber scooped her right up, and then a couple years later when Jen came to town, their event-planning coven was formed. They were sending each other Snaps all day and wearing matching outfits and deciding to give up dairy and I never knew about any of it. She just stopped being my friend. And I never forget that when my dad died, I waited for her to reach out to me, to give me a hug, to do anything to show me she still cared or understood at all what I was going through. But she never did.

I don't know if there's any coming back from that.

It was kind of awkward when Leah started working at 66 with me a few months ago, but Brenda's been scheduling us for different shifts, and Leah hasn't said anything. I'm pretty sure she doesn't care.

"What are you going to be for Halloween?" Leah asks Jen.

"Sam and I are going as Thing 1 and Thing 2."

"A solid choice."

"A little basic, but I want to be warm. I freeze my ass off every Halloween and I'm not in the mood this year. How about you, Ju?"

"I don't know yet," I say. "I'll probably just whip out my trusty old cat ears."

Halloween was my dad's thing. Since he's been gone I try to work if I can, and just stay away from any festivities.

"Cool," Leah says. "You've had those since sixth grade."

"I always forget you guys were elementary friends," Jen says. "Cute."

We stand around and are just about to dive into another embarrassing silence when Dax Furlong appears, a white kid holding a red cup that appears to already have been put to some use.

Dax Furlong.

Leah and Jen and I all exchange looks and for once I'm not on the outside of this. Dax is. Because he is Sam Sloane's biggest rival, one of the Denver Rockets and the only person to easily dominate Sam. An actual bona fide Sentinels enemy. In fact, Dax is the one who almost beat Sam last year. It went into OT. Sam escaped in the last millisecond and won on points. If Dax hadn't been so busy hamming for the audience, he probably would have taken the title. I feel like a traitor just having the thought, but it's true.

Dax seems to have no idea he's causing any kind of stir. He merely presents his cup for refilling. "Hey," he says to us generally.

"Hey," we all answer.

He glances at me, then does a double take and smiles. It's of the gleaming variety. "Hey, I know you. You're the scowly one from the matches." He extends his hand. "Dax."

"I know who you are." I shake his hand anemically.

"Ouch," he says. "Did I murder your cat or something?"

I snort and semi-laugh. This is the first non-terrible moment I've had at this party so far, so I soften a little. "It's my job to be scowly at the likes of you." I lean toward him. "You're the enemy."

"I know, right? I wasn't sure I was going to make it in the door, but no one's said anything so far. I mean, except for you, of course." He grins.

"Of course."

He takes a sip of beer. Jen and Leah gawk and he definitely doesn't notice. "You know, you're kind of scowly right now," he says to me. "Is it because this party sucks and everyone is boring?"

A laugh forms in my belly but I manage to repress it.

"Ah," he says, "the corners of her mouth *do* move in an upward direction." He squeezes his eyebrows together. "Noted." He looks around. "Well, I'd better get on with my exploration of rival culture. As you were."

He saunters off like he's got nothing to do and nowhere to be, and I'm filled with questions. Why is he here? Who the hell brought him? And mostly, why is he so sure of himself?

"You want to dance?" Leah asks Jen suddenly.

"Sure," Jen says. "Let's go."

Leah hesitates, Jen's hand in hers. "You can come with us if you want," she says to me. I could almost laugh.

Dax was an effective momentary distraction, but now I'm right back to wishing a portal would open up and suck me literally anywhere else. I'd take a planet of starved, brain-sucking zombies over this. Curse me for insisting on driving.

"No thanks," I say. "I'm going to do a little stargazing."

"Um, weird, but . . . okay?" Jen says, with a little laugh.

Leah waves goodbye and follows Jen.

I slump down around the corner in the shadows where hopefully no

one will see me ever again. After a few minutes, during which I do genuinely look at the sky, which is *amazing*, Sam shows up. "Here you are! You
okay?"

"Yeah, totally." I consider. "Wait, why did you come find me? Did Jen
say something to you?"

"Leah," he says. "She just said you seemed a little upset or something."

"Nope, I'm excellent."

Feelings are such a drag and right now I have way too many of them.
"Sam."

"Yeah?"

"I'm not totally excellent."

"I know." He takes my hand.

I don't know why I get like this. I could go play beer pong or pool or
get in the hot tub and maybe I would have fun. But my stomach is cavernous and my heart is hollow, and I don't know how I got here.

Even with Sam there are things I don't want to talk about, and I'm too
raw to let him in on the extent of all this. "It's like I'm never going to fit
anywhere, except maybe in that stinky gym."

"Which is why we're going to keep you there permanently."

"Ugh, may I escape such a fate. By the way," I say, grateful for the
change of subject, "you know Dax Furlong is here?"

"Yeah, we played some pool. He seems all right. A little full of himself, but whatever." Sam shakes his head, then nudges me. "Come on, it's
cold. Let's go play! I'll let you win."

Sam pushes himself off the wall to stand up, hand still in mine, but
before he can, Ty and Amber stroll out in front of us like they have all the
time and space in the world, feet kicking softly against the grass.

I don't want to stay but I also don't want to emerge from the shadows of the wall, so I tug on Sam's arm for him to keep still and be quiet. It only takes me half a second more to realize that by not moving I have now become the creepster I was trying to avoid being, but it's already too late. We'll have to wait them out.

Amber settles on a swing, and Sam gives me a look like if swinging is involved it could take a lot longer than it seemed it was going to a few seconds ago and also that I'm potentially ruining his life because Jen will be looking for him and he's stuck hiding with no beer.

"Did you bring me out here to watch me swing, Tyler?" Amber's voice is the voice of all the girls who have ever known a boy was into them and also knows how to tease it out of them.

Ty watches as she twirls the swing from side to side. "No, I didn't bring you out here to watch you swing." The aw shucks in his tone reminds me that all boys are just as scared of everything that can happen with a girl as we are of them. He's nervous. I can tell by how he shoves his hands in his pockets then grips the side of the swing set like he's looking for somewhere to put them and they won't stay still.

Nausea rolls through me and I focus on my breathing. It's bad enough knowing this is happening without having to witness it in person.

"Actually," he says, "I brought you out here to see if you might want to hang out."

"We're hanging out right now." She lets her fingers trail over his wrist.

"Well, yeah, but you know that's not what I mean."

"No, I don't." She's so smooth and soothing.

I cringe thinking about Monday afternoon in Ty's bed. We were so close. We gazed into each other's eyes.

Mental note: *This* is what it looks like when a boy has his heart caught in a net. He's watching her as she rocks herself as though he's in exactly the right place with exactly the right person. I wish everything wasn't so illuminated by floodlights.

"I have tickets to a show this Friday at the Ogden," Tyler says.

"A show?"

"Yeah, I got VIP tickets to Lucy's Diamond. I thought . . . if you wanted to . . . we could go to dinner before. There are some good places in that neighborhood. One of them has a menu that's all based on famous book titles. A Tale of Two Sliders, Catcher in the Pastrami on Rye." He trails off as she watches him. "Never mind, it's stupid."

"No, it's not. It's super sweet."

It *is* super sweet.

"What about Jo?" Amber says.

I start at being brought into this situation when I'm in full voyeur mode. But also, yeah. What *about* me?

"Jo?" He looks completely perplexed at the mention of my name. "You mean Beckett?"

"Yeah. I thought you guys were maybe a thing, but then it didn't seem like it . . . I don't know . . ."

"No." He cuts her off quickly.

Sam squeezes me and I am caught between wanting to slap him away and lean in closer to him.

"No?" she prompts.

"Definitely not."

No? Definitely not?

"No. I swear. I mean we did hook up but it's not like that."

We hooked up several times. And we had sex.

"Well, last time I checked, people hook up because they like each other, so . . ."

Tyler leans against the green frame. "It's complicated."

Amber laughs. "Try me."

It seems like even the grass under me is waiting for his explanation. "She's just a . . . practice girl. You know?"

Practice girl?

Amber narrows her eyes. "A what?"

Yes, a *what*?

"Okay . . . well, a practice girl is someone you practice, you know, hooking up with." Ty seems to check Amber for disgust level. She's listening carefully so he goes on. "So you don't get emotionally attached and you aren't going to ever get in a relationship with them. That's what Beckett is. And it's totally different than you. You're someone to . . . you know . . . date. And it's over with Beck, I swear."

Amber furrows her brow. "But you did sleep with her, right?"

His shoulders deflate.

I'm still trying to understand what I just heard . . . *you don't get emotionally attached and you aren't going to ever get in a relationship with them.*

Every fear I've ever had about myself and how I'm perceived is being confirmed in real time and I can't absorb it fast enough.

"Yeah." He delivers this admission like it's going to end his life. "I did."

"But you aren't into her?" Amber says.

He perks up. "No! I'm into you."

Oh my God, I'm actually going to die. I can't breathe. I can't feel anything except my entire body pulsing.

Amber pulls herself up and wraps her arms around his waist. He hugs her, and his eyes flutter shut, like it's sheer bliss. "I'm going to need to have a little chat with you about this practice girl situation, but okay."

"Okay?"

"Yeah. Okay, I'll go to the show with you."

She looks up at him and then they press their lips together and a little sound escapes me, a breath of pain.

Romance isn't dead. Romance is only dead for *me*.

A crash comes from inside the house and Ty groans.

"We'd better go in," Amber says.

"Yeah, I can't leave those animals in there unsupervised."

She makes a sound of consent and they disappear from view.

Another silence follows and I can feel Sam searching me for damage.

I look at him and his sincere green eyes and all at once I realize: He *knew*. He isn't surprised. He's just worried.

"Sam, did you know he calls me that?" I say.

Sam doesn't say anything. He looks down. I swallow.

"Sam."

"Jo."

Uh-oh. Sam never calls me Jo. A new and terrible thought is occurring to me now. "Does *everyone* call me that?"

He looks like he's about to dissolve, like he's trying to crawl out of his own skin. It's all slowly coming together. Joost, Luke, Ty . . . All of it, total and complete nothing. Every time my heart leapt at the idea of being with them, every time I held them close to me and reassured them when they were uncertain, every time I guided them to the right places and told them what they could do to make it even better. Every time I smiled and laughed and shared and gave. Every time I let them in.

Garbage. Fake, disgusting garbage.

I might as well be a blow-up doll.

"Joost and Luke called me that too, right?"

Practice girl.

He nods reluctantly. "Yeah. I've heard them say it too. It's just a thing guys say. It doesn't mean anything."

"You didn't tell them to stop? Point out how incredibly disrespectful and demeaning that was of them to say *about your best friend*?" I wait. "Nothing? What? Did you laugh along at my stupidity?"

He's like an animal caught, frozen and looking for a path to escape. "It sounds bad now but it didn't seem . . . In a way it was kind of like what happened with us," he says. "I thought . . . You said you just wanted it to be practice."

That was years ago. We were so brand-new at this. I can't believe he thinks this is connected to that. "Sam, we mutually lost our virginities to each other for the sole purpose of not being virgins anymore. It was a practical decision. How is a bunch of guys passing me around, acting like they were into me when they were just using me for sex practice until girlfriend material came along *anything* like what happened between us? This is *not* the same."

"I wasn't thinking of it like that. I knew you liked them. I didn't want to upset you . . ."

I am so filled with rage I could set this whole place on fire with a flick of the wrist. "You let them turn me into nothing." My voice darkens so much Sam actually takes a step back.

"Jo," he says.

"You let them make a total fool out of me. And you never said anything to me, ever."

"I was trying to keep it separate, not interfere."

"No." I hold up my hand. "Stop talking. You don't get to say any more words. I need to think." But I can't think. Not now. A new round of people spills out of Ty's house, hooting. Someone throws someone into the pool. It's all such a blur I can't see. Everyone around me is having the best time ever, and meanwhile it's like I'm not even here, like my feet are not on the ground, like I could just float away. And then it hits me, and I look Sam square in the face. "Shit. You are not my friend."

"What?" Sam is an emotional kaleidoscope. "I only heard the guys say it a few times . . ." He trails off weakly.

I don't know what else there is to say. I need to get out of here.

"Find another ride home." My voice cracks.

Before he can respond, I speed through the house and out the front door, back to the shaky rumble of my car. I need to be alone right now.

No one is going to see me cry.

CHAPTER FOUR

Obviously, I don't go to the meet on Saturday because I'm still trying to figure out how I'm going to show my face or if I even want to. I don't call Coach. I don't call Sam. Sam calls me, over and over and over. Actual phone calls, not just texts. I can only stare at my phone screen and watch it vibrate across my side table. I don't know what I would say to him. In fact, I don't think I would say anything. I would just shriek at him until he exploded from the pitch and volume.

Because *practice girl*? What the actual fuck?

I keep thinking about it, about that blank, panicky look spiraling over Sam when I asked him if he knew and why he didn't do anything about it, about Ty's casual ease when he told Amber how I was nothing to him. About how my dismissal and commiserating about my worthlessness actually helped them get together. I can't help wondering things, like did Coach know? It's not likely, but what if he did and he let them do it? Worse things have happened on sports teams. Did the guys all sit around and make plans about who was going to be next? Did they give each other tips about how to get me to think they liked me?

But the worst thing is that it all feels true, like they saw the most vulnerable, softest part of me, found it lacking, and treated me how I actually deserve to be treated.

I'm sure as hell not walking into the meet after that, and I'm definitely not staying home to bake cookies with Tiff and Mom and Kev-Kev. So I call Brenda and ask her if I can pick up an extra shift at 66. Unlike most diners, this one is only open at night from five to ten, six days a week, because its owners, Brenda and Ralph Abernathy, are there for every shift. They never miss, and 66 is always busy.

Brenda says *hell yes* to an extra shift for me so she can do some paperwork instead of running around on the floor the whole time, and it's the first moment since last night I feel even the slightest bit normal. Because I'll embrace anything that gets me out of the house and out of wrestling and out of reliving Ty's party in a loop.

The diner is almost as much a home to me as the gym at school. I used to come here with Dad all the time. He would get a bacon double cheeseburger and a chocolate malt, and I would get a grilled cheese and a cream soda. The walls are covered in pictures of old, brightly colored trucks, music is playing all the time, and there's a seemingly never-ending menu that's fifteen pages long. I've never even thought about getting a job anywhere else. Brenda and Ralph had been telling me since I was eight that they were ready for me to start working whenever I was, so that's what I did as soon as it was legal. I get internship credit for it at school, so it works for everyone.

"Hey, sweetheart," Ralph says from behind the stove in the kitchen. His salty hairs poke out from under the gray watchman's cap he wears at all times. He's long and skinny with kind, watery eyes and a mustache that covers his entire mouth.

"Hi, Ralph."

"How's the wrestling?"

"It's good," I lie. We have this exchange every day when I work, but today it carries more weight. "How are the burgers?"

"Good enough, hon. Good enough."

I get my apron and book from the cubbies in the back room and exhale for the first time since last night. They have no idea about anything here. I'm just good old Jo in for a shift. Plus, the changing room is comforting, with its pink chairs and cacti and curlicue cream-colored vanity.

Brenda steps through the beaded curtain. "Hey, Jo! How's my girl?"

I force a smile. "I'm good."

"No practice today?"

Practice. "There's a match." I hesitate. "But I'm taking a break."

Her eyebrows scrunch. "Huh. Well, all right. Not going to get much of a break being here. We've been busier than moths in a mitten."

"That's okay," I say. "It's good."

I'm tying my apron when Leah walks in and I almost drop it on the floor. I totally forgot she would be here when I asked if I could pick up a shift.

It's not that I hate Leah or anything, but now it's impossible for me to pretend coming here tonight is anything other than me trying to escape the truth of who I am. For all I know, Amber told Jen and Leah and everyone else at the party what Ty said, and they all sat around talking about me after I left. Leah's face doesn't register anything I can see, but I have no idea if she knows.

Practice girl.

I give Leah a quick hello and walk out into the dining room, where I grab a tray of ketchups and mustards and the big bottles to refill them. I'm squirting a yellow stream of mustard into its plastic container when I realize Leah has joined me.

"Do you want to do the ketchups?" I ask.

"Okay." She's in her 66 T-shirt and apron just like me, but with her beautiful black hair and flat silver shoes, she looks fresh as a peach and smells like one too. You would never know she spends every spare second on a horse.

"I'll be on counter and in back when you need me to run booze," Brenda calls. "Otherwise I'm in the office. Got so much to do and cannot keep up."

"Yep," I say, trying to make my voice sound chipper. "I've got it!"

"Sure," Leah says. "Sounds good. Thank you, Brenda."

When Brenda is gone and it's just the two of us, the silence gets heavy and long.

"So, did you have a good time at Ty's party?" Leah says as she squeezes the last of the ketchup.

"I guess." I slice through a lime, checking my peripheral for any signs that the question is a jab.

"Me too," she says. "I guess."

"We should do silverware next," I say. "We need enough for the restaurant to turn over three times."

"Yeah," she says. "I know."

This pretty much ends the conversation and we roll setups together in silence. When we're done with that we brew fresh coffee for the guys who sit at the counter every night and only eat pie.

Of course, as soon as Brenda pulls the string on the open sign the place is chaos. Everyone loves 66. We're pretty small, twenty tables, but we have everything from sweet tea to whiskey, steak to Caesar salad. It gets hot and full, and I can't think of much except getting the food to the people who need it. I like that being here almost lets me forget about Ty and Sam and everything else. I'm too busy to fuss over it too much and that's exactly what I came for.

But as much as I try to bury them, those words keep coming back to the surface: *practice girl.* I keep going over all the times little things have been said in the locker room. Mason's constant references to my servitude take on another meaning. Maybe me giving them blow jobs and letting them practice sex is just an extension of that, or that's how they see it. The fact that I've always laughed at all their jokes and adored them blindly makes me so angry.

Then shit starts going seriously wrong.

I forget a straw for someone's Coke. I take someone a regular burger instead of a veggie burger. I forget to write how someone wants her steak. Even Ralph seems a little frustrated with me. Finally, for the grand cherry on top of my crap sundae, I drop a tray of twelve waters all over a little kid.

I fall to my knees and start picking pieces of ice off the ground. The people are so nice. The toddler's dad is crouched down next to me trying to clean up. Brenda and Leah are trying to help me too. And meanwhile, tears I can't control anymore are dripping down my cheeks, over my nose, and landing on the floor.

"Excuse me," I manage, and run out of the dining room.

I'm just glad this is our last table of the night. Soon everyone will be gone and I can begin to make sense of my life.

I sink onto one of the pink poufs in the changing room, tuck my knees under my chin, and just let myself cry. I can't stop myself anyway. I cry for myself, my dad, for being a practice girl, for not having real friends, and I cry for Sam. I don't know how I can be friends with him anymore, and I don't know who I am if I'm *not* friends with him.

Leah's head pops through the doorway.

"Hey." She lingers, doesn't come all the way in. "Are you okay? You seem . . . not okay. Tell me everything."

"I'm fine." I lean back and rest my head under the Dolly Parton poster.

"Okay, because if you're not fine . . ." She doesn't sit next to me, but takes a couple steps into the room and lingers next to a picture of Brenda and Ralph from the 1990s in full biker gear standing in front of their "ponies."

"What?" I say.

"Well . . ."

"You'll be here for me?"

Leah flinches.

"Sorry," I say. "It's been a super, super bad day."

She nods. "Well, if it makes you feel any better, that little girl was covered in chocolate before you dropped that water on her. Her dad said she needed a bath. She's laughing now and is totally fine."

Brenda pokes her head around the corner. "I gave the girl a T-shirt. Fixed her right up."

"I'm so sorry, Brenda," I say. "You can take it out of my check."

"Never!" She sighs. "We've all been there a time or two. Sometimes it's impossible to leave the day at the door. The last of the customers are paying. I got it. You girls take a few minutes. Come on back out when you're ready."

"Yes, ma'am," I say to Brenda.

When she's gone Leah gets her phone out of her cubby. She scrolls like she has one million messages waiting for her. Then she looks at me. "You really okay? I mean, you want to talk about it?"

For a second, I actually consider telling her everything. It's been so hard keeping all my anger and frustration and hurt bottled up inside, and it would feel so good to just let everything out. But then I remember: Leah and I aren't the same as we used to be, and I still don't think I can say out loud the words that have only been ricocheting around my head. It might destroy me.

"Yeah. I'm okay," I say.

She looks like she's about to ask another question when the song coming from the speaker changes. From the first bars our eyes lock. I am instantly in her living room and we're doing eighties dances as Elton John's voice blasts across the house. It's like being thrown into a bathtub of ice. That's how fast I get hurled into a memory and remember how deeply and tightly I loved her. We were best friends once. It wasn't always only Sam.

Leah smiles and we trail back into the dining room. We don't talk, but we start to sing parallel as we work, circling each other.

CHAPTER FIVE

When I get to school Monday morning, Sam's by the huge double doors that lead inside, dressed in his usual hoodie, navy vest, and jeans combo, talking to Jen, who's sitting on the wall. I knew I would have to face him today, I just didn't know it was going to be the second I got here.

I guess I shouldn't be surprised. He's been trying to reach me all weekend, even with the storm that blanketed the whole town in a foot of snow. Mom said he came by the house too, but I made sure to be gone as much as I could during the day and worked every night. Obviously I thought about everything I was missing, but every time I started to worry about the team, I stomped my guilty feelings down. I should not feel guilty. They should feel guilty.

Jen is leaning into Sam, but when she sees his expression change as he catches sight of me, she joins in the stream of people going inside.

My chest balloons with emotion I definitely can't deal with right now, so I try to get past him, but he intercepts me. It makes me feel slightly better to see that he looks completely miserable. Slightly better, but also slightly worse.

"Hey," he says, blocking my path to the door as people push past us.

My face fills with blood. "Get out of my way, Sam." I mean this to sound strong, but my voice shakes. "Please," I say.

"No. You have to talk to me." I note that his voice also shakes.

"I don't have to do that at all."

"Please, Jo."

I let out a deep breath and move around the corner, out of the way toward the track where the guys run on conditioning days. Sam follows me. Over here everything is quieter and there's no one around.

"Jo—" Sam begins, but I cut him off.

"If it was Jen saying something like that, I would have warned you, even if she was my friend. Because you have always been more important than everyone else."

"I felt like I should stay out of your business, like I was caught between the guys and you."

"That's bullshit. Just total bullshit. It's me and you first. Or it was."

"I know," he says. "I know and I'm sorry."

"I'm not coming back," I say. "To the team. I'm going to let Coach know today. I'm done with all of it."

"Not coming back?" Sam seems to need to speak the words to make certain he heard them right, to make them real. "Not coming back . . . *ever*?"

"Right. Ever."

Sam is frozen and everything goes totally still around us. There's not even the hint of wind. I adjust my backpack and start to turn away. The conversation seems over.

"You can't do that." Sam stops me with his unusually low timbre.

"Why?" I demand. "Because the next douchebag waiting in line will miss his regularly scheduled blow job?"

He flinches like I've hit him. "Don't say that."

"Let's be real. Let's take the discussion of you and me and our friendship totally out of the equation." I look at him now, really look at him. "I thought I was a part of the team on every level, but I'm not. I understand that now, and now that I do, I can't ignore it. I can't pretend it isn't there."

"That's not true," he says. "You're giving up."

"I'm not giving up. This is about respect and the team's total lack of any, at least when it comes to me."

He is completely silent and totally still.

"You can't just leave us," he says. "You're one of us."

It's true the only thing besides Sam that helped after my dad died was being a part of that team. But it's also true that I've never actually been one of them. I'm on the sidelines. I fetch and soothe and organize, but mostly I'm used and unseen.

And then there's Sam. Whatever there was between us is broken and I'm not sure I can ever get it back. Sam betrayed me with his silence. He let me be diminished, was witness to it and didn't speak up, maybe even encouraged it. "I thought I could trust you."

"You can," he says.

"I can't, so don't say that. You've proven I can't and I'm having a hard time adjusting."

"Beck," he says.

"Yes, Sam?"

A freshman fitness class trots out onto the field, crunching through the snow behind us.

"I . . ." He fumbles. "I tried to tell you. I tried to tell you not to go to that party."

Pizza and pineapple upside-down cake?

"I know you're embarrassed and I did the wrong thing. I know the guys were awful, but Jo . . . wrestling?" he says. "That's something else. That's not even about the guys, or me. It's your history. It's . . . who you are."

He's talking about my dad. He's talking about all the weekends I spent holding the stopwatch, studying the rules for a proper takedown, reversal, and pin, my dad by my side.

"I don't know if you can ever understand, but I convinced myself that . . . stuff . . . wouldn't matter to you," Sam says to me now. "I convinced myself it was the same for you as it was for them. Sexwise. I mean, I know I was wrong," he corrects quickly. "And I knew it would hurt you if you knew about the name, but I just couldn't. I couldn't say any of that to your face. I couldn't tell you they were calling you—"

"Practice girl," I say softly.

"Yeah," Sam says. "I couldn't." There's something desperate in his eyes, begging me to trust him again, to put all the pieces back where they were.

She's just a practice girl.

I hear it over and over. Since the party at Ty's, it's ever present, worming its way into every potentially pleasant second like prying, uninvited fingers. I can't make it stop.

"I'm sorry, Sam, that you couldn't. But that's not good enough. And now *I* can't pretend you didn't completely screw me over. I can't just go back to normal."

I leave him there, not because I'm all that angry anymore. My rage has sunk into a dull despair, and I can't stand seeing the hurt expression on him, the one I know is mirrored on me. I want to go back and throw myself in his arms and tell him everything is going to be okay, but I don't turn around, because this whole practice girl thing is not something I can just let go of. Until I can make sense of all this, Sam is going to have to find his own way.

CHAPTER SIX

It's amazing how fast we adapt. By Wednesday I'm in some kind of twisted routine. I go to my classes and speak to no one. I skulk off campus for lunch and come after everyone is inside, just in time for the bell. My last period is study hall and attendance is only mandatory based on GPA so I leave before anyone sees me. After the first couple times I ignore Sam when he talks to me, he quits trying.

And I think and think and think.

I said I was going to tell Coach I was quitting, but when I went to find him on Monday afternoon, he was all excited about how Barney performed at the meet I missed, and how no one saw him coming, and I got excited too. I was so sorry not to have been there to support him. And then I remembered how Coach has always honored my dad and been so proud to have me standing next to him, and I couldn't get the words out. So, I told him a straight-up lie: Brenda had an emergency and needed me at 66 this week, so I hated to miss practice and everything, but I would probably be back soon.

He looked suspicious and asked me if anything was the matter, and later Mrs. G pulled me aside to check up on me, but I told her everything was fine.

And it all goes on. I don't know what I want to do or how I'm going to do it, so I put one foot in front of the other and try to get through the days.

There's only one really fraught piece to my survival plan. Lockers. The entire team and I lobbied for and got lockers all in a cluster and now that's something I can't undo, so when I have to go to my locker, my stomach pretzels right up.

Which is why when I discover I'm missing my copy of *Stamped* and have to get it from said locker cluster, my throat goes dry. This is prime after-lunch time, when everyone is getting ready for their next classes. It's not private or quiet or strategically secluded. Skulking is not an option.

Just keep your head down and get through it, Jo.

I've gotten the book and am shoving it under my arm when Leah appears before me, blocking my path to leave. I'm dimly aware of strange looks and lockers opening and closing around me, but I purposely refuse to bring them into focus, keeping my eyes slitted softly instead.

"Hey!" Leah says. "Are you going to ELA?"

"Yeah." I half-heartedly wave my book at her. "You?"

"Yeah."

"Okay." I make to pass her, but she stops me.

"Hey, wait. I just wanted to see how you were doing. Like, after work the other day."

I shrug. "I'm okay."

She nods. "I know we haven't . . . hung out in a long time. But I wanted you to know that I'm here, in case you ever do want to talk. About anything . . . everything."

I don't know why Leah is being so nice to me. Maybe I'm right, and she has heard about the practice girl stuff. But whatever the reason, I have to admit that I actually really appreciate it.

"Thanks, Leah."

Suddenly there's shouting down the hall and a crowd of rubber-neckers immediately gathers, obscuring my view.

"What the hell?" Leah says.

We automatically follow the flow of traffic until we can see what's going on. Sam has Ty pinned against the locker.

"Oh, shit," I whisper.

Sam shoves Ty hard so there's a clanging noise as his head connects with metal. That's not good.

"Ouch! It wasn't like that," Ty says. He scans the gathering crowd forming behind Sam and tries to lower his voice. "I didn't mean to hurt her feelings, dude."

Sam's face is contorted by fury. He's barely recognizable and is breathing hard. "She thought you liked her. You didn't tell her any different. You took what you wanted and then fucked her over. You're a piece of shit. She's worth more than that."

Leah looks over at me. *Oh no.*

Sam—who always maintains his pleasant exterior and who never cries except at movies—is losing it. If this was the real world and not some parallel universe, I would get between them and make Sam stop. But I can only watch them, knowing that everything Sam is saying to Ty is something he's also saying to himself.

"How could you call her that?" Sam says, still clutching Ty by the collar. It's like Sam doesn't know they're making a scene, like it's just the two of them fighting in private. There's an awed hush in the hallway. The whole school worships Sam and no one's ever seen him like this, including me. "How could you do that to her?"

Ty seems to think for a second, then growls. "You were right there, man. You could have said something, but you didn't. You didn't say shit."

My sentiments exactly.

Sam loosens his grip and looks like he's going to step away, but then without any warning rears back and punches Ty square in the jaw. The crowd goes wild, of course, but Sam doesn't stop. Ty isn't really even fighting back. Maybe Barney broke his spirit.

"Didn't mean to hurt Beckett?" Sam yells, punching him again. "How could it not hurt her? You don't deserve her. You should have realized what you had."

Oh no. He said my name.

"Stop it! Stop it!" A whistle blares through the hall. "Samuel Sloane, step away from Tyler right now." Ms. Anaya is a terrifying woman and she is constantly on patrol. She is the first female director of this place and she takes it very seriously. With her angled bob firmly in place as she sends her wheelchair down the hall at full speed, cross glinting in the light, she uses her most commanding voice. "Not in this building, gentlemen."

The sea of students parts. Sam hears her and lets go of Ty, but is still eyeing him like he might re-attack any second. He rubs his wrist and Ty cups his jaw. Ty's lip is bleeding but other than that he doesn't look too bad.

"Are you kidding me?" Mrs. Anaya says, bringing her chair to a stop, looking between them. "Samuel and Tyler, this is completely unacceptable behavior. Do we not remember the school's mission statement? Leaders in our community and in communication?"

They both watch her blankly.

"Disappointing, gentlemen. I expect more from our athletes. Come on." She opens her arm toward her office. "Let's go have a chat."

Sam lets Ty go ahead of him and then follows, shoulders hunched, not looking up until he passes me. Then he stops, raises his head and one corner of his mouth, and shrugs as if to say, *What else could I do?*

I know everyone is watching us, but right now it feels like it's us again, that secret space we occupy together where we share complete understanding.

And I can't help it. I smile back.

"Mr. Sloane," Mrs. Anaya calls.

"Yes, ma'am," Sam says, and lopes down the hall.

I'm in my room after school, trying to digest everything that happened with Sam and Ty earlier today, when Mom barges in bearing a pile of folded brightly colored clothes. She always comes in and out of my room at will. This is why I do not journal.

"Oh!" Mom says, that super-annoying note of surprise in her voice. She glances around as though looking for signs of what I'm doing, but when she doesn't find anything, she creases her brow. "Don't you have practice?" She puts the pile of clothes onto the dresser top and sits down beside me. The depression she makes in the mattress throws me off-balance and I tip toward her, have to tense myself to keep from flopping onto her lap, which I kind of want to do. When I was little and terrified of thunder and lightning, I used to bury my face in the safe darkness of her middle and stay there in her warmth until the drama outside stopped.

I scoot away from her.

"Yeah. I decided not to go."

She reaches out a hand and grazes my shoulder, but then quickly retreats. "Is everything okay, honey?"

I consider giving her the monosyllabic answer I normally would, but the reality is there's not one single person on this planet I feel like I can have a completely honest, soul-baring conversation with, certainly not my mother, but she's probably as close as it gets right now and I need, *need* to talk.

"Yeah, I'm fine," I say.

She sighs and puts her hands on her thighs, ready to hoist herself to her feet.

"I mean—"

"Yeah?"

Oh boy, our communication is hella rusty.

"Well . . ." I say.

She lifts her feet and settles onto the pillow next to mine. I can't remember the last time we were this close to each other. I smell her Ivory soap and French face cream. Neither are perfumed but both have a subtle scent that's so her.

"I think I have to quit the team." And just like that my voice goes wobbly and the waterworks threaten my lower lids. I swallow it all back down and stare hard at the picture of Sam and me at the beach two years ago when we went on our wrestling trip to Maui. "I don't want to be manager anymore. I can never go back."

I say this last part with more passion than I mean to, and I feel my mother looking at me closely. "Are you safe? Did something happen with one of those boys? Because—"

"No!" I say, even though something did happen with one of those boys. But if I told her it would be like the end of the world and anyway it's nothing like what she's thinking. "It's just . . . I don't want to do it anymore. That's all."

She's quiet for a while. She flattens my comforter with her hand even though it doesn't need to be flattened. "You know, Josephine, I know you preferred your father—"

"*Mom!*"

"No, no." She waves me away. "I'm not saying that to be passive aggressive or anything like that. I just know things were . . . easy between you. Easi*er*, I mean. And it was because you had the whole wrestling thing in common. Or maybe you two were more similar. I don't know. Things don't always turn out the way you planned them."

I know that. And I also know that she may not be saying any of that to make me feel bad, but it does make me feel bad so I wish she would stop.

She turns toward me. "Your dad and I didn't work out as a couple. Our marriage was . . . well, it was what it was. But I loved him. It's just sometimes that's not enough. What you two shared though was special. For a while there it was like the two of you shared a heart."

For the first time ever, I'm thinking about what that meant for Mom. If every weekday Dad took me to school and picked me up and we didn't come home until nine at night, and then we traveled to meets on weekends, what was she doing? She always left a plate for us and we'd eat sitting at the kitchen counter. Sometimes she was already asleep when we got home.

"The point is," she says, "wrestling is your birthright. Now, I don't know what happened with the team, and if you really feel like you have to quit, I'm not going to stand in your way. But you already gave up on wrestling once. Are you really sure you want to give it up again?" She holds my hand, and this time I let her. "Heart wins, Jojo."

The words ring out into my room. I haven't heard her say them, maybe ever, and they fill the space between us with all the memories and hurts and hopes we never talk about. Maybe we don't need to. It's possible we just did.

The door to my room swings open and Tiff charges in, fully outfitted in princess gear. There is glitter all over her face. "Daddy says it's time for dinner."

Kevin and Tiff and Mom are all home together all day, but Kevin is only here for dinner a couple nights a week and he always fixes food even though you'd think he'd be sick of it after cooking all week at his job. Mom blinks.

"He made a pupu platter," Tiff says. "Are you coming, Jojo?"

"Jojo's busy." Mom pats her hair back into place and smooths her shirt as though to bring herself back to herself. "Let's go, Tiffany." She stops in my doorway. "You want me to bring you a plate, sweetie?"

It's been a long time since she called me sweetie. It's been a long time since I let her.

"I'll be out in a few minutes."

"Oh? Good!" She lingers in the doorway. "Don't forget to put these clothes away."

Ah, well. Family bonding time is over, I guess.

She shuts the door and I hear Tiffany telling her all about the different appetizers they made as they pad down the hall.

I can't get my mom's words out of my head. She's right. I gave up on wrestling all those years ago, even though I loved it more than anything. And to do what? To bring water and towels to a bunch of jerks every day. And now I'm going to quit because of them?

No.

No. The word comes quickly and urgently. No, I'm not quitting the team that's my primary source of joy so a bunch of assholes who treat me poorly can feel more comfortable and forget about what they did. They may have forgotten that I used to kick their entire asses, but I haven't.

But, but, but . . . now a new voice starts up, chattering at me about my poor conditioning, my lack of postpubescent experience, and how no one anywhere near here has a girl on their team.

I slap that down, bat it back like a bothersome pup. All of that may be true, but so is something else: I am my father's daughter and he taught me everything I know. That's got to count for something, to make up for the physical piece of this I'm lacking. I picture myself, a crowd on all sides, people standing up in the bleachers screaming my name.

Okay, that may be a little lofty, as lofty as, say, going on a real date with someone who likes me and treats me like an entire, real person. But I'm not sure I even care. I want those guys, every one of them, to have to watch me fight, to understand that what's inside of me is more than just their water girl. Even if I fail, I want them to have to see that I'm a survivor. And I want to make them very, *very* uncomfortable.

I glance at my silent phone. I haven't gotten a single social media message since the fight when everyone I've ever had a passing conversation with in the school sent me shots of Sam's contorted face as he slammed Ty against the locker. Sam hasn't tried to reach me in days, which is too bad because if this were any other situation, he would be the person I would be telling about all of this. But hey, looks like it's just me and me these days, so it's either fall into a pit of despair until this annus horribilis is over, or start clawing my way out now. I unlock the screen and scroll through my contacts until I find Coach Garcia, then linger over his name, heart clanging before I hit the phone icon.

He doesn't pick up. I almost press the end button, but then I think about everything that's happened and, like my mom said, who I want to be.

"Coach," I say after the beep. "This is Beckett. I need to talk to you about something."

CHAPTER SEVEN

Coach gets in early to warm up before the guys arrive for conditioning, and since I didn't hear back from him last night, I've decided to come in person. It's 5:30 in the morning, which is probably too early for what I'm about to propose, but here we are, me clutching my homemade coffee, wrapped in a hundred scarves, shuffling through the gym door. Buzz is setting up cones and raises two fingers in a bleary greeting.

"If you're here then what the hell am I doing?" he grumbles. "You want to take over so I can go home and crawl back into bed?"

"I would but I need to talk to Coach. You can have some of my terrible coffee though."

He waves me off. "Got a liter of it on the bench. Don't worry about this old guy." He pauses. "Coach is in the office."

"Thanks, Buzz."

It's a chilly morning, still dark outside, and the gym feels cavernous and cold.

I round the corner and knock on the open glass door.

"Come in," Coach says without looking up. He's examining some paperwork, making notations with a pencil.

"Coach?"

He does look up then, obviously startled, but immediately goes back to studying the file in front of him. "No," he says, waving me away. "Nope. Bye-bye."

"No?"

"Yes, no." He stands up. "You go take care of whatever you need to and come back when you're ready, but I will not accept your resignation so goodbye and have a nice day."

"No, Coach. I wanted to talk to you before the guys get here. I'm not quitting."

His level of anxiety shifts palpably. "Oh, thank the Lord. I've been a mess without you."

"Yeah?"

"Yeah. Yes. Absolutely. Even with Buzz and Santi around I feel like my good luck totem is missing."

"It's true, I am extremely lucky," I say.

Coach doesn't miss the sarcasm. "You know what I mean. You always know what we need to focus on and who should go to a meet. You know all the other players and their patterns. Hell, your spreadsheet is so damn perfect I wish I could pay you." He sits back down into his old leather roller chair. "This last week without you has been a real eye-opener and I feel I owe you an apology. The boys are falling apart. Their performance levels have dropped. I'm sure you know Sam and Ty got into a fight and I had to make deals for them to be able to stay on the team. Ms. Anaya wanted them removed and only got talked out of it because she appreciates our title. Camille has started having nightmares and no one is sleeping at my house. Mrs. G is starting to look at me all twitchy-like. If one more thing goes wrong . . ." He seems to realize he's digressed. "But that's not what we're talking about here. You have real, natural wrestling intuition and I haven't been giving you credit where it's due. I apologize, Beckett." His face crumples. "Now for the love of God, please come back to me."

My eyes fill a little. I never expected anyone to notice what I do for this team, but it still feels good to be missed, not because of who my dad was but because of my own accomplishments. I sit down across from him. I don't want to tell him all the things I have to tell him, but I am going to have to put my big-girl pants on. I am a warrior like my dad always said, and now is the time to actually act like one. Or at least I can try.

"Coach, I need to tell you something."

"Great!" He hands me a file. "Can you add these stats from last week? They're on Post-its. I'm sorry."

"Um, yeah, no."

"No?"

"No. I don't want to be your statistician anymore. Like, at all."

Coach furrows his brow. "Okaaaay. I thought you said—"

"I would like to join the team."

"You are on the team."

"No, I mean, I'd like to wrestle."

"Wrestle," he says, as though tasting the word for the first time. I can see what follows, what's playing through his head. A girl on the wrestling team. Interesting. He's also instantly assessing my lumpy form under my coat. I have noodle arms and haven't done cardio since I don't know when.

"You know I wrestled from basically when I exited the womb through seventh grade. Anyway, I was pretty good. You can ask Buzz. He was there. I know I would need work but—"

Coach Garcia makes a steeple of his fingers from where he sits across from me. I can't read his expression. "Does this have anything to do with Sam and Ty?" Coach meets my eyes. "Level with me."

I think. I could lie to him, but I don't want any more secrets. If he's going to take me on he's going to have to do it knowing who I am. I want to be honest. "I was . . . involved with Ty and it got kind of messy."

There's a low-key rule about me and the guys. At least I think there is. It's never been discussed but I definitely feel like I crossed some sort of line. But it happened and there's no point denying it now.

Coach raises his eyebrows.

"But I'm not seeing him anymore," I say quickly.

"And the fight?"

"The guys said some things about me. Sam didn't like it. So I think that's what happened with Ty."

"Ah," Coach says. "Both of them were like steel traps when we had our meeting after the incident. Couldn't get a word out of them even when I threatened to bench them for the rest of the season. Should have figured it was something to do with you, considering your disappearing act this week."

"Brenda didn't really need my help at the restaurant either. That was a lie."

"Okay." He puts up his hands. "That's enough honesty, Beckett."

"Yeah, okay. I've been trying to figure out how I wanted to handle everything, you know?"

"And what did you decide?"

"At first I wanted to go to the desert and dig a hole until I disappeared or it was time to go to college, but then I realized I actually really, genuinely love this sport and I want to be a part of this team."

He shakes his head, his eyes lighting up with recognition, then just as quickly shutting down with denial.

"Coach," I say, letting all the emotion I've been feeling bubble to the surface. "I need to kick some ass so I can get revenge for the shit they talked."

I wouldn't usually talk to an adult like that and the words leave my cheeks flaming, but this is something he doesn't want to do and I need to make him do it. His movements are slow and measured as he watches me. "Go on."

"This is my birthright." As I repeat my mom's words, I think about my dad, hand on my shoulder, showing me how to execute a perfect flat-man pin. I could barely even walk. "Wrestling is my inheritance, not something I think I'm entitled to, not like that . . . it's something I've worked on and been around and been passionate about and *loved* my whole life. I practically fell out of the womb in a hold."

"Aw, Beckett." Coach wrinkles his nose. "There's no need to—"

"I will work hard for this. And I promise I won't ever get romantically entwined with anyone from the team again." Easy promise to make. I'm definitely not going back down that treacherous shit show of a road.

Coach leans back in his chair. It creaks and whines. He never takes his eyes from mine and I don't back down. "You'd be coming to wrestling cold, after years of not doing it at all, jumping in mid-season with a bunch of guys who think of nothing else. You may know everything in your head, but that's really different than doing it for real. I wouldn't be able to send you into a tournament or anything unless you proved you were actually ready. And you would have to trust me to make that decision." He taps a pen on his desk. "You would have to know I would not go easy on you, nor would I make any decisions about competitions that I couldn't absolutely stand behind."

I look at him levelly, determined not to betray any of my fears. "I don't care about any of that. I will give it everything I've got and if I have to be on the bench all season, that's what'll happen. But I will have tried. I will have stood up instead of cowering."

"Once you commit to this there's no backing out. You're doing this until February. This is your life. I'm not competing with Brenda for your attention. If 66 is in crisis you have to say no. You're here five days a week at six a.m. and you are here until six p.m. when practice is over, and you're at every meet and tournament on weekends. No excuses. If you have pneumonia or a broken arm I don't want to hear about it. You're here. End of story."

"Yes, sir." The pit in my stomach is slowly becoming air, open space, potential. This is hope.

Buzz knocks on the door. "Heya, I don't mean to interrupt but the boys are here."

"Yeah," Coach says. Then to me, "We'd better get out there. You good?"

It hits me that Coach is nervous, not for him but for me.

"I mean, I'm totally going to hurl but other than that it's cool," I say. "I'm good."

"You tell anyone about your idea yet?" he asks. "Sam?"

"No one," I say. "I haven't talked to anyone."

"Let's go then," Coach says with a whistling exhale. "And get ready because those chicken arms need work."

"Yes, sir."

We walk out to the mat where the guys are stretching, everyone in their shorts and hoodies looking haggard and half awake, but they come

to attention when they see me. They look at each other, then from Ty to
Sam and back to me again.

She's back, someone whispers. I don't look to see who.

"Hey, Jo," Barney says. No matter how much drama there's been, I can
be almost certain Barney knows nothing.

"Hi, Barney."

"I need everyone's attention," Coach says.

The room goes quiet.

"The meet this last weekend was rough for some of us. Frankly, overall that tournament was an embarrassment, except for you, Barney. Good
job. This week hasn't been much better so far. But I have an announcement I think might change things a little, remind us we're a team and we
take care of our own."

"Ooooo . . ." Mason makes spooky arms. "What could it beeeee?"

"Mason, put a sock in it," Coach says. "We have a new team member."

"Another ninth grader?" Luke asks.

"No," Coach says. His face betrays nothing, not a hint of the nervous-
ness or doubt I saw during our meeting. "Our amazing and recently
missed manager is going to be joining us . . . as a teammate."

Sam lets his arms fall to the side and takes a step toward me but stops
himself.

The guys groan and laugh, and the rumble gets louder. Ty blanches
and I meet his eyes until he looks down.

"Who's going to wrestle her?" Luke asks. "And no offense, Jo, but how
are you going to do this? Physically, I mean."

Coach runs a hand over his hair. "There are no official gender requirements. She'll wrestle in her weight class."

"But she isn't in shape. She never works out."

"That's true but I'm going to *practice*," I say, deliberate emphasis on the syllables. "I'm going to be the best *practice girl* anyone has ever seen."

Coach looks puzzled. Luke and Ty each only meet my stare for a moment before looking away, down, anywhere but right at me.

There are more murmurs of protest and I catch a couple of snarky comments. I really hate them right now and for a second I don't know why I'm doing it at all. The blinders are off and however much I loved them before I now despise them in equal measure. They're awful, and I'm going to have to spend the next three months dealing with their bullshit. I raise my chin and fold my arms across my chest.

Sam steps forward. "Jo knows this team and sport better than any of us. She knows every tactic and move there is. She knows exactly what it takes to win."

"Dude, all due respect," Mason says, "she hasn't wrestled since we were kids. We have titles on the line."

"If she sucks, what does it cost you? Nothing. If she isn't good enough to compete, she won't compete. She deserves the chance to try."

"Well said, Sam," Coach says.

"Yeah, don't be a bunch of pissants," Buzz grumbles, coming to my side.

I have to admit, I'm basically beaming. Sam coming to my defense is one thing. But Buzz? No one is going to go up against Sam or Buzz on this front. And it looks like no one wants to talk about the practice girl issue either, which is good because I'm not ready. I don't know if I ever will be.

"Okay, time to run." Coach surveys the room. "Three miles outside."

No one moves.

"Get out of here right now or it's going to be five. Remember . . ."

"Heart wins!"

━━━━━━━━━━

I practically fall into the girl's locker room. My legs feel shaky and I'm less fueled by pure rage now that I'm alone and don't have any of their sullen, pouty faces to look at. Now I have to get out there and actually run.

It's peaceful in here, but the walls are covered in a sickly pink, not the bright My Little Pony kind I like but the kind that reminds me of upset stomachs. The last time I tried to run, it was because Mason was trying to throw me into a pool and I only ran around said pool a couple of times and was so out of breath my lungs stung. I collapse onto a bench and put my head between my legs. I still can't believe how angry I am with people I once called friends. There's no going back now. I'll have to stick with it until the season's over, like Coach said.

I force myself outside, willing one foot in front of the other.

We run.

I die.

I am so out of shape, but I push through even when I am completely sure I'm going to puke and cursing the black coffee gurgling in my stomach.

I take an extra ten minutes to run the last mile, and Sam runs it with me in silence, letting his steps fall in with mine. After, when practice is over and everyone else is showering, I take a second to sit on the bleachers, look at the mountains in the distance, the sky above. My entire body is screaming at me. It's beautiful right now with the sun coming up over the ridge—cold and crisp and quiet, and I feel quiet inside too.

Sam comes out of the building, spots me, and walks across the field. The sight of him churns something achy. Before I can say anything, he holds up a hand.

"I was an asshole," he says.

"Was?"

"Sometimes I'm a blockhead."

"Sometimes?"

He waits and I wait.

"Okay," he says. "I should have told you right away." He takes a deep breath. "I didn't listen to you when you said how much it hurt you. I didn't want to believe I was that much of an ass. But even worse than that is I didn't defend you. I never should have let anyone talk about you like that. No excuses. I know you wouldn't have. I'm so sorry. You're right. It's me and you first."

It took us a few weeks of hanging out in fifth grade to realize we were both on the outside in our own homes. At that time, things weren't great with my mom and dad and Sam had older parents who tried but couldn't ever understand him. We found each other. We stuck by each other.

He slides his arms around me and I let him.

"I have hated every second of the last week," he says into the top of my head.

"Me too," I say.

"I probably need to work on that. It's probably codependent or something."

"Probably."

He pulls me in tighter. And then tighter. He's holding on like he's never going to let go, and I feel both our hearts accelerate.

"You want to know the weird thing?" he says.

"Do tell."

"I think I wanted Ty to fight back. He knew he deserved what I gave him. But I deserved it too. I wanted him to hit me. I wanted to be hurt the way I hurt you."

We're still clutching each other. "Thank you." I loosen my grip.

"Anytime." He releases me and takes a step back. "Damn," he says, looking me up and down.

"What?"

He shakes his head at me. "Don't take this the wrong way, but your muscle game needs serious work."

"Hey!" I smack him and he follows me to my car.

"Seriously though. You want to do this, you're going to have to bust hard. Tomorrow is weights. It's one thing to watch and another trying to keep an opponent from turning you inside out. We're going to have to work extra."

"You're going to help me?"

"Who else is going to do it? I know you're not going to push yourself, because you're a lazy person." He pats his stomach. "Want to get a bite? I'm starving. Sausage biscuit sounds excellent." He gets in my car.

I get in too, smile, and put the key in the ignition.

"Hey, Jo." Sam stops me and gets quiet. "You know how we . . . practiced with each other?"

Just when I think I can relax, he has to bring this up. "Yeah?"

"I wanted you to know . . . It wasn't just practice. To me. It was . . . more than that."

He lingers on me, blushing so I can see it in the light of the new day.

I have absolutely no idea what to say.

He smiles at me and I smile back.

"Start the car," he says. "I'm freezing."

We pull out of the parking lot and head for Starbucks. And . . . I don't know . . . Maybe I feel like things are going to be okay.

CHAPTER EIGHT

Pretty much the only thing that stops 66 from cranking like the dining machine it is is Halloween. This town takes Halloween so seriously I sometimes wonder how we came to this, what strange feud led everyone to battle each other over whose yard is going to dominate. My theory is that it has to do with the American Dream. Everyone who lives around here has worked hard to try to make that fantasy come true and this is one way to show the world they've made it. Witness the shrieking, frightened children! Behold the giant chocolate bars! We are the land of plenty.

The subdivisions are all highly decorated with everything from snowboarder scarecrows to lowriders with skeletons inside. On my block alone there's a house that turns into a pirate ship every year and another owned by an artist who makes creepy sculptures and at Halloween puts them all on display for everyone to see. It really is terrifying. I don't like walking by her house at all whatsoever.

Tonight is slow and quiet because every single person in Coyote Valley is occupied by Halloween endeavors. Well, everyone except Mr. Salieri, an old friend of Ralph's, who doesn't miss a night of the daily soup special or his coconut cream pie, come rain or snow or shine. Under normal circumstances there's hardly ever a second to gather myself in this place, and considering this is a once-a-year occurrence, Brenda has invited Leah and me to sit at the bar and have something to drink until all the kids are done trick-or-treating at 7 p.m. and the huge rush begins.

Brenda has decorated the place with porcelain pumpkins and witches, each table has its own supply of candy, and we've got a few special kids' drinks on the menu tonight, like Candy Corn Surprise and Ghostly Hot Chocolate. When the parents come in, they're going to be ready for some extra-special beverages with a splash of Kahlúa or a dash of bourbon, since the kids are usually crying from sugar overload and need real food their parents are too exhausted to cook. It's nice to have a minute to rest before the hammer comes down.

Leah's sipping on a Shirley Temple, cheating on the costume front since she's wearing her cowboy hat, a bandana, and boots, which she wears when she's on the ranch anyway, and I'm having soda water with several lemons, regretting my decision to come as a clown. All things considered, that's not what I'm going for. Poor decision-making due to extreme hunger and Leah disrespecting my beloved cat ears at Ty's party.

I have my steamed brown rice, broccoli, and baked chicken breast in a Tupperware container in my locker, and I would like to murder whoever came up with the wrestler's diet I am now on. I would feel guilty for trying to impose it on the guys all these years except I hate them so I'm not sorry. I wish they would all choke.

Leah's Shirley Temple has extra cherries just like when we were little and she flips through her phone while I try not to be entirely steeped in dread over tomorrow's practice. I'm already so sore that sitting on the toilet is a whole thing, and it's going to be another leg day.

After a few minutes, Leah slaps her phone down and sucks on her straw.

"So," she says, "you going to tell me about this whole fight that occurred in the hallway the other day? Or are we supposed to pretend that didn't happen and that it wasn't odd the way Sam stepped up for you? Tell me everything."

A flicker of electricity skates through me. It happens every time I think about Sam's face when he punched Ty. The fury. The intensity. I've been having trouble getting that vision out of my head and now that Leah's mentioned it, here it is again. Sam, cheeks flushed, eyes flashing, muscles tensed. Because of me. And what he said the other day. That when we had sex it was more than practice. I don't know what that meant but I've been chewing on it ever since.

"We're best friends," I offer.

"Uh-huh." She looks unimpressed. "Fine. But don't think Jen didn't notice. That's all I'm saying."

She goes back to flipping through her phone and slurping on her drink. I suddenly want to slap it out of her mouth.

"Jen's insecurities are not my problem. I didn't make Sam do anything. Totally not my responsibility." I know I sound like a bitch, but Jen grates on my nerves. Everything coming out sideways like she can't just say what she's thinking. That's why I can't deal with girls.

Well, now you can't deal with guys either so where does that leave you, Jo?

Leah glances up, one eyebrow cocked. "I think if you put yourself in her shoes you might be able to see how your boyfriend battling for someone else's honor could be a little awkward. Especially since that person has a—"

"Reputation?" I cut in. "It makes me sick that people still talk like that. Totally sick. Haven't we moved past the double standard? Would a guy ever get called into question for having sex? Like I'm supposed to let misogyny—especially coming from other girls—control me?"

Leah looks up and we hold each other in a stare. "I was going to say it can be a little awkward if that person has a vendetta against you, but okay, cool." She shrugs. "I don't know why anyone dates in high school. Looks like the biggest nightmare, I swear. Handing your body—or even worse, your heart—to a starved, humping puppy." She shudders.

"Every single person in that school that flaps their stupid gums about everyone else's business can suck it. Sam and I have been best friends since fifth grade and I shouldn't have to explain what that means. Not to you."

Everything is implied. Her abandonment. The ways she has never been as good a friend as Sam. That things with Sam are so completely strange right now.

"The fact that everyone wants to make everything about sex all the time is just pathetic," I add.

Leah's eyes narrow, but before she can say anything else Brenda pops her head through the beaded curtains, gives us both a look, and then steps behind the counter to refill Mr. Salieri's tea.

"And also," I hiss, when Brenda is gone. "Do you know why Sam did that? The couple of guys I supposedly dated who were on the team, including Ty, have been calling me a practice girl. Do you know what that means? It means I'm a blow-up doll, a hole in the wall. A practice girl," I say again.

Maybe if I say it enough times the words will become nothing but syllables, meaningless letters placed in random order. Maybe they'll stop feeling like razor blades. To my surprise her eyes grow wet.

Crap. I forgot how emotional Leah can get. Crying at *America's Got Talent*, getting teary when she eats really good food. And don't even get me started on what prolonged eye contact with a horse does to the poor girl.

"I almost hurled Hazel Lupin into the wall when I heard her whispering about it the other day," I say. "I'm so sick of it. So excuse me if I don't really give a shit how Jen feels. I'm glad Sam kicked Ty's ass. I wish I could have done it myself. Actually, maybe I will."

I picture myself with Tyler pinned on the mat between my thighs, powerless against my strength. I like that idea very much.

"I'm not trying to start anything with you," she says, in a way that makes me sorry I swore so much. "I want us to be okay."

She waits.

I wait.

"I did hear something about that practice girl thing." Leah puts her phone facedown on the counter.

"I'm sure you did."

"I think it's completely messed up. If I were you I wouldn't want to be anywhere near those guys. I'd do anything I could to avoid them. They suck. If I were you I'd be glad Ty got his butt kicked too. That's not even what I'm talking about. I just wish your life wasn't all about guys, that you'd make room for a girl or two."

"Oh, right. Like you?"

I expect her to balk but she only eyes me levelly, then goes over to the computer where we control the music that filters through the speakers. "Country or indie?" she says.

"Indie," I say. Everything she's said has made me grumpy. Or maybe it's that all I've had to eat today is a protein shake and some greens.

"Look, I think you're great, okay?" she says. "A little weird and angry sometimes—"

"Hey!"

"But once upon a time you were *my* weird, angry friend and I liked it." She hits the button and music starts playing. It's old indie, perfect for this kind of night, and I recognize the song as something my dad used to play sometimes. "Can we please get over all the rest of it?"

"Your friends suck." I grab a rag. "I'm going to clean some tables."

"No." Leah stops me with a gentle hand. "Real talk. Those girls are not just 'those girls.' They're people. They have problems and do their best just like most of us. You don't want to get put in a category based on the way you look or what people think of you and you're doing exactly the same thing to them." She pauses. "I know you're repelled by anything other than sneakers or combat boots but they're more than a shoe choice. And so am I. I don't want to be judged for wearing cowboy boots and curling my hair any more than you want to be judged for having some sex."

"Fair," I say.

"I have other things going on. The ranch means everything to me, you know? It's my heritage, my connection to the land. I want to be me, all of me, and my friends understand and appreciate that when some people wouldn't. So they aren't cookie cutters. They're way more than that."

"Okay, I get it." And I do. Even though they can be monumental jerks, I can accept that Leah wouldn't have been hanging out with them for so long if they were jerks to *her*. They must be positively contributing to her life.

"Not that Ty isn't a total asshole," she says. "What he did was terrible and I can't deal with how cutesy he's being with Amber."

That stings, but right now I'm not sure Ty actually is an asshole. What

Ty did hurt my feelings and embarrassed me but I slept with him in the first place, without ever having had a discussion about what would come after. That part of it wasn't me being victimized.

I don't like the idea that I'm this small person that anyone can do anything to, who is so thick she can't even tell when a guy is using her for sex. I tried to read the signs instead of verbalizing anything. I interpreted Ty's laughter at my jokes, the way he wanted to be with me, how he wanted me so badly physically—as being so much more than horniness. That's not fun to think about. It's complicated and messy and dirty.

It's too hard to explain though, easier to nod and say, "Yeah. He's a complete hoser." But now I'm thinking about Amber and Jen and Ty and Sam and my very own assholeness. Stupid self-reflection.

Brenda comes in bearing a plate of fries and another with two little packages wrapped in plastic with small orange-and-black ribbons attached. "Ralph made you a snack and I baked up some Spooky Boo Brownies for you. Better eat up. The trick-or-treaters are probably just about done and then they're going to descend on us madder than wet hens and hungrier than bears just out of hibernation."

I want so badly to eat those fries. I want to shove the whole plate in my face, and I can't even begin to express how much I love Brenda's brownies, especially these ones with the marshmallows on top.

When Brenda's gone I push the plate toward Leah and say, "You take them. You can give them to your dad or something." If Leah's dad hasn't changed too much he'll be in front of the TV in his recliner right now and until such time as he falls asleep. He's a rancher and a sunup-to-sundown kind of a guy.

She takes the brownies and eyes me suspiciously. "Are you kidding?

Since when do you ever turn down the chance to eat sugar?"

She remembered. I tend to face-plant into a bag of Sour Patch Kids whenever I can. Put them in the freezer. That's the best. Up until last week they were about the only green things I ever ate. I liked it better that way.

"Since nine days ago," I admit.

I wrote up a whole nutrition plan that involves a lot of egg whites and protein powder. I know it's the only way I'm going to be able to build muscle in the amount of time I have, which is basically no time at all, if I want to compete this season or even survive grappling at practice. So my plan of spending the entire year eating only Oreos and soft-serve ice cream with fudge is out the window. I hate to admit how much I miss sugar.

Leah raises her eyebrows and makes a "well, tell me the rest" motion. She reaches for several fries and shoves them in her mouth. They look crispy and perfect.

"I joined the wrestling team," I say. This is the first time I've said it out loud to anyone outside of the team.

"'Bout time," she says. "I been wondering what the hell you were doing all these years." All of a sudden I love Leah more than anyone because yeah. *About time.* And of course she thinks that way. She'd probably lose it if she had to stand there watching people ride horses and recording their jumps instead of getting on one herself.

Her mouth full, she inhales rapidly to stop the fries from burning her. "Ow!"

"I'm going to be an actual wrestler on a high school team."

"Yes!" She swoops me into a hug. "I can't wait to watch you kick some serious ass. It's going to be the best to watch those guys crumble in awe."

I haven't gotten past the air of total dismay coming from the guys at practice, or how hard I'm going to have to work to be in any kind of shape. I've only been able to get to the place where I can vaguely imagine a time when I might be wrestling instead of curling into a cashew formation and whispering frantic prayers to myself until the two minutes is over.

"I'm going to be there every time, serving those boys some evil eye while you absolutely crush."

"You're going to come to the meets?" I say.

"Of course!" She slaps my shoulder and I remember the Leah she used to be, so nuts about horses she always smelled like one, prone to loud laughter and random dancing. "I'll be there whenever I can. It's about time someone did something about that stupid boys' club."

"Yeah!" I say.

"Double yeah!"

We're being goofy now and Mr. Salieri is half frowning, half smiling at us. He holds up his cup of tea to show us he needs a refill but we're too busy laughing our asses off. Leah makes a howling noise and I start cracking up, and even though I'm still mad about not being able to eat the fries and especially the brownies, I make a howling noise too and then we're both howling and Brenda comes in and stands in the doorway, giving us a tired look.

"Couple of werewolves, I guess," she says, and leaves us to laugh and howl alone.

Once we quiet down and get ahold of ourselves, I get Mr. Salieri his tea and take away his dirty plates as the kids start filtering through the front door, so high on sugar their eyes are wide and flashing, their haggard parents trailing behind.

CHAPTER NINE

I failed, flailed, and my butt hurts.

Coach is giving me a wide berth, like my angry aura is messing with his flow.

I'm flopped onto one of the practice mats breathing, staring at the ceiling, and willing myself to get up and do something. Buzz and Santi want to go home. Everyone has a life. I lick my lips and taste salt, try not to think back to five minutes ago when I had to grapple Mason and he decimated me, then lectured me about how vegan athletes are actually superior and probably I should try that diet if I really want to slay. He wasn't even a little bit breathless.

I'm two weeks in and I can feel some things changing for me physically. I'm building muscle and everything is tightening around my bones. It's nothing dramatic yet, but I understand in a whole new way what it means to eat carbs before a workout and protein after, the difference on muscles between a cardio workout and lifting, discovering that I really like pushing weights around, focusing on muscle groups, big and small. I like being sore. I like burning. I had forgotten and now I remember. That part feels good, excellent, even. But it's not enough.

I never wanted this kind of a body, have never been the girl to ask whether her ass looks good in jeans. I like the way I look just fine. But I have to admit I've been getting into the feeling that I can do push-ups without landing on my face after five, and that even though I'm still slow it's not quite so painful to run three miles in the morning. I kind of look forward to it now, rolling out of bed while it's still dark, making my smoothie while my car warms up, leaving the house with purpose.

Other than Sam, the guys don't really talk to me, and I don't care. Not in the morning when everyone is kind of grouchy and Mason is barely awake and Blue Feather doesn't even talk to anyone, just listens to death metal on his headphones while he works out.

But at night? Those practices have been grueling, more emotionally than physically. It's harder to be around them than I thought it would be. My new strategy is to picture them like they were when we were all little. They were scrawny, not very skilled, and easy to dominate. But it's been a long time since then. They're not quite men but while I've taken a four-year hiatus, they've been working at it, getting better and better every year using tricks I've helped teach them.

I get mad every time I think about it. I have been helping them while they have been treating me like garbage, and meanwhile my muscles have been growing steadily more floppity.

And tonight.

Oh.

Tonight.

On top of getting schooled by Mason I had to grapple Ty. Coach, who has been doing a good job of keeping us apart, was out of the room when Santi paired us up. Ty's chest pressed against mine, his arms were around my waist. He was on top of me. And he destroyed me.

So I'm lying here in part because my body hurts, in part because that was really stressful, but mostly because I want to be in this space where I've so often felt completely myself. I want to feel that way again, like the smell, the air, this particular cocoon are all made exactly for me.

"Uh," someone says.

I peel my eyes open. Barney is standing over me, damp from a shower. He has a hoodie on and his glasses slide down his nose as he peers down at me.

"Hey, Barn."

"Hey. I wanted to make sure you're okay and everything. I know it can be a little rough sometimes."

"Yeah. I'm okay." I sit up painfully.

"You're not giving up or anything, right? Because it's hard at first but it gets better."

"There is no part of me that is planning on giving up. Anyway, how could I give up with you as my role model?"

"Yeah." He chuckles and I suddenly see what Barney is going to look like in twenty years. Some people are born middle-aged. "If you start feeling bad about yourself for any reason, just remember my first month and you'll be all good."

"You all right, kid?" Sam says, coming up behind Barney.

I was kind of hoping Sam would slink out, go on a hot date with Jen or something, but here he is. I guess if we're trying to pretend everything is normal, the usual thing would be for him to make sure I'm good after I got my ass beat. I brace myself for more awkwardness. Even though it seemed like maybe everything would just revert to the way it was before, after that first morning we tried to meet and work out, but there was still too much between us. Turns out that kind of hurt isn't so easy to block out and we've both been making careful excuses.

Plus there's the other thing. I keep going back to that hug in the parking lot, to what he said about when we lost our virginities, how it was more than practice. Because now it's like a spell has been cast and all of a sudden I notice where he is in the room in a different way and I want to be away from him instead of next to him.

"Good night, Jo," Barney says.

I don't think Barney likes Sam very much. He always looks at him with a measure of suspicion. We watch him leave and Sam sets his gym bag on the floor.

"You want to practice some moves, Beckett?" Sam says.

This is charity. He knows I'm not really getting the chance to develop myself because of the way the other guys are approaching me and the way they're tearing me down.

"It's okay," I say. "You don't have to do that."

My discomfort is a pit.

"You tired?" he says.

"So tired," I admit. I don't add the word defeated. At this rate I'll never get to actually wrestle in a competition. I also don't admit I thought the fact that I am descended from my mighty paternal lineage would give me superhuman wrestling abilities, because that seems so ridiculous now.

Sam pulls up his knees. The room quiets and a new weight settles between us. "You know what will make you less tired?"

I continue staring at the ceiling.

"Winning," he says, with an emphasis that gooses my skin.

Because it's exactly what I want.

I snort. "Oh, come on. That's never going to happen." I look around. "Anyway, don't we have to go?"

"Nah. Henry's here so we don't have to worry about locking up. We can just split when we're done."

"Done?"

"Yeah, wrestling. You do want to practice with someone who will let you get some muscle memory in, don't you?"

I want to shower, shove a chicken breast in my mouth, and go to bed. I can't say that to him though. He was at practice just like I was and I don't want to admit how tired I am.

"Here." He hands me a snack pack of pretzels. "Eat this."

"Aw, thanks, Sammy boy." I sit up and try not to snarf them, but I can see him grinning at me anyway.

"Slow down, Tex, you're going to hurt yourself."

"Shut your piehole," I say, spitting crumbs.

"I'm proud of you," he says, as I'm licking the bag. "I know how much you like your Twix and Snickers and you've done a really good job cleaning it up."

"How dare you say Twix to me? What kind of monster are you?"

"And look at you, showing up to every practice, beating our dummy all to heck, practicing singles, doubles, even getting on the mat with Ty."

"That was unpleasant."

"For both of you. I'd wager that's why he tipped you so fast, why all the guys are. I don't think they're trying to be dicks."

"And yet . . ."

"I'm just saying I don't think Ty wanted to be manhandling you any more than you wanted to be manheld by him."

"Manheld?" I feel myself coloring. "Is that even a word?"

"Drink," he says, handing me his bottle. "But not too much."

I take a few sips of heaven water and pass it back to him, then flop back.

Sam laughs. "This is truly a pathetic sight."

"Fuck off."

"You know what? Forget doing more moves. I can let you give me a sound thrashing next week. What you need is a stretch. Stretching is an important part of the sport."

"Oh, Sammy, I love it when you mansplain things to me."

"Oh, har." He takes one of my legs and puts it on his shoulder and leans forward.

"Yow!" I whine. My muscles have hardened to concrete. Thus, I want to quietly die in my sleep instead of whatever this is.

"That's not what we're looking for in terms of flexibility," Sam says gravely, eyeing my hamstring like he's just discovered a new enemy. "Seriously, you can't underestimate the importance of stretching."

I'm about to make a joke when I realize Sam is totally serious.

"Relax," he says. "Let me do this. I won't hurt you, I promise."

He goes slowly, gently, pushing into my hamstring until it starts to release.

"This is not good," he says. "You're going to have to give some real time to your flexibility."

"I'm flexible."

"Maybe, but with the amount of working out you're doing it needs to be a regular part of your exercise routine. Otherwise you're going to retract and lose the flexibility you have naturally and you'll never be able to do the splits."

"Splits? You have totally lost it now."

"Oh, you don't think it's possible? Anything's possible."

"Is it?"

"Well, I don't know. Isn't that what you're trying to prove?"

"Among other things I suppose."

"Right," he says.

What he's doing is starting to feel really good. He switches legs and I have to try hard not to groan.

"So, you ready for tomorrow?" he asks.

Everything tightens up again and pain shoots up my leg. The meet is at 9 a.m. tomorrow and aside from throwing around a rubber doll I've barely gotten to do anything. It's going to be a very public disaster.

I pull my leg off his shoulder.

Sam rests a hand on my ankle.

"It's going to be fine. You'll probably be out in thirty seconds but you'll get the experience of being on the mat with a real opponent. It's great Coach decided to let you compete. It'll be good for you. Then we can set some goals . . . if you'll let me help you."

This is something Coach Garcia and I do with all the players. Set goals for the season. What they'll improve. How many matches they want to win. What kind of shape they want to be in.

"I'll set my goals right now," I say. "Number one: not die. Number two: not die."

But I'm thinking about actual goals, dreams, and schoolgirl fantasies. One: kick everyone's asses. Two: prove girls can compete with boys at wrestling. Three: prove I deserve better than to be a practice girl. Four: prove I deserve everything good.

"Hey," Sam says, distracting me back into the moment. "I'm going to be right there. I'll have your back, okay?"

"Yeah, okay."

"I'm serious." His voice has more heat in it than I would have expected. "I'll never not have your back again, okay? I know that's hard for you to believe but I mean it."

"Sam—"

"I don't want you to say anything," he says. "I just want you to know it. I'll be there, every practice, every match, and when wrestling season is over I'll be there then too."

I give him a look.

"Flip over," he says. "Here." He hands me a face towel. "Put that under your cheek."

I do what he says, let my face rest on the soft cotton. My heartbeat accelerates and I can feel my palms getting sweaty. Even though Sam and I are always kind of on the touchy-feely side, it's not like he regularly massages me like he's doing right now. Also, we've been really careful not to touch each other since that long hug and now he's, like, *on* me. He presses into my shoulder muscles and I gasp.

"Tight," he says.

"Um, yeah."

He doesn't stop, just keeps going until I shrug him off. This is a little, I don't know, intimate for me. "My turn," I say.

Sam stays sitting up while I rub his shoulders. Even though we're still touching, now I have control over it and I start feeling a little less odd.

"You're a goddess," he says.

I snort. "You're so dumb."

He reaches for me and for a second I think he's going to pull me against his back and hug my arms into his sides, but then in a flash he twists and I'm flat on my back.

"How the hell did you do that?" I say, right into his face because now he's hovering above me, and seems to be slowly leaning in.

The sound of a mop bucket being dragged across the floor is enough to send Sam reeling back so he's sitting on his butt, looking at me, dazed.

I want to ask him if we just almost kissed, but Henry the custodian is looking at us. "You kids supposed to be in here? Who's watching you?"

"No one is, Henry," Sam says. "We were just about to leave."

What would have happened if Henry hadn't come in here?

"Coach let us stay for some open mat," I say, voice breathy. "There's a meet tomorrow."

"Here?"

"No, Littleton," Sam says.

"Littleton. Good team. You two better get back to practicing," he says.

"Actually, we'll leave you to it." I don't know what that moment I just had with Sam was but I want to get away from it.

Also, I can see Leah and her arched eyebrow looking at me accusatorially over time and space and I curse her for getting in my head. I don't know what I'm even doing here all alone with Sam. I don't know why it feels strange either. It just does.

"You need a ride?" I ask him.

"Yeah," he says. "Actually can you drop me off at Jen's?"

"Of course!" I say. "I would love to drop you off at Jen's."

"Hey," Sam says, holding onto my shoulder. "You okay? You seem . . ."

"I'm fine," I cut him off. "Perfect."

"Okay, cool," he says, but he's watching me carefully.

I grab my bag from the corner.

Sam and I are friends.

Just friends.

That is all we have ever been and is all we'll ever be. For one thing I promised Coach I would never get involved with another wrestler on this team ever again, and for another he has a girlfriend and I'm not going to add teenage home-wrecker to my list of accomplishments. Also, I'm still not sure about him and who he is when I'm not there. I want to be the kind of person I can face when I look in the mirror. I'm barely starting to be able to hold my head up again. I'm not going to give myself another reason to look down.

That's it. End of story.

Over and out.

CHAPTER TEN

Kevin is behind the kitchen island when I get home, still in his chef blacks and clogs after a day shift, while Tiffany sits in front of the TV watching *The Voice*, pretending she has a buzzer. She has a plate of tropical fruit in front of her that she munches on as she watches, completely transfixed.

"Hi," I say, because it seems rude to walk past him without saying anything. I already know Mom is in the guest room on her Peloton. It's basically where she lives right now because she just started working as a real estate agent and she's stupid stressed about her competition in the market.

"Hey!" Kevin says. "I made you some snacks. I thought you'd want something after practice."

He remembered I had practice. He noticed when I walked in.

"Here you go!" He presents me with a plate of pineapple.

I'm allergic to pineapple.

"Thank you," I say.

I make like I'm going to head upstairs to my room and Kevin says, "Sit, sit!" I look around, seeking help and support, anything to get me out of this situation, but Tiff is slapping the table and yelling at the TV and the person on it who is presently yodeling. I haven't gotten to shower yet and sweat has turned to salt crust. I would normally refuse but I think about the moment I had with my mom the other night, when it appeared she actually gave a shit.

I settle in across from Kevin and he beams at me.

"So, tell me about the wrestling. Do you get to wear those cool masks with lightning bolts on them?"

"What?"

"You know? They go over your head?"

"That's Mexican wrestling, not high school wrestling," I say.

"Oh, yeah, right . . . I forgot." The look he gives me tells me he was just messing with me, like we have a funny little secret between us.

Stepdad jokes?

He opens up the oven and pulls out a quesadilla. He may have forgotten that pineapple could kill me, but he has remembered that quesadillas are my favorite thing. He even has condiments prepared at the ready. Sour cream. Salsa. Guacamole. My mouth waters. He reads something in my expression and retracts the plate.

"Oh gosh, I completely forgot," he says. "You're on some kind of diet, right?"

"I have a meet tomorrow." I force the words out. "I can't."

"I understand," he says. He takes the plate and puts it in front of Tiff. "No problem!" he calls from the living room.

Abort Mission: Fake Family. I know he means well, but he's not going to understand the weight pressures or how any of it works, and he's certainly not coming to my meet tomorrow, so I'm better off leaving.

"You okay, kiddo?" he calls from the bottom of the stairs.

I don't answer, but go directly into my room, into my bathroom and the longest, hottest shower ever. My life has turned into a series of horrifying moments, all of which I replay in my mind. There's Kevin, of course. So awkward. Then there's Ty straight-up slapping me onto the mat with his pinkie finger. Then Sam. What even was that? That . . . almost-kiss. That massage.

I'm out of the shower and in my dad's Radiohead T-shirt when I feel the room warm up ever so slightly. I feel the stress leave my chest. This is what I can't explain even though I tried to tell Sam about it once. I know my dad is dead and I'm not someone who believes in ghosts, but I do believe in this because I don't know how else to explain it. Sometimes, when I'm alone, I feel him there. I can almost hear him. I just *know* he's with me, that he's telling me everything's going to be okay, that he loves me and he isn't gone.

He definitely wasn't some TV dad. There was the goofing around that exasperated Mom, sure. There were his long hours and his avoidance of family life and the way he could never sit still. But there was more than that, a wound he couldn't explain to me, and once or twice he told me wrestling had saved him. I think his heart was always a little hurt. That's why "Heart wins" was his motto. He had overcome his own history to be this guy, my dad.

I hope he knows I'm thinking about him, that I haven't forgotten about him. I open my closet, which has been mommed since the last time I was in it. All the clothes have disappeared from my floor. My scattered jewelry is organized and in place. My scarves are all hanging from their hooks. Up above all that is a box squeezed in next to the blankets Mom keeps there in case someone ever decides to sleep over here. I haven't looked at it in a long time. I pull it down, open the green velvet, and the warm spot in my chest pulses.

One of the things my dad was big on was positive affirmation. He said that was how he coped with his childhood. He would look himself right in the eyes and tell himself he was worthy and could do whatever he wanted. So when he had his own team, he started writing affirmations on Post-its. If one of the guys was trying to gain a few pounds he would stick a Post-it inside his locker that said EAT MORE SANDWICHES AND BELIEVE IN YOURSELF. If he knew one of the guys was going to ask out a girl, he might say MEDITATE ON THE YES.

He did it for me too. I let my fingers run over the pink and blue and yellow slips. In this box is every single note he ever left for me on bathroom mirrors, next to my bed, on the passenger dashboard of his car, in my wrestling bag, on my pillow. He always knew when I needed one. I hate the way they're fading, curling in at their edges. I used to look at them all the time, when I needed his voice in my head, when I couldn't stop crying. Then I put them away because I had to.

I'm not trying to make him into a mythical creature. I know he wasn't. He also wasn't much of a writer. But he was really good at being my dad.

KNOCK HIM DOWN

HEART WINS

NEVER LET WHO YOU ARE BE DEFINED BY OTHERS

ALWAYS REMEMBER I'M HERE

I LOVE YOU, JOJO

YOU'RE MY DAUGHTER FIRST

DON'T LET THOSE BOZOS GET YOU DOWN (LITERALLY)

There are piles and piles of them. I thought it would make me sad to look at them after all this time, but instead I feel like this is as good as the videos I have stored in the cloud. This is a box of pieces of him, pieces of myself too. Maybe someday I'll leave notes for my own kid. Make it a family tradition.

I'm almost to the bottom of the box when I see a small green spiral notebook with my dad's writing on the front. MOVES, it says. I haven't seen this notebook in years. I'm not sure I've ever read it properly. I flip it open and it's full of diagrams, but more than that. Notes about me, Mason, Sam, Blue Feather . . . all of us who were in Little Wrestlers.

JO, it says, CAN'T ASSESS OPPONENT.

I gasp and lean back against the bed. It's like my dad saw right into my soul and figured out my fatal flaw when I was ten years old.

There's a knock at my door and I scramble to put the box back up in the closet like I'm guilty of something.

"Yeah?" I say.

"Can I come in?" Kevin knocks again. Two short raps and then a pause and one more. "Hello?" Kevin does this on the rare occasion when he comes up here, like he thinks I'm always naked when I'm in my room alone.

"Come in," I say.

"I thought this might be a little better," he says. He presents me with a bowl of salad. His faded crab tattoo peeks out from under his cotton shirt. There's good stuff in it like peas and onions and some broccoli and the marinated chicken breast we always have in the fridge. I'll admit Kevin makes the best dressings around too.

"Thanks," I say. Kevin's too nice to be real. I want to tell him to run, that I'm a mutant.

"You okay?" he says.

"Yeah. I'm just tired."

"Okay, then." He makes to leave but then turns around, looking at me with an expression that's hard to pinpoint. "You know you can always talk to me if you need to, right?"

He doesn't wait for me to say anything back, and I'm grateful for that.

After I've finished eating, I sit at my desk, open the green notebook, and read.

CHAPTER ELEVEN

First thing I see when I walk into the Littleton gym is Leah holding a sign over her head that she waves about wildly as I enter with the rest of the Sentinels. Brenda and Ralph are next to her too. I can't believe they're actually here. Most of the parents from Coyote Valley are here and they make some noise, but nothing as intense as the boos coming from all around us. This is not our home turf. Brenda looks squirrelly as hell and like she needs a smoke real bad. Her blond hair's piled like soft-serve ice cream on top of her head. I want to run up and give them some hugs and kisses but I'm too out-of-body right now.

The lights are bright in the gym and it's so loud I can't hear myself think. Outside the high windows hangs a stark gray sky, as flat as I'm about to be on the mat.

A bunch of the Sentinels are about as far away from me as they can get and still claim to be on the same team, so I'm saved by Sam and Barney, who hover on either side of me. I force my hands to my side, worrying the leg of my shorts.

"Okay there, Beckett?" Sam says. He seems almost as nervous as me.

"Oh, yeah," I say. "Peachy AF."

Barney puffs out his chest and presents his shoulder. "You can lean on me if you need to."

"Man, she does not need to be leaning on anyone," Sam says. "She needs to do some power posing, positive affirmations, whatever it takes for her not to pussy out right now."

"Sam!" I scold. "The vagina is powerful."

"I'm insulted on behalf of the female sex," Barney agrees. "Or gender. Whichever works as the case demands."

"Dude, you can't be personally offended about something you can't even relate to," Sam says across me.

"What?" Barney says. "I've been oppressed. You think I haven't been picked on for my slender physique? I understand being dissected and judged."

"Is this really what we need to be talking about right now?" Sam edges in even closer. "We should be focusing on us."

They probably have no idea how happy they've made me. I almost forgot for half a second how totally screwed I am. The high school jumbotron across from us lights up and the match order is announced. Sam is up first and his name flashes across the screen.

"Sam." I tap his shoulder and he stops arguing with Barney and glances over.

He's wrestling Dax Furlong, who I automatically search for and find bumping fists with a super-attractive Asian girl with a septum piercing and baggy pants. He doesn't look the least bit nervous, has that gleaming open smile glued on.

I squeeze Sam's shoulder so he'll know I'm here for him. Everything but this falls away. The match between Sam and Dax was so close at finals and this is the first time they've seen each other on the mat since. Friendly game of pool and the fact that it's the beginning of the season notwith-standing, for Sam this is war. It's everything.

He takes a couple of deep breaths then exhales fast and jumps up and down. I'm not the only one who's nervous.

"You're going to totally kick his ass," I say.

"*Please welcome to the mat, Sam Sloane and Dax Furlong!*" the voice calls over the loudspeaker. Coach takes Sam by the shoulder, talking in his ear as they head over to the mat.

The crowd goes absolutely ballistic screaming Dax's name.

"Sam!" I yell, but my voice gets lost in the din. I'm right behind him so he knows he has my support.

Sam doesn't need me though. As I try to get his attention to let him know I'm here for him I spot Jen in the bleachers with his parents. She's beaming at him.

Right.

She beams at him because she's his girlfriend and that's what they're supposed to do.

I've done an excellent, professional job of compartmentalizing since the other night in the gym with Sam, but I can't now. I can't get the image of our chests touching, of our lips almost grazing, out of my mind.

The gym gets really quiet. You can hear people breathing. Even the parents at the concession stand are focused.

There's a pause as both boys get ready, Dax's black hair poking through his head gear in tufts. He's bent over doing some stretches, making silly faces, hamming it up for the crowd when he catches sight of me. He pops straight up and blows me a kiss.

The crowd goes bananas and the gym fills with the sounds of hooting and hollering. I flip Dax the bird, which may or may not be considered poor sportsmanship, but he only grins in response.

Who does he think he is?

Now he and Sam are in it. They shake and the bell sounds. They circle each other for a solid five seconds before Dax tries to go in for a single. Sam sprawls, pushing Dax's head into the mat before spinning around him for a takedown, then driving him to his back. Dax arches his back to prevent getting pinned. Sam sinks the reverse half, slowly lifting Dax's head, forcing his shoulder blades to the mat. The ref slaps the mat to confirm the pin.

That's it. Done. Epic.

My mouth is wide open.

Like, dropped.

I've seen Sam do some cool shit in my time but that pretty much takes it. That was a sweeping, *decided* victory. Like, I'm feeling a little sorry for Dax right now.

Dax, on the other hand, seems just fine. He congratulates Sam, then goes back to his team and sits on the bench after bowing several times while his teammates give him a hard time.

The next match flashes on the screen.

It's me and some guy named Chad Collier. I remember this kid from last year. He has greasy, blondish-brown hair, bird eyes spread far apart, and a nose that pushes off his face like a hawk's. He's skinny and mean as hell. I wouldn't be surprised if he pulled out some brass knuckles at the last second or stabbed me with Wolverine claws during the match.

He's only in tenth grade, he's only in tenth grade, he's only in tenth grade.

My mantra is not helping.

Sam comes off the mat, sweaty and beaming, and pulls me into a tight hug. Over his shoulder Jen's face goes sideways, her expression sour.

"You did it!" I pull away, give him a pat on the back.

"Yes," Sam says. "Victory! I didn't want it to be close and it wasn't. Had to get last year's curse off me." He puts a hand on either cheek to force eye contact. He brings his face close to mine. I wish I couldn't see over his shoulder. "Hey, now it's about you and only you. I want you to go out there and do your best. This Chad asshole deserves everything you give him."

"I'm going to get my ass kicked," I tell him. "I'm not ready."

"Yeah," Sam agrees, transferring his hands to my shoulders. "You probably aren't. But this is the first of many times you'll have on the mat in front of these people. So give them a show and don't go down easy. And remember, 'Heart wins.'"

Coach signals to me from the side. When I get to him, he looks up from his notes.

"You needed something?" I say, all jitters.

"Yeah. All you need from today is to know you did your best. That's it. If you win, great. If you don't, that's great too. Remember, no one woke up one day knowing how to wrestle and it's been a long time for you. But you can do this."

I'm grateful he doesn't mention how I've been doing at practice or anything about the doubts that keep pushing through the back of my mind, about whether there really is something to the idea that girls simply can't beat boys once they've gone through puberty. Boys have the upper-body strength, a muscular advantage. I hear my dad say wrestling is about being quick, limber, and smart.

I nod, then step onto the mat and the referee tries to keep a calm expression, but the intensity's ratcheting up. I'm running through drills, trying to keep my breathing steady, not looking at the crowd. Chad steps on and an odd hush falls over the crowd.

Buzz and Santi watch from the corner with the rest of the team. Ty looks more petulant than the rest of them, deliberately drilling his eyes into the space in front of him, hands locked at the knuckles. I'm glad he's the last thing I see before the ref tells us to shake because I am filled with rage at the sight of him. I remember how I opened myself up to him. And how much of a joke it was to him.

She's just a practice girl.

Hell no.

Hell no.

I go to shake Chad's hand and he holds it out limp and snarls, "Go somewhere else to prove your point, like the bathroom to change your maxi pad."

My eyes skitter to the ref but he seems oblivious and it's unclear to me whether or not he heard.

"Go Jo, go Jo, go Jo!" It's only a few people, but I hear them, Brenda and Ralph, Leah and Sam. A few more people jump on the bandwagon as the bell rings, but even with the way Brenda can throw her voice, the sound of hisses quickly rises up and swallows them.

It really pisses me off.

I go in hard. I may suck and I may not be ready, but I'm not going out like a punk. I try to get him in a fireman's carry but he spins me around and I'm on my back almost immediately, staring at the ceiling, trying to figure out how I got pinned in less than ten seconds.

The ref slaps the mat.

Just like that, the ref is raising Chad's arm to indicate his victory to the crowd. It's over.

My back stings and then I'm up and moving off the mat so they can get it ready for the next match.

"You did great!" Sam says, hugging me.

"Yes, solid job going in at his legs like that," Coach Garcia says. "You didn't freeze and you didn't stall. That's saying a lot for your first match."

"Yeah?" I say.

"Absolutely," Sam says. "I'm going to go check in with Jen, but great job. Seriously. Really great." He pats me on the back before taking off.

The rest of my team is sitting there, ignoring me. They don't say anything at all. Ty keeps studying the floor. Mason focuses on his Rubik's Cube.

Coach Garcia makes a sucking noise and shakes his head. I have a feeling there's going to be more about this later on, probably lectures about teamwork in the locker room, but right now he has other things to think about.

I jump when I feel a hand on my back, and when I turn around it's Dax.

"Shit, sorry. I didn't mean to startle you," he says.

"What is it with you and traipsing all over enemy territory?" I say, annoyed that he touched me.

"Oh, come on. You guys always beat me so it's practically a walk of shame."

Dax is incredibly good-looking in a goofy way.

That sounds wrong.

The last time I saw him, aka The Worst Night of My Life, he looked sort of done up or something. Now his hair shoots goofily in all directions and I can see a bunch of little moles on his shoulders, which are larger than they appear in a shirt, which I had forgotten until now.

"So you got through your first match."

"Yeah," I say. "Speaking of walks of shame."

"Why would you talk about your fierce performance like that?"

"Fierce." I sputter and snort.

"Scoff if you want but we were both out in ten seconds. You were truly stupendous out there. You know how many people have been wrestling for years and keep to the corners as long as they can?"

I know he's right. I didn't even think to do that. Not the way Ty was looking at me.

"You earned street cred. Forty points. Level up. Anyway, just came over here to tell you great job, Jo."

He remembered my name.

"All your practice paid off and now everyone's talking about you."

Practice?

A tide of emotion rises up and claws at my chest and I try to push down the sudden burst of shame. I can't think clearly. I wonder what he's heard about me. In a panic, my mind scrambles, sure that he's over here talking to me because he knows I have sex with wrestlers and am an easy mark.

"Have a good one," I manage to say as I start to walk away.

In my peripheral vision, Ty and Mason are openly staring.

"Did I say something—" He trails after me uncertainly.

"Everyone's talking about me?" I snap. "What does that mean?"

He looks around and sweeps across the gym. "Uh, you're the only girl here today in a wrestling capacity? Did you not know gums were flapping?"

"Oh, I knew." I grab my water bottle angrily and take a healthy swig. "I knew all right."

"I came over here to tell you I think you did great and to shake hands as double losers, but I'm getting the feeling there's something going on in your head that I have absolutely no idea about."

I credit him for not accusing me of being on my period. "It's been a stressful few weeks."

"I get it," he says.

"No, you don't."

"Okay," he says. "Are you good?"

"I'm fine!"

The next match starts nearby and I don't pay attention.

Dax looks at me uncertainly.

"Do you need something?" I ask.

"Uh . . . yeah. So, I know I'm wearing this extremely attractive outfit at the moment, but I was wondering if I could get your number or your Snapchat or IG? Name your preferred form of contact." I can't assess whether or not this is a joke. "I mean, I don't need *all* of them . . . that would be excessive." He looks down, then back up, meets my eyes. Not a joke. "One point of contact would be good though."

My stomach somersaults, and I force eye contact with him. I'm not sure of him and even if I was, this beast I currently am is not about to start dating a major competitor while I'm trying to do something that requires utter focus on my part.

"I thought we could hang out or something . . . sometime," he presses.

Images of myself giggling at Ty, of my head getting pressed downward in that movie theater with Lucas play like a reel. "You want to hang out with me?" I say, trying to get control of myself. I can't make sense of it. If Dax wants to hang out with me that must mean everyone in the entire Denver metropolitan area has heard I'm a practice girl.

"Yeah." He grins. "I only hang with incredibly impressive female wrestlers you know."

That's when I remember. I'm not the only one with a reputation that may or may not precede me. Dax has one too. Last year when he was being such a dick to Sam, Sam told me Dax has literally slept with everyone at his school. He's a total girlanizer.

"I can't," I say. I wish I had some kind of snappy comeback or ironically witty thing to say, but right now it's hard enough to get my breath under control.

Can he see my hands shaking?

"Cool," he says, disappointment wringing his features. "Hey, it's okay. No pressure, I swear. I just thought I'd ask."

I look at him for signs of a joke, of some deeper knowledge, of a trick, but he only wrinkles his brow and then smiles. "But so you know, you really did look totally badass out there today." He eyes the bench. "Don't let the tiny pricks on your team make you feel otherwise." He waves to Mason aggressively. Mason flips him off. "Huh," he says. "Interesting. Is that like a team hand signal or something?"

That makes me smile and the gargoyle that has possessed me for the last few minutes relaxes and gets out of striking position.

"I'll see you, Jo," he says.

"Yeah."

I watch him walk away, thinking several things at once: He didn't call me a bitch or ask me if I thought I was too good to give him my information, which is what usually happens when I politely decline. He seemed genuinely saddened that I said no but took it at face value, thereby having actually listened to what I said, and he left me with a compliment that's making me feel a little tingly in the belly button.

I allow the fleeting thought that Dax Furlong might, in fact, be a real person, then I shove it back where it belongs, deep in the netherworld of my subconscious. I look over to the bleachers for Leah, and instead, I catch Sam's gaze, and it's intense enough to make me avert my eyes.

CHAPTER TWELVE

The next morning, Leah and I meet at We All Scream for Ice Cream in the strip mall by the school. In order to be more accurate, I should say I hobbled into my car and then moaned every time I had to hit the brakes. Also possibly whimpered. This is due to the fact that when I woke up I discovered I can no longer walk properly. I've grown used to being sore, but this is a new level. Something about clenching everything at once as though your life depends on it while someone flips you like a Parisian crepe does different, experimental things to your muscles.

Meeting Leah here is like a first date. I paid attention to my clothes, made sure to apply concealer and a little highlighter, and put my hair in low pigtails and a ladybug barrette. And this is the first time other than yesterday and a couple of awkward hallway moments that we've seen each other outside of 66. She continues to hang out with Jen and Amber, and I continue to loathe them for their mere existence. But what I would usually do on a Sunday morning, i.e., hang out with Sam in some form or fashion, doesn't feel right after our maybe-perhaps-near make-out session the other night or the long, intense hug yesterday. Rather than entering into yet another surreal situation with him, I've elected to step into this one, which, while no less surreal, is a little less uncomfortable right now.

The place is pretty empty except for people coming in from church to get a cone, such as Leah. Hence, the timing. Once we get our ice cream, Leah leads us to a round table set off to the side. I'm so excited for my scoop I don't care where we are. She's her usual put-together self but the conservative church version: lighter mascara, lighter lipstick, black shoes. Me? I'm in my saggy jeans and a T-shirt and I'm looking more forward to this than I have anything in a long time. I'm so sick of smoothies. Also, take your steamed greens and shove them high and hard. I've been so measured and careful and soft serve with hot fudge is my favorite and I make sure they don't skimp on the whipped cream either.

"Don't you wish they had table service in here?" she says, licking at her chocolate hazelnut sugar cone. "It'd be nice to be the one getting served, right?"

"Totally. Maybe we should go into Denver and get lunch sometime. Like, if you ever come back to one of the meets down there." I pause and force the words from my lips. "Hey, Leah," I say.

"Yeah?"

"I just wanted to say thank you for being there for me yesterday. You didn't have to do that."

She waves me off.

"You and Ralph and Brenda are the only ones who showed up."

"I bet it wouldn't have been easy to deal with all those boys by yourself," she says crisply, "and I know that historically speaking your mom isn't exactly active in your wrestling life."

"But you came all that way just for me. Right?"

"This week's snowpocalypse wrecked my riding plans." We both pause for more ice cream. "What else was I going to do? Stay in pj's and watch Netflix all day? No thank you. Not this girl. Anyway, if you don't stop making everything so heavy every time we see each other I'm going to start avoiding you again."

"Heavy is my brand." I give her a scowl.

"I'm kidding." She nudges me with her shoulder, right in a bruise that has been developing since yesterday. I try not to wince. "You totally killed it, by the way."

"Why is everyone trying to give me a participation trophy? It's embarrassing. I was thoroughly stomped."

"No, you weren't. You gave him a little bit of a challenge."

"Only because I didn't just roll over and beg for belly rubs when the match started."

"I don't know," she says. "That's not what it looked like from where I was sitting. Anyway, that's not why I asked you to come here."

"Ulterior motives. I knew there had to be some reason you drove all that way and sat in that stinky gym all day."

"I'm offended," she says. "I just have a teeny favor to ask you."

"Spit it out. What do you need me to do? Wash your car? Like an Instagram post?"

"No. I was thinking maybe you could join the dance committee."

I actually stop everything. I almost forget I could potentially scrape a last bite of vanilla/fudge mixture out of this poor, abused cup I'm holding. I'm sure I look completely confused because she bursts out laughing.

I join her, laughing along with her. "I knew you were kidding."

She puts a hand on my arm. "I'm not kidding at all, but the look on your face is amazing."

"Wait, you're being serious right now? You want me to join the *dance* committee? Leah, my dude . . ."

"Hear me out, please." She puts her half-eaten cone into my empty cup and leans forward. "I know you look down on that stuff."

"I don't know if I look *down* on it. I haven't been to a dance since eighth grade—"

"Precisely, and you're running out of dances. Don't you want the school experience? To be on a committee?"

"I've literally never even thought about this."

"So think about it now. It would be a personal favor to me. Also, if you don't do it, Casey Bennington will, and every time words come out of her mouth I feel like a piece of my soul dies."

I am the girl that ladies on dance committees flee from out of fear that whatever I am will rub off on them. And you know what? I don't mind that at all. Plus it occurs to me that there's a high probability that Jen and Amber are involved, and after the look Jen was giving me yesterday I don't think I need to be around her any more than necessary.

"I'm too busy, and with school and practice and work I don't think it's a good idea."

"Let me ask you this: What does your social life currently consist of, now that you're not hanging out in jock hell?"

My life looks like this: wake up, practice, school, practice, sometimes work, bed. There's been no Sam, no nothing.

I don't have to answer her.

"That's what I thought." She leans forward, chest grazing the table. "Also, it's like five or six hours total and it would give us a chance to hang out again."

I don't hate the idea of hanging out with Leah again, but this is a bridge too far. I know my place and it may be on a mat when no one else thinks so, but it's not on any dance committee.

"Oh, I see." She wipes the crumbs from her cone off her pants. It's clear I am the crumbs.

"What do you see?"

"You're too cool to cut out paper hearts?"

"Leah. I did not say that."

"You hate pink."

"Not anymore. I've grown as a person—"

"You don't want to be friends with me?" Something in her tone stops me from any further protest. She said it like it was a joke but there's something behind it, some deeper hurt. "Because I'm definitely too cool to go to wrestling meets instead of Netflixing. And yet . . ." She makes a flourishing motion with her hand.

"All right, the emotional blackmail is unnecessary."

She gives me a flat, triumphant smile and leans back.

"But," I say, "there's a caveat. I'm super busy so I might not be able to do all the things. I'll help when I can."

She lets out a little whoop.

"And," I insert, "if Jen and Amber are heinous beasts, I'm out."

"Sure."

"I mean it."

"Yeah," she says. "Okay, I get it."

I've really been enjoying hanging out with her even though we're from two different planets sometimes. There's something about her exuberance and utter lack of interest in guys that's still a decent counterpoint to my internal darkness. With Leah, it's like being with someone who has a totally different vision of the world than me, and it's . . . nice.

Maybe it won't be so bad after all.

"Yay! I knew you would say yes. There'll be glitter bombs and tracing and coloring, and you know I'm going to get a horse in there somewhere! Aren't you so excited?" She looks over my shoulder. "Oh, look!" She waves. "Amber and Jen are here."

"Here? Now?" I sputter. I need more time to mentally prepare for this, but sure enough when I turn around, Jen and Amber are getting out of Amber's Toyota, which is somehow shiny in spite of the recent storm. "You ambushed me. I've been had! Bamboozled!"

"Okay, drama."

Jen pulls a box from the back of Amber's car.

"What is that?" I say, panic rising.

Whatever it is glints in her arms.

"Supplies." Leah frowns at me. "Oh, come on. No time like the present to get over your bullshit." She waves them over to the table.

Amber motions to the line, letting us know she's going to get a cone. Jen follows her, not even looking my way.

Meanwhile, I'm trying really hard to pull it together, to think of Jen without Sam and Amber without Ty.

"Be your best self," Leah suggests.

"Um," I manage, my only protest. There's really nothing left to say. I eye my car outside in the parking lot and consider the various consequences of fleeing vs. those of staying here and dealing with whatever social dynamics are about to turn my day into a dumpster fire. What would actually happen if, high on the power of fudge, I vaulted over

Leah's head and straight through the window, thereby escaping whatever is about to happen to me?

"We need to get started. Time's a-wastin'."

"Leah."

"Jo. I know it's been a lot, but please trust me. Please." She smiles, then reaches across the table and squeezes my hand, so tightly I can't run away.

CHAPTER THIRTEEN

"Can I get everyone's attention?" Miss Pike calls across the room. She's a tall, lanky, white woman who seems too young and too pretty to be a teacher, and who is passionate about helping us to be good leaders. I am not in the mood to lead.

I want to crawl under my desk in the fetal position. It has been the longest day. My combination of insomnia and grueling morning workout has left me feeling more like a zombie than usual and now I need to go to practice again.

We've been working with partners for the last hour. Since we're seniors we all have to do a final project that shows we're involved in our community. Sam and I got paired up and we've decided to work at the Stray Hearts shelter and to collect donations of pet supplies from the school. It hasn't been weird so far, but I'm not quite comfortable.

"Everyone is required to put in thirty hours before the end of next semester and must make a video journal about the experience," Miss Pike says. "In a few weeks you'll be presenting the beginning of your process to the class along with a self-assessment of your projected positive impact on the community. Given our class size, I think we can do good things, even in relatively low numbers."

I could not be more delighted. Even though my mom's mission in life is to fulfill her white middle-class fantasy of a happy home life in suburbia, she has never liked pets of any kind, wouldn't even hear of getting me a golden retriever. Dad said he was too busy when he moved out, so I've been bereft of animal companionship. Same with Sam. Ollie goes everywhere with his parents but is definitely a fishing dog and stuck to Sam's dad like superglue.

"I can't wait to roll in a pile of puppies," Sam says as we leave class.

"And to pet kittens."

"And feed them and love them and hold them."

"I saw on social that Stray Hearts found ten puppies in a dumpster."

"Yeah," Sam says. "They need some extra love for sure. People are awful."

Leadership is our last class of the day so we start walking together since we're both heading to the gym. We stop when we get to our lockers. All that's normal but it feels tense. It's hard to believe how much difference a month has made, how much distance it's put between us.

"So when do you want to go over there?" Sam gives me a side-eye. "They said we need to schedule an orientation so we can see how the shelter works and everything. We don't have practice tomorrow, so how about after school?" He smirks heartily.

"Why, no, Sam, I can't go tomorrow after school."

"Whyever not?" The smirk, impossibly, is growing.

"Because I have a dance planning committee meeting." The words stick in my mouth, mostly because I know how much shit I'm about to get. "With Jen and Amber and Leah."

Sam points at me accusatorily. "Ha! So it's true what they say. Jo Beckett has defected, she's morphed into something unrecognizable and terrifying . . . a high school committee planner!"

I shove him lightly. "Shut your dirty mouth. Your girlfriend is part of that crew."

"Oh, I'm well aware," he says. "I know all about active school participation and event organizing."

"Don't be jerky." I bristle. "It's how things actually get done."

He looks over, surprised. "I know. I just never imagined you doing it. Doesn't seem like you. I don't remember ever seeing you at a school event that didn't involve wrestling." He slaps his locker shut. "I just want to make sure you're not concussed or something, that you didn't suffer a worrying blow to the head on Saturday."

The match comes back to me in a blur of overexposed color and humiliation. The smell of sweat and fear, the feeling of getting winged onto my back by Chad, the embarrassing but intriguing conversation with Dax, the bad vibes from Jen, Leah and her sign. I don't know why I'm doing any of this. Maybe because the alternative is home with Kevin and Tiffany while Mom whales on her Peloton.

"So was it the worst thing ever?" Sam says.

"Awkward at first, I guess," I say. "Definitely not ideal. But it wasn't as bad as I thought. You know, Leah's been cool lately and she asked me to do it. Well," I amend, thinking of the unexpected turn of events at the ice-cream shop, "she did ambush me a little. But it turned out okay."

"Seriously? How many fingers am I holding up?" Sam says. "Do I need to get you to a hospital?"

His joke is starting to piss me off. I imagine Jen going to his house after ice cream, telling him how bad I am at planning and/or being the kind of person who hangs out with girls. The truth is I was a little baffled

about some of the conversation they were having in between coming up
with ideas since I don't really know most of the kids at school and they
seem to know everything about everyone. It made me realize how much
of a bubble I've been in and what it might be like to actually be interested
in what other people are doing.

"What did Jen say?" I ask. "Was she talking about me or something?"

"No! Nothing! She didn't say a word!"

"Nothing at all?"

"Nope."

"She must have said something."

"No, seriously, she just mentioned that you met up. I straight-up
thought she was kidding at first but that's cool if you and Leah are hanging again. I can't wait to see you putting up streamers, Josephine."

"Speaking of Jen, where is she? Doesn't she usually show up for your
after-school make-out sesh?" In actual fact, they used to be seen daily
sucking face by the pillars out front between school and practice, but I
haven't seen her out here lately.

Sam flinches and pulls a string cheese out of his bag. He offers it to me
and when I shake my head and wave him off he tears into it.

"Jen and I haven't been hanging out as much as usual, lately."

"I'm sorry," I say.

"No, it's okay. She's super busy running the school, and with wrestling
and everything else . . . I don't know . . . it's not like it was. Things are
changing for me."

He meets my eyes and then quickly looks away and something starts
thumping frantically under my sternum. Again I think of the long hug
with Sam at practice, about the look on Jen's face from across the room

at the meet. I've never understood her low-grade hostility or the way she thought my friendship with Sam was so annoying, but now suddenly I do.

If I could speak to Sam honestly, like I used to, I would tell him how cool it is that Jen eventually warmed up to me while we were planning the dance. After about twenty minutes of discussing possible themes, Jen stopped talking to me like everything I was saying was some kind of attack on her and her planet of girly girls and I could kind of see why Sam loves her.

Lie.

I've always been able to see why Sam loves her.

I don't know if I could have been as understanding and mature as her if my boyfriend was flirting with his supposed best friend right in front of me, or if he always made me second, or if he laughed more easily with someone other than me, someone who thought she was one of the guys.

Even though I'm mildly blinded to boys and their ultimate intentions with me, I do think I know when someone's flirting with me. And why can't Sam meet my eyes?

"I didn't know there was trouble in paradise."

"Not trouble," he says, "just changes."

"Sam," I say earnestly.

"What?" He looks worried.

"I've been meaning to talk to you about some physical changes that may occur in these teen years. You see, son, it's called puberty. You may begin to see changes in your body, hair may appear—"

Sam cracks a smile. "You're playing with fire messing with me. I'm about to run your workout, remember?"

"I shudder inside," I grab my shoulders and chatter my teeth.

I'm grateful the serious moment with Sam is over. While we've always had depth to our friendship and I would tell him almost anything, it's nice to have it back on a level I can comprehend. Plus, even though I'm already wrecked, I do feel like I need to work out extra hard. I don't ever want to be in another situation like the meet on Saturday again. I don't mind losing, but I don't want to be that easy to lay out.

"Bring it," I say.

"Hey," he says, shifting his gym bag from left to right. "After we finish working out maybe we can go up to the Peak and check out the stars or something . . . if you want to."

When I first got my car we used to go there all the time. It's this one spot above town where you can see all the lights, few though they may be, and you get the clearest, most star-filled skies.

"Yeah," I say. I want so badly to go back to being Sam and me, the one place I ever felt totally right. "Let's do it."

―――――――

As we lift weights and do squats, we talk through what happened on Saturday. I'm probably never going to win on strength, even in my weight category. Guys have more upper-body strength than girls and more muscle mass in general and now that I'm lean the key is going to be to build muscle strategically and then practice the sneakiest moves possible, along with speed. I need some of whatever Barney has going on, a little unpredictability and a whole lot of tricks up my sleeve.

I can also learn as much about my opponents as possible. Like Sam pointed out, he learned from his mistake with Dax and that Dax's goofiness is just a front for a really high level of skill. He won't underestimate him again and thanks to the Rockets YouTube channel and the high school website he has been able to study him, which is why he decimated him so easily on Saturday. Preparation, he says, is the key to winning. That and being ready for anything.

When we get up to the Peak, Sam grabs the blanket I always keep in the back of my car. It's a habit to keep the same kit my dad always had in his trunk. Firewood, emergency blanket, extinguisher, flashlight, matches, Fix-a-Flat, and playing cards, plus a couple hoodies, gloves, and hats. You never know what'll come in handy if you break down on the side of the road somewhere in Colorado where there's potentially no cell service. I mean, read the news.

"Scoot in," he says when we're settled on the hood, blanket just out of my reach.

I'm purposely keeping a respectable distance from him but now he pats his chest and I lean on it obediently, relieved to be back in such a familiar spot.

"I'm glad you showered," I say.

"Irish Spring, baby."

I sniff at the air. "Maybe you should have showered twice."

We watch the sky for a bit and I tell myself that the way my pulse has sped up is indicative of nothing.

"Hey, Beck," he says.

"Hey, Sam."

"I think Coach would have been really proud of you."

"Garcia? I think he's had about enough of my antics. I'll probably never actually wrestle again."

"No, not Garcia. Your dad."

A lump invades my throat, fills it up, tries to escape it.

"Maybe. I hope so." I hesitate, thinking of the warm, haunted feeling I got when I was in my closet, like my dad was all around me. "I found a book of plays that he'd been keeping."

"No shit?" Sam says.

"No shit. It was in my closet up in this box where I kept all the notes he used to write me."

Sam gives me a little squeeze, which bolsters me enough to go on.

"But, I don't know . . . it was weird. There are all these notes about us."

"Us, like you and me?" Sam's body seems to come online, suddenly alert. Sam and wrestling. Wrestling and Sam. He wants more than anything to unlock the secrets to his own potential, wants a formula for it.

"Like all of us who have been together all this time. Me, you, Mase, Ty, Blue Feather . . . everyone."

"What did it say?"

"We were pretty little, right? So it's trippy, like a time capsule or something."

"I bet."

"It made me feel a little sad, actually."

"I know. It's sad he's gone. It's so sad what happened."

"But it's more than that."

"Yeah?"

"Yeah, like what has changed and what hasn't. He was talking about us as wrestlers but also just as human beings. And it made me think . . . maybe there isn't much difference between how you are on the mat and how you are in general."

"Meaning?"

"He said he thought my biggest problem was that I couldn't read my opponent. And then I started thinking maybe that's because I'm too focused on myself and what my opponent—"

"Or guy—"

"Or guy. I can't read my opponent because I'm too focused on what they're thinking about me. But like, what do *I* think? Does he have the qualities I actually want in a person?"

"So we're not talking about wrestling anymore." Sam squeezes me.

"But seriously. Maybe if he had just told me that I'm blind to what everyone else can see it would have saved me some trouble."

"Yeah," Sam says. "I think a lot of things would have been different if he was here."

There's a warm but dense ball forming in my chest. "My entire sexual history would be erased. No one would ever have slept with me if he was around. They'd have been too scared."

"Yeah," Sam agrees. "Of his very lengthy and emotional lectures."

We both laugh a little at that, and I have visions of him sitting on his desk, leaned over some poor soul, dispensing wisdom while the kid tried to disappear into the chair.

"What did he say was my wrestling flaw?" Sam asks after a minute.

Ambivalence.

"You?" I look up at the sky, all those stars. "He said you were perfect."

Sam chuckles. "And you?"

"Me what?"

The endorphins from my workout are wearing off now and they've left a pleasant exhaustion in their wake. It's so peaceful up here without any cars and no way to reach the outside world. It's crisp and cold but I'm snug in the crook of Sam's arm, which he shifts now to pull me in closer.

"Do you think I'm perfect?"

"Nah, you're not perfect," I say. "You're just right."

"You say the sweetest things," he says, drawing me closer still.

I allow myself to lean into him, only vague thoughts of Jen and how she would feel if she were here filtering through. It feels so good to be warm on a cold night, safe with Sam again, not thinking overmuch about the practice girl thing and how he may not be the friend I thought he was. We all make mistakes. We all fail sometimes. Sam and I will be friends for life and that means mistakes will be made. Again I think of my dad's note and feel myself rolling off the tracks of my own thoughts. *Can't assess opponent.*

Oh, Dad, if you only knew.

I can't even assess if someone is an opponent in the first place.

CHAPTER FOURTEEN

We're currently in the bearded dragon section of Petco, shopping for my leadership project.

By "we" I mean my mom and me, and of course, Tiffany.

All things would have been simpler had Mom listened to me and let me come alone. For one thing, Tiffany could have stayed at home instead of being here standing in the cart, begging Mom for literally every animal she sees followed by every treat for every animal she sees.

But Mom wanted us to "spend time together" and she also wanted to "contribute" so here we are, Tiffany causing an absolute ruckus while I try to steer us toward the cat food and dog bones.

This is not working.

Mom is texting, holding up one finger, telling me to wait for her to finish before I say another word. There's some real estate staging thing she has to do and she's stressed out by people who keep sending her texts about it, which she apparently can't wait ten minutes to answer.

Finally she looks up, everything about her on edge. Other than the zombie-suburban-wife version of my mom, this is my least favorite. She holds onto her phone and pushes the cart, eyes darting from the outside world to the one she's clearly occupying on the inside.

"Mom," I plead. At this rate, we're going to spend all weekend in here. The cloud of guilt hits her like a summer rainstorm.

"I'm sorry," she says. "This is just a really big opportunity for me and I don't want to mess it up. But what does that matter?" She shoves her phone in her pocket. It begins buzzing immediately. "This is supposed to be our time together . . ."

"Mom, look at that one! Let's take him home and name him Lucifer." Tiffany points to a mighty handsome ball python who slithers toward her and seems to be waiting for her to pick him up. Her hair is in pigtails brushed tight off her face, and she has a plastic tiara wedged across her forehead. With the adoring gaze she's giving the snake, I wouldn't at all be surprised if she busted into Parseltongue.

The Petco reptile guy stands by, long and loose-jointed himself, at the ready, excited to open the tank. My mom shakes her head at him and he wanders away, disappointed.

"I don't know where she's getting this stuff," Mom says. "Lucifer?"

"TikTok," I answer. "May I suggest parental controls?"

"Okay!" Mom straightens. "Let's go get some supplies for all those needy doggies and kitties."

Her phone bleeps and bloops. "Honey—"

"It's cool," I say. "Answer." I want to be resentful but she looks so miserable I can't muster it. All the hairs on her head seem individually frayed and out of order. "Go deal with your thing. I'll take Tiff and meet you back here in ten."

She squeezes my wrist. "Okay." She looks around. "But can we meet near the front register?" She eyes Tiffany warily and lowers her voice. "I think she really wants a snake so let's keep her out of this area."

"I do want a snake!" Tiffany says. "And also a puppy."

"Or just some Honey Nut Cheerios and a seat for your butt." I take the cart from Mom.

Tiffany scowls at me but sits. She and I both know she's really too old to be in the cart and if she argues with me she's going to be walking at my personal choice of pace.

"Here." I hand her the portable snack cup filled with Cheerios and her juice and we trundle across the store. Tiffany is a pretty good kid, but when she's with Mom she becomes a total asshole.

"You stalking me?" I hear from behind me.

There stands Dax Furlong, hands in his pockets, blue Petco T-shirt on.

Tiffany looks up, distracted from her efforts at pulling Cheerios out of her spillproof cup.

My heart immediately starts racing. "You're the one who keeps sneaking up behind me," I say. I definitely had a little bit of an emotional meltdown the last time we saw each other. I'm pretty sure he asked me out and I reacted very badly.

"So what brings you all this way?" he says.

"There's no Petco in Coyote Valley. Lest you forget, there is naught but a coffee shop, ice cream, and a diner."

"Why are you talking like that?" Leave it to Tiffany to point out that I'm about two octaves above normal.

I give her a warning look.

"And who's this?" Dax says, peering around me to Tiff.

"I'm Tiffany." Tiff points to herself. "That's Jojo."

"Jojo, eh?" he says. "I like that. It suits you." He extends a hand to Tiff who wipes her sticky one on her shirt before grinning heavily and shaking his hand. "I'm Dax, a friend of your sister."

"Or her team's sworn enemy," I amend. "Too soon to tell."

"Oh, come on," he says. "After the sound thrashing I took on Saturday, I'm hardly a threat."

"Too early in the season to draw any hard and fast conclusions."

He nods, then stands there like he wouldn't mind hanging out in an aisle all day.

"So you work here?" I ask.

"I do."

I don't know why but I pictured him as another rich boy with a fancy car and a cleaning lady to do his bidding. Those kinds of guys usually don't work at Petco.

"And what brings you here this fine day? Cats? Dogs? Rabbits?" He looks at Tiff. "Hamster?"

"I'm getting a snake," Tiffany says.

I shake my head over hers.

"I'm going to name him Lucifer," she adds.

"Excellent," he says.

"You are not getting a snake at all," I tell her. I lean against the dog food shelf, then decide against it. I am the person who knocks everything down. "I'm doing a project for school, volunteering at the shelter in Coyote Valley. Mom wanted to donate supplies so . . ."

"How noble," he says.

It could be a sarcastic comment, but it's not.

Mom barrels around the corner like she's on wheels. She's practically out of breath as she moves me out of the way and takes hold of the cart.

"It's empty," she says, nearly hysterical. "I thought you would have this done by now."

"It's not empty," Tiff pipes up. "It has me!"

"I need to go," Mom says quickly. "You were supposed to be getting supplies."

"I ran into someone," I say, numbly realizing Dax is watching. "I'm sorry. Did something happen?"

"Yes. The Winters want to look at the house on Full Moon Court."

"The big one?"

"Yes! And their son is flying in later so they can only meet me in an hour and then . . ." She makes a defeated sound and throws up her hands. "If I can't do it then someone else will and then who knows what will happen."

"But—" I point to my empty cart.

"This is Dax!" Tiffany says.

Mom seems to realize someone else is present for the first time and her eyes move shiftily back and forth between us. "Dax?"

"Yeah," I say.

"Hi." He extends his hand. "It's a pleasure to meet you."

What even is he?

Mom's like a cat that's had its fur repeatedly stroked backward. "Nice to meet you," she says, eyes flitting to the front door.

Dax puts his hand in his pocket.

"Jo!" she says. "We have to go. Right now."

I didn't expect her to spend super quality time or anything but this still sends a lurch of disappointment through me. It's just so typical. The atypical part was coming here in the first place.

"I can give you a ride," Dax says. "My shift just ended. You could get what you need. No hurry."

"I usually have a car." I don't like having other people drive because then you're at the mercy of whatever they have going on.

"I'm sorry!" Mom flaps her arms in a hurrying motion.

"It's no problem. Plus I know my way around here pretty well," Dax says.

Mom's eyes flicker to his vest, connecting the dots. "I guess maybe—"

She pauses her frenzy long enough to look from me to Dax and back again. She takes a breath. "You know each other from school?"

"Dax is a wrestler," I say, like that answers her question in any way.

I assess him through her eyes—his wild black hair, his one crooked tooth.

"You're safe?" Mom says. "No weapons?"

"No, ma'am," he says.

"It's not going to ruin your day?"

"Not at all," he says.

"Okay, excellent." Mom reaches into her purse and pulls out a hundred-dollar bill. She shoves it at me. "Get what you need."

"Mom," I say, but I take the money.

"And you'll bring her home?" she says to Dax.

"Absolutely," Dax says.

"Okay. Should I get your number just in case?"

"Simmer down, Mother. We're good."

And just like that, she's blazing through the store with Tiffany cranking herself at a dangerous angle to watch Dax and me while shoving a lone Cheerio into her mouth.

It takes a second for the energy in the aisle to recover from Mom's madness. Mom, who just left me at Petco with Dax, a person I hardly know. Dad always said to pay attention to those kinds of signs—when a text gets bounced or social media won't post your picture, or when a person just keeps showing up . . . like it's fate.

Dax is already moving quickly to the carts stacked along the side of the store. He rolls one over and starts putting things into it. "It's a regular shelter, right? No big animals? Just cats and dogs?"

"Yeah," I say, grateful that he's broken the silence.

"Excellent." He grabs some trays of canned food. "This is good stuff and it's cheap so you get more for your dollar. Let's get them some snacks." He pulls some trainer treats and pig ears, then moves deftly to the cat aisle and continues slapping things into the cart, which is filling rapidly. He looks my way and then back to the shelf.

"Thanks for doing this when you're off work and probably don't want to hang out here anymore," I say. "Especially since you have to drive me twenty minutes out of your way."

"Twenty-five, actually, so let's round it up to an hour both ways."

"Oh, great."

"Kidding. It's no sweat."

"It's Saturday so you probably have all kinds of things going on—"

"I have nothing going on." He holds up two fluffy toys. "I'm hoping maybe you'll fix that. Bells or squeakers?"

"Squeakers mimic the sound of prey trying to escape." I'm trying to focus on the cats and dogs but did he just ask me out again? "I mean, not that that's a good thing," I amend.

"Squeakers it is." He turns to me. "Okay, that ought to do it."

The cart is now completely full.

"I only have the hundred," I say. I stupidly thought I'd be with Mom the whole time so I didn't even bring my wallet.

"*Only* have a hundred?"

"That's not what I meant. Just . . . that looks like more than a hundred is all."

"Oh, I pride myself on being able to do some serious pre-counting. Been practicing for years."

He rolls us to the front where a Native girl with dyed orange hair and a name tag that reads POLLEN is waiting at the cash register. "Hey," she drones with no inflection at all. "You getting out of this hellhole?" She begins scanning. *Beep. Beep. Beep.*

"Why would you call it that, P? We're surrounded by toys and treats for all our furry friends! Plus you get to operate a forklift."

"Does it hurt being that perky all the time, Dax?" the girl says. "Because my soul suffers from your brightness." She glances over at me. "Do you ever get sick of it?" She says this, but there's the glimmer of a smile under her grimace, a little light in her eyes.

"We don't—" he starts.

"I love it," I say.

The girl cocks an eyebrow and the nebulous smile intensifies.

"Nothing wrong with being happy."

Dax gives me a look that makes me feel naked, makes me want to clasp my hands over my chest, my face, to hide myself.

"That's ninety-eight forty-six," Pollen says.

"I am king!" Dax shouts, raising his hands into victorious fists. "And you can use the other dollar fifty-four to buy me a hot chocolate on the way home. Just kidding! Hot chocolate is five bucks," he says. "But if you have the time maybe we could stop and *I* could buy *you* one."

He *is* asking me out again, or at least to *hang* out. Maybe he knows my answer the other day was one born of stress or maybe he's persistent. I don't know. I run through all the things I have to do today: taking supplies to the shelter, my English paper, my workout, eating more steamed broccoli and sweet potato and (ugh) another chicken breast. It all fades into one gray "have to." And tonight? Nothing that I know of because even though Sam dropped the "things are changing with Jen" bomb and we had some time watching the stars, I haven't heard from him since. Leah will be with her horses and at 66, my family is what it is, and Kevin works weekends.

The seconds bend and weave between us and I search Dax for signs of knowing about the practice girl thing, of seeing me as an easy mark. My dad said my problem is that I can't assess my opponent, but I really don't know how anyone assesses anyone accurately. The truths and complications we hold inside us can't be known by another person. That's what makes being human so lonely. So I can't know what Dax is thinking, or who he really is. Not yet. I remember all the things I've heard about the long list of girls he's been with, the trail of broken hymens and broken hearts, and I cast them aside. We're talking hot chocolate. That's it. And maybe two people with fraught reputations can enjoy a warm beverage together without the world falling apart. Maybe, briefly, it will all be less lonely.

"Hot chocolate sounds good," I say.

Dax exhales like he's been holding his breath. "Yes!" he says and makes a little fist in the air and pumps it, then high-fives Pollen, who's been watching us while counting her drawer. "Yes. Best Saturday ever. Really." He grins widely.

I laugh because I can't help it and there's a hummingbird in my chest flapping, flapping.

We're in the Marshmallow Maven, which is a little coffee place along the highway between Denver and Coyote Valley. There's country music playing but the baristas are more rockabilly than new country and anyway the music is Johnny Cash, which can go either way. There are only a few tables made of dark, raw wood, but there's a long line to get one, so Dax and I get hot chocolate from the counter and wander outside to the bench. For a while we watch the traffic like it's TV.

"It's a nice day, right?" He breathes deeply. "Smells like winter."

"I hate winter. Wrestling is the only redeeming thing about it."

"What?" He clutches at his heart. "What about snowboarding? Candy canes? Snowmen? Come on!"

"Cold, cold, cold, and cold. I do like a candy cane though."

It's freezing today, but I don't mind right now. This place is cute and Dax is cute and for the moment I don't feel the weight of everything. He throws up his hood. Even though it's only early afternoon, the sky is darkening. The hot chocolate is rich and velvety with a satisfying, salty finish.

"Tell me something real," he says.

"Whoa, can I get a little foreplay?"

"All the foreplay you want."

My insides flop.

"I'm actually serious," he says. "I need you to start us off, because as you already know I'm very self-centered and if I start this conversation I will entirely dominate, whereas if you do I'll be able to listen and learn."

"Uh…thank you for your candor?"

"What? I'm working on myself and growing as a person daily."

I snort but his expression doesn't change. He's still watching me, waiting for my answer. "That's a lot of pressure," I say.

"Right? I know. Let's work through it, step-by-step."

"Something real, huh?" I say.

"Take your time. I know in this slapdash world of ours it's hard to think past all the plastic."

We both gaze back out to the highway where the cars are zooming and the billboard promises a bushy-haired lawyer will come to your aid if you get into a car accident on this road.

"I don't know who I am," I say, parting the air between us sharply. I take a sip of my hot chocolate and welcome the scalding.

"I get that," he says, after a minute. "There's so much noise."

"Exactly. So many billboards."

"Yeah."

"I feel like I'm going to explode all the time lately. Like I *need* to explode. I mean, look at this!" I open my free arm wide toward the animal smashed on the side of the road across from us, nothing but a splotch of black-and-white fur. "Everything is so brutal. Trying to be happy is brutal. Figuring out what the fuck to do in life is totally brutal. You think you have it figured out and then *bam*, you're roadkill."

"Okay, okay, I'm picking up what you're putting down. Existential crisis? A little early from what I understand, but I get it."

"Yeah, so that's my real."

He watches me for a second. "I may have a solution."

"Yeah?"

"Hot chocolate."

"Hot chocolate?"

"Yeah, and that." He points to a single pink wildflower growing out of the asphalt at our feet.

"You planned that," I say. "Over the top. On the nose."

"Mm-hmm," he agrees. "I went too far. Put it right there for this precise occasion when I'd be able to show you the world has beauty despite the pain, through the existence of a single flower."

"Man, you're cool," I say.

"You're right. I'm also super wise."

I take another sip of my hot chocolate and now my hands are as warm as my belly.

"But if you need to explode I have just the place," he says.

"Yeah? Can we break stuff?"

"Just our throats."

It's not far and this time it doesn't feel so strange to be in the car with him. I like his music and the way he asks me if I'm comfortable or if he should adjust the heat. I remember back to that first time I saw him when he beat Sam, how he seemed like such a doofus, hamming it up for the crowd. He pulls into a parking lot by an abandoned warehouse.

"Don't worry," he says when I give him a look. "It's not a meth lab or anything. Just far away enough from houses and other people." We get out and step over old bent nails and piles of broken concrete. "They supplied construction materials or something." He shrugs. "My dad used to work here. When I'd get pissed or sad he'd bring me out here and tell me to yell."

There are so many questions I want to ask him now. Where's his dad? Where does his dad work now? His car's kind of old. Where does he come from? Who is his family?

"So do it," he says.

"What?"

"Yell! You said you needed to explode. There is no better place for it."

The sky is a sheet of ice above us. I've always sort of had this sense that there's something up there, something is watching over us. I could yell at that, whatever it is.

"I'll go first." He smiles so joyfully at me I'm not expecting him to blast so hard when he yells. I blush, uncomfortable as his face contorts. It's animal and kind of scary, and then it's over. "Oh, yeah," he says when he's done, patting his belly like he just ate an amazing meal. "That felt great."

I almost go back to the car, get in, ask to go home. This is so stupid. I'm not standing in the middle of a warehouse parking lot and yelling at the universe. But then I look at Dax, his happy face and ridiculous grin, and I think, this is it. This is the secret to him being able to get in front of people and fail or win and not be affected. You have to be able to look a little stupid sometimes.

"Look away," I tell him.

"Seriously?"

"Yeah. Turn away."

Because it does feel like I'm getting naked, like if he's watching he'll see too much. It comes out more like a howl than a yell, and he's right. Something shakes loose as it echoes out into all the open space, and afterward I'm vibrating, free.

"Can I look now?" he asks, hands over his face.

"Yeah."

He beams, resting against the side of his car, and I skip over to him and hug him. It starts as a thank-you for showing me this place and taking me away from my regular life, but then his arms tighten and both of us are holding on so hard. I take a step back.

"You ready to go make some puppies happy?" he says, face flushed.

It takes me a second to realize he's talking about the food and treats in the back of his car. I pull myself together, get my brain back online. "You don't have to do this. You can take me home and I'll deal with it later."

"Ridiculous!" he says. "I will not rest until we see this through to its conclusion. You're going to have to give me directions though."

We get in the car. I'm shivering and my face is almost numb from the cold outside. As soon as he turns on the heat it begins to prickle. We thaw.

He moves the vents so they point in my direction and then says, "You're fun to hang out with."

"You too," I say truthfully. While this has been a super unexpected turn of events, I genuinely like Dax, and I like being surprised. "When I woke up this morning I had no idea I'd be yelling at a busted-up building site with my best friend's mortal enemy."

"Mortal enemy? Damn. I didn't know I had one of those." His eyebrows shoot up. "Wait, you mean Sam Sloane?"

I shrug.

"Aw, man, you were serious at the party? Because I was kidding. I don't give a shit about any of that. It's totally not how I was thinking about you. Or him. That's how you think about me? Sam's enemy? But . . . we played *pool*."

"I . . . no." It sounds so petty now. And silly. "I used to. You did almost beat Sam last year, which makes you a threat."

"Not currently." He smirks. "He took care of that last week, right? Who got destroyed?" He points to himself with both hands. "This guy."

I nod uncertainly.

He checks my expression. "But it's just a sport."

Wrestling is so much more than a sport. When you're a wrestler, that's everything. I'm not sure he's telling the truth.

"Sam needs the scholarship. It's not just a sport. It's a potential life, an education paid for, a mindset, a culture." I flick the vent back in his direction. "It could be the difference between success and no success. The stakes are high."

"I didn't mean it like that," he says. "I think it's great you're doing what you're doing. I think it's cool you want to play the sport." He scoots so he's facing me and turns the heat down. "I used to be the most dedicated guy around, but I learned I have to keep it in perspective and put it in its place."

"What place?"

"I used to be so competitive I would get pissed if I lost. I couldn't control myself. I made it so important I would throw tantrums and kick stuff."

"So you're bad at losing?"

"I used to be. Now I'm excellent at it."

I grin, remembering him getting thwapped onto the mat and handling it.

"I told you, I'm very self-centered and I inherited a shitty temper. I almost got kicked off the team a few years ago. Anyway, if I got myself all messed up in the head every time I lost a match I wouldn't be able to deal. We can all have our passions, but for me, personally, my whole life can't be centered around the team. I need other friends, to be with my family, a job, and to remember that wrestling is only one part of me." He turns back so he's facing front and puts his hands on the gears. He doesn't move to reverse. "But I'll admit I have an ulterior motive for being invested in you not thinking of me as an enemy."

"Yeah?"

"Yeah." He glances at me briefly. "You see, if you think of me as a rival, you probably won't want to hang out with me again and I'm really hoping you will."

"Oh."

"No?" he says. "That's a no, right?"

"You want to go on a date?" I ask.

"Yes. A date."

"Why?"

"Why?"

"Yeah." I break out in a light sweat, a rush of unexpected anger. "Is it because you want to have sex with me? I would rather know up front if that's what you want so we can have an honest conversation about it."

He looks like he's going to choke for a second.

"You all right?" I feel satisfied that those words came out of my mouth, and now I want more. More honesty. More straightforwardness.

"You would go for that?" he asks.

I think about it. Dax is very attractive and I wouldn't mind having sex with him. I'm sure his body is nice and pleasant and would be fun to explore. But I don't want anyone touching me ever, ever again unless they love me—*all* of me—and respect me as a person.

"No, I wouldn't have sex with you if that was your primary motivation, but I would rather know right now if that's what you want."

He pauses, and I sense his stress levels rising. Good. He wasn't expecting this and I love it.

"Honestly, I think you're totally beautiful," he says.

So at least I know I'm being objectified.

"But it's not that. Every time I see you it's like . . . boom. I just want to be near you or something. I like your vibe, your look, how you seem all wound up like you're about to spring any second. Look at this, right now. You're just like, here I am and this is what I want. I'm into the whole package." His eyes flicker to mine. "Too intense?"

"No, not too intense." I hesitate, trying to absorb everything he's said, dissect it all in milliseconds. I, or my heart, decides he's telling the truth and I relax back into the seat. "Can I tell you another real thing?"

"Always."

"Something happened that first night we talked."

"At the party?"

"Yeah."

His eyebrows knit together.

"No. Nothing like that. No rape."

"Okay, then what?"

"The real thing is that I'm not ready to talk about the specifics of what happened, but it kind of fucked me up and I'm not sure I'm over it yet. That's why I reacted the way I did at the meet."

"You mean when you acted like I was mortally offending you by asking you out?"

"Yeah, I guess. But that's all I want to say about it right now."

"Fair enough."

"I just feel like it's legitimately crap timing for me to be dating anyone. Because I also think you're super attractive and I get a boom too. I'm just trying to be different than before and I'm still too confused to deal. Working on myself like you said you are. Trying to be honest and straightforward, which seems like something no one is capable of, ever."

"I'd say you're doing pretty well so far."

"Thank you."

"Okay then, I get where you are. Just promise me you'll let me know if that changes, okay? Text me anytime, day or night. Text me from a plane, train, or automobile."

"All right, all right," I say.

"Hot air balloon, parachute, motorcycle…."

"I get it." I laugh.

Something is nagging at me though. For all my talk of honesty, there's something I'm not saying and not being straightforward about at all. All of what I said is true and real. I don't want to date until I feel stable and until I know I'm dating someone who actually gives a shit about more than what's under my clothes. But there's something else behind it all, something I can't get out of my head, something I don't want to share with Dax.

Sam.

I keep thinking about his face, what it would do to him if he thought I was dating Dax. And it's not just because of their wrestling rivalry, though it would be convenient if it was. I'm not sure I can go out on a date with Dax because it would probably eliminate any possibility of something happening with Sam, like, forever.

This little burst of internal honesty almost makes me gasp out loud. What the fuck?

Sam? Since when do I care about whether or not I can ever date *Sam?*

Dax turns on some music. "We better go if we're going to make it to the dogs."

"Dogs. Right. Of course," I mutter.

Damn. It seems like no matter how much work I do to try to understand myself better, there's always some new layer, another lie I've been telling myself. I'm grateful Dax doesn't make too much conversation as we drive the rest of the way, because my mind is whirling with brand-new truths, and I kind of hate it.

CHAPTER FIFTEEN

It's Sunday night and Sam and I are watching *Transformers* for the fortieth time. He came over unannounced like he used to, and while that normally wouldn't make me feel anything at all, after yesterday's admission to myself I'm totally nervous and probably acting erratically. I've spent the last twenty hours or so mulling over whether or not I actually have feelings for Sam or if I'm just possessive of him and our friendship in a way that isn't altogether cool, considering Jen. Either way I'm an asshole and I probably need more processing time before we're spooning on my damn bed (why *do* we spoon so much?) so I'm crouched away from him like a shadow creature, staring at him nervously, and instead of watching the movie *at all* I'm trying to look and act normal when I have no idea what that even means anymore.

We're in my room with the door closed and copious amounts of popcorn since we don't want to be in the living room watching *Peppa Pig* with my family, but it's like I don't know where to physically put myself. Sam seems to have no such problems and has plopped himself right into the center of the mattress, hands behind his head, waiting for me to lie down next to him and rest in the crook of his arm like I usually would. After what happened the other night and then the whole afternoon with Dax yesterday I'm the tensest person ever. I want to ask Sam why he isn't with Jen tonight even though I suspect it's because Jen takes like three hours to plan her outfits for the week. I would also like to ask him exactly what the

fuck is going on between us, and why when Dax asked me out yesterday
I felt like if I said yes I'd be cheating on someone.

On screen, robots have landed.

Sam looks at me for my reaction like, *Isn't this the coolest thing you've ever
seen? Isn't Michael Bay a genius?* And I'm sitting there munching on a kernel
of popcorn like a neurotic mouse.

"Okay, what the hell is this?" He bursts out laughing. "What are you
even doing?"

I realize I haven't exhaled in a minute.

"We're supposed to be chilling before another week of getting
smacked around and being stressed out," he says. "Whatever this is that
you're doing needs to stop." He takes the remote from where it's buried
in my covers and hits pause. "Tell me what's going on, Beck, because
you're killing my vibes."

"Okay," I say, but unlike yesterday in the car with Dax when things felt
clear, now I'm tongue-tied, words chaotic and unwieldy. "Ugh. Why can't
people just talk to each other?"

"There's something you don't think you can talk to me about?" he
scoffs. "Come on. That's not how we roll. You can tell me anything." He
raises his hand and makes flames. "Fire-promise."

I try to gather myself, channel the me from yesterday. "Okay, fine.
What'd you do last night?"

"Umm"—he sits up, grabs one of my pillows, and hugs it—"I went
to Ty's with Jen."

"A little date?" I say. "Like a couple date thing?"

"I guess." He shrugs. "Why? Do you think I shouldn't be hanging out
with Ty?"

No. I think you shouldn't be hanging out with your girlfriend. I think she shouldn't even be your girlfriend anymore. I think that's what I think.

"Actually it has nothing to do with Ty, except I do still kind of hate his ass." I want something to fidget with, anything. "Dax asked me out yesterday."

Sam digs into the pillow. "Dax?" he says. "Dax *Furlong*? Jesus, where did that guy come from? He was someone I used to have to see a few times a year and now he's *everywhere*."

Sam is clearly freaked out, which relaxes me.

"I ran into him at Petco when I went shopping for Leadership, which thanks, by the way, for not coming with me."

"Not fair. You said you were having mom time or something."

"Yeah, well, she had a thing and Dax was there to pick up the pieces."

"So . . . so you guys . . . what?" he stammers.

"I don't know, he gave me a ride. He helped me drop off the stuff at the shelter and then he brought me home."

"That's it?" Sam demands. "He just brought you home?"

"Uh, not that it's any of your business, but yes." I hesitate. "We also went and got hot chocolate and screamed at the universe—"

"What? You screamed at the what?"

"You know." I indicate all the space around us. "The *universe*."

"What the hell are you talking about?"

"And then he asked me out."

He flings the pillow to the side. It almost makes me laugh. "Are you serious?" he sputters.

Sam is short-circuiting and I don't hate it but I didn't imagine a reaction of this magnitude.

"I don't ask you every detail about your romantic life with Jen."

"What did you say? Did you say you'd go out with him?" It's like Sam can't hear me, like he's lost the ability to focus.

"No," I say. "I told him no. I told him it was bad timing." There's so much more I could add.

"But you were what? In a car? Did you hold hands? Did you kiss?" He glares at me. "Are you starting to fall for him, because you know you get confused and—"

"I am *not* confused. And are you mansplaining my own feelings to me?"

Sam's expression changes, softens. He slumps back into the bed.

"No. Sorry."

I've finally calmed down enough to think, to say the things I want to say. "Sam, are you jealous?"

There's a pause. "Why would I be jealous?"

He's lying and I know why. Sam's not someone who would ever cheat on his girlfriend and he would also never take a chance on anything if he wasn't absolutely sure of it. The only place Sam appreciates a risk is on the mat.

"Yeah," I say. "Exactly. Why would you be jealous?"

He turns his head so his cheek rests on a pink fuzzy square.

I hold his gaze until he breaks it.

"Not super cool to be hanging out with someone on a rival team, Jo," he says flatly. "We don't need that right now. We need solidarity." He slides off my bed, pulls his jacket off the chair in the corner of my room, lingers under a picture of the two of us on the roller coaster when we went to Disneyland with his parents a couple years ago.

"You know what's not cool?" I am suddenly exhausted by all of this. The tension oozes out of me and all I feel is depleted. "This constant head trip is what's not cool. And don't make me explain myself because you know exactly what I'm talking about."

"I really don't," he says. "You're the one with the head trip lately. I'm just trying to be the way we've always been."

I want to argue with him, but I think he may not know he has romantic feelings for me, just like I didn't really know I had them for him until yesterday. Sometimes you have to lie to yourself to keep all the pieces of life together, and I know how much Sam wants to keep what he has: wrestling scholarship, stable girlfriend, and mostly his status as a nice person. I've been wrong before, but never about something having to do with Sam. I'm always right when it comes to him. And there's another thing: Just because you have romantic feelings doesn't mean you have to act on them, but I don't want to be caged by things that are hard to admit or inconvenient. It's inconvenient to be used for sex, inconvenient to admit I was at least partially complicit. This is inconvenient too, but it's true anyway. On both our parts.

"I'm going to head out. Guess I'm not really in the mood for *Transformers* after all," he says, looking like he suspects I might thrust myself upon him at any second. "Enjoy that popcorn though."

And then he's gone.

I turn up the volume on the movie and stare at the screen.

CHAPTER SIXTEEN

We're in the old town hall, which is where all the dances happen because the gym permanently smells like sweat and tears, and dances are supposed to be a cheerful and inspirational delight. Liberty Township erected a shiny new building a few years ago, so now this is where lots of people get married and where the Christmas craft sale happens at holiday time.

It's got this dark red carpet that's kind of heinous and reminds me of murder. It's got cool windows though, and some big glass doors that lead out onto a huge patio with views of the mountains. The town donates the space to the high school on the condition that we get a committee to do as much of the cleanup as we can and that we treat it respectfully. As far as I know this never happens but they keep giving it to us anyway.

Leah, Jen, and Amber are unleashed like fairies, dancing across the hall, discussing the stage and whether to have a band or a DJ, and whether it would be worth it to blow some of the budget on renting those heaters for outside so everyone doesn't have to be stuck in here. They are basically in heaven. What's not to love? There are snacks to be decided upon, and ticket prices, and we haven't quite nailed down the theme, only that there will definitely be a lot of glitter involved and bunches and bunches of hearts.

I can barely even look at Jen and feel like Amber is analyzing everything I do so I wander behind them and stay quiet. Unless Sam said something to Jen about all the unspoken tension lately (ha, unlikely) there's no way she knows anything about what's been happening between us, but I still feel it like a rope around my neck. I smile and nod when they say things. Much as I've always thought Jen was a bad seed and a troll, the more time I spend with her the less I think that's true and the more I think maybe the reason I feel that way is because I've been harboring feelings for Sam this whole time.

I don't know if I'm a fan of self-awareness.

Eventually we settle on the stage, where the band or DJ would be set up. We naturally take up a circle formation, the paperwork and permits we've been working on spread out on the floor between us.

"What do you think?" Jen says. I have no idea what she's asking me about.

I briefly consider the possibility that she's asking me about Sam, and pulse with cortisol.

"About the dance theme?" she says.

"I think Under the Sea and Snow Ball themes are way overdone. We've had both in the last two years."

"Not that you've come to any dances, or any school events that I can recall," Amber snipes. "Other than wrestling, of course."

Okay, fine. Here goes more radical honesty. "Because the events are uninteresting. Especially dances."

"Jeez, Jo," Leah says.

"I'm not trying to be harsh, I'm just saying the reason people hate these dances is because they're boring and only geared toward heterosexual cis couples. Oh, sorry. *Traditionally* beautiful, conforming heterosexual cis couples. Do you know how many breakdowns happen because people are trying to find dates to these things? They're popularity contests, which doesn't feel great when you're just a person trying to survive high school."

"I mean . . ." Jen starts to argue but then slumps back. "I guess you're right."

"They feel exclusive and like they're going to be filled with shitty, judgmental people."

"We just try to set standards," Amber says, looking up from the paper she's been studying. I feel like a cockroach under her gaze.

"But . . . could the standard encourage people to be who they are?"

"Well, aren't you progressive and enlightened?" Amber clacks her red nails against each other. "Lecturing me."

"We're not going to change the entire culture around school dances in an hour-long planning meeting," Jen points out. "And we haven't decided on a theme yet."

"What about Come as You Are?" I say, thinking out loud.

"That's not a theme," Amber says, but she looks interested in spite of herself.

"Let her finish," Jen says.

They all wait expectantly, fake eyelashes fluttering. It's like some kind of audition or something. I've broken their fairy circle and now they're trying to decide whether to cast me out, which, you know, wouldn't be the worst thing.

"Come as You Are," I say. "Nineties rave-slash-grunge theme. Everyone welcome. No formal anything required. All LGBTQ+ expressions welcome. Just be yourself and have fun."

"It's too much to ask people to dress nicely a couple nights of the year?" Amber says. "God, this town is pathetic."

"No," I say. "But it would also be nice to have a school event where people can just have a good time and be silly and weird instead of taking everything so seriously. If you want to wear a prom dress, go ahead! Be you!"

I'm flashing to Dax, thinking how his goofiness makes him free.

"Nice?" Amber says, a small smile playing across her mouth. "Is that what we're going for? Nice?"

"Yeah, why not?" I say. "The mean girl thing is so over."

"Calling me a mean girl?" Amber's tone is still playful but her hands clench again.

"I'm saying it would be a good thing to have everyone in this school feel like they can leave all the negative things that have happened in high school behind and just come to a dance and have a good time."

"Yeah," Jen says. "Like reputations and people talking shit on you?" She looks straight at me.

"Whoa, hey," Leah says, sitting up taller. "Let's take it down a notch, people."

"No. I've been wanting to say something since that practice girl thing happened," Jen says.

Here's where she tells me how gross I am, that I'm flirtatious with Sam. I brace myself for a fight.

"It needs to be said," she goes on. "The whole thing is bullshit. Those guys are assholes for that, including Ty for sure, and Sam too. We went over to Ty's house and I honestly wanted to slam his face into the table."

"Jen!" Amber says.

"No, really," Jen says. "It pisses me off. Do we have practice *boys*? Would we do that? No, because it's shitty as hell. It's misogyny on so many levels and I'm so sick of dealing with it. We all have to filter it one way or another all the time. And if it happens to you, it's happening to all of us."

I couldn't be more shocked if the bag of carrot sticks in my purse came to life and started singing me a ditty.

"The way the guys treated you was not okay," she says. "And I want you to know I gave Sam a really hard time."

"You did?" Sam said things had changed between them. I wonder if this has anything to do with it. Guilt slaps at my cheeks and I feel myself reddening with it.

"Yeah. It could have been any of us. It could be any girl at any time, getting treated like that."

She looks at Amber meaningfully.

Amber sighs. "Yeah, I mean I think you're unintelligent for trusting a bunch of boys in the first place but I don't approve of what happened. I've been educating Tyler as often as possible."

This whole time I've thought of Amber and Jen as enemies, competition or something. Except they don't feel like enemies now.

"Thanks," I say.

"It's important to remember boys aren't mythical creatures filled with wisdom and magic," Amber says. "Some of them are nice to look at and are fun to hang out with sometimes, but in a lot of ways they're babies with wrong ideas about what it should be like to be with a girl, or what that girl should be like, how she should act, what she should wear."

"Preach," Leah says. "I'm not riding anything except a horse."

"Wait, you're a virgin?" I say. I didn't think those were a thing by senior year.

"You bet, and I'm going to stay that way until I get out of high school and meet someone worth my time. And speaking of hetero," she says, eyes flashing. "I am not. I'm pan and I'm patient."

I wait for this revelation to inspire a reaction. It does not.

"I like dating," Amber says. "I like dressing up, going to dinner, to shows, getting to know someone. I'm not in any hurry to hop in the sack though." It's impossible for Ty not to flash through my head and exactly what it was like to be twisted up in sheets with him.

"I get it," Jen says, looking over at me. "The sex part? Wanting to have it? I want it a lot and I don't know why I shouldn't. Sam and I hooked up almost right away, so fast I had to take emergency birth control. We used condoms but I was still scared. And he wasn't my first either. I get what it's like to want that, for it to feel like it's bigger than you and like you're out of control."

"I didn't want to get laid," I say. "Or . . . I didn't want to *just* get laid, not that there's anything wrong with having a sex drive when you're a human person. But that's not what I wanted, or hoped for."

This stops all of them cold. The sound of the wind outside is newly noticeable.

"It's embarrassing, but I fall in love really easily," I say. "I get these huge feelings for guys the second they pay attention to me. I've slept with four people and I thought I was in love with three of them when it happened. One was . . . different." My eyes flicker to Jen who gives a slight nod to show she knows what I'm saying.

"That's tragic," Amber says, and she doesn't sound mean at all. "At least you have feelings though. I don't know if I'm ever going to fall in love."

"You don't love Ty?" I can't say I've ever been behind this particular curtain, talking to other girls about boys. I like it. Very useful information back here.

Amber lets out a throaty laugh. "I like him. I like having someone to spend time with."

"But you don't get butterflies every time he looks at you? You don't stay up nights hoping he'll text you? You don't count the times he looks your way to try to figure out if he feels the same as you?"

"No, I don't." Amber looks at me. "If that's how you felt about Ty, I'm really sorry things went down the way they did and I'm even sorrier that he called you bullshit names."

"It's dehumanizing," Leah agrees, "and I think what you're doing with the whole wrestling situation is commendable."

"Yeah," Jen says, "except also gross. I think you should drop the whole wrestling thing and come to our side. We smell better and we're not assholes."

I laugh and let my head slump against Leah's shoulder.

These girls definitely smell better, but until now I would never have said they weren't assholes.

I was wrong.

"They're the ones who are practice," Amber says. "They just don't know it. And I say if you want to have sex then have sex and fuck 'em if they can't take a fuck."

"Ew, Amber," Leah says.

"What? Just don't let them have anything else," Amber says.

"I don't think I'm built like that." I wish so much I was.

"I get it," Jen says, shooting Amber a dirty look. "You want to be someone's girl. You want someone to love you and those guys took advantage of that."

"I don't just want someone to love," I say, barely getting the words out past my swollen throat. "I want a best friend who really knows me and who also wants to introduce me to his family and wants to spend Valentine's Day with me."

Jen flinches and I want to tell her I don't mean Sam, that I'm not after her boyfriend, but I also don't want to lie to her.

And then I decide.

I won't have to lie to her because whatever is between Sam and me, slithering below the surface, is dead as of right now. From this moment forward, Sam is strictly a friend, and not the kind you cuddle for hours either. From now on, I'm doing this correctly. Just friends. Friends with boundaries.

The room sits quiet, and I feel like we're all probably mulling our own boy stories, our own sexualities too.

"Come as You Are," Leah says, leaning her head against mine. "I like it. Let's do it. Everyone, come to the dance and leave all your baggage behind."

"Or bring it with you," Jen says. "Nobody cares!"

"Are you fucking serious?" Amber says. "Oh my gosh, *fine*. But you're going to have to tell me how this makes for fun decorations."

"Are you kidding?" I say. "DJ playing all nineties music, glow sticks . . . it's going to be great!"

"You guys are dorks," Amber says, but I think I see a spark of something in her. "Although I do have this really cool choker."

Now I'm excited. I, Josephine Beckett, am over the moon to be semi-officially on a decorating committee. If this is possible, anything is. Literally anything.

"Wow," Leah says. "This place is so nice."

She's looking around with wonder at the cream-and-taupe decor, Mom's new countertops, the long, heavy drapes in our living room. If her house is anything like it was when we were kids, it's all dark wood and her mom's collection of porcelain kitchen ducks and china plates with horses on them. I guess it is a departure from the house we had with Dad and all the woody man things. Here there are flowers Kevin buys for Mom every week on the table, everything is immaculate, and the temperature is a perfect 70 degrees Fahrenheit at all times.

"Your dad had all those wrestling posters, remember?" she says. "Hulk Hogan and those heavy metal bands."

Oh, I remember. He and Mom were always arguing about how she didn't want to look at Axl Rose and his bandana anymore.

"Yeah."

"Sorry," she says. "I don't know if it's okay to mention him."

"No, yeah, it's totally fine."

How we got here is Leah said we should iron out some of the dance details, but we both know this is another step back to the friendship we used to have where the two of us existed in our own world.

"You hungry?" I say. Mom keeps an impressive array of pantry snacks around here.

"Nah, I'm going to eat dinner at home. My mom is making calabacitas."

Calabacitas are summer squash and corn with green chile and are perfect for crappy days like this one. I don't blame her for wanting to save her appetite.

No one's here right now. Kevin is working and Mom took Tiffany to ballet so the house has this empty, museum feel to it. Not once we cross the threshold into my room though. It's still colorful and kidlike in here, the bed covered in the pink-and-red afghan my grandmother made for me, pictures all over the wall, multiple stuffed animals and cozy pillows, my collection of Converse, and my rows and rows of bright books. It might be a little more organized than it was the last time Leah was in a room of mine, but it's basically the same.

"Oh my God, you still have Mr. Cuddles!" Leah pounces on the patchy elephant my dad gave me when I was five. She holds him in the air. "This is amazing!"

My kind of chaos works for me, but I guess it also makes me feel like I still carry a piece of my dad with me, like his messy charm still exists in my life.

"Good ole Mr. Cuddles," I say.

Leah rolls over onto her stomach. She looks just like she used to except now she's long enough for her feet to flop off the edge of the bed. She lays Mr. Cuddles down in front of her and I sit in Dad's old easy chair that Kevin moved in here for me after he died.

"Can I ask you a question?" she says.

"Sure." Why not? Heavy conversations seem to be trending lately.

She looks up at me. "Why did you stop talking to me? I mean really?"

Me stop talking to her? I only had her and Sam. I would never have ditched out. "I didn't. You stopped talking to me."

"Shut up," she says. "You don't really think that."

"Yes I do! You totally bailed when my dad died. I waited and waited to hear from you and you never reached out."

"You're not messing with me?" Leah throws Mr. Cuddles to the side and I retrieve him and deposit him on my shelf. "You're being serious right now?"

"Leah," I say. "I am definitely not messing with you."

"Okay," she says, nodding. "That explains a lot I guess. I sent you like a hundred texts and waited for you to write me back but you never did. You really think I didn't try? Did your phone fall in a lake or something?"

As she's talking, I remember a glimmer of something, some distant fog of seeing a couple of half-hearted attempts to talk. "You texted. You didn't call. You didn't come over. You didn't even come to the funeral." This last cuts the deepest, makes it hard to breathe. I remember standing there with all those people, trying to find one person to lean on.

And I did.

Sam.

Leah's face falls and she comes and sits at my feet. "You're right," she says. "I know I wasn't there for you. Would you believe me if I told you the funeral terrified me?" she says. "My dad is everything to me and the idea of losing him was more than I could take. I was a seventh grader, okay? I had no idea how to be bigger than that fear. It felt like a vertical that was too tall for me to get over. I thought you would text me when you wanted to see me and then you didn't."

"You had Amber. By the time I was strong enough to reach for anyone the two of you were too close for me to get past. And she seemed so mean."

"She's not mean. She came to this place at the worst time in middle school and is literally the only Black person in this entire town. She had to have her defenses up. And anyway, you had Sam."

The quiet settles over us like a weighted blanket.

"Amber was strong. She had attitude," Leah finally says. "She made me feel like I was protected."

"Or dominated."

"Maybe, but with the two of us, you and me, it was the blind leading the blind. I didn't know how to help you. I knew I'd do the wrong thing. I'm better with horses than people."

"Well, that's true," I say. "But I'm glad you're here now."

"Yeah," she says. "Me too."

CHAPTER SEVENTEEN

I'm cleaning cages at Stray Hearts when Sam comes in. I haven't seen him since Sunday, which, granted, was only two days ago. We've been released from class to come volunteer and neither of us made plans to meet or go together. I didn't even expect him to show up, but here he is in his usual sweatshirt and jeans, looking all sporty and attractive. He definitely showered this morning and he smells really good, especially compared to me who is covered in a thin layer of dander and desperation. As soon as I see him I remind myself of my personal pledge to have good boundaries.

"Sorry I'm late," he says. "I got held up in Trig."

I point to the empty cages. "It's doggie socializing time so they want us to pull out all the stuff and put the clean blankets in the crates. I'm also bleaching the plastic toys and washing the cloth ones because gross."

"Okay." Sam crouches down next to me and starts working on the next cage over. "So do you want to do some extra training tonight?"

I'm ready for this, have rehearsed it in my mind since yesterday afternoon.

"I don't think so," I tell him, trying to keep my voice light. "I have to work."

"Oh, right. Well, tomorrow then, after practice?"

"I don't think so."

He looks over at me, totally surprised. I finish wiping down the cage and spraying it with the sanitizer, don't face him directly.

"Can you hand me that blanket?" I point to a maroon fleece.

"Sure." He watches me as I tuck it into place. "Why? I thought we were going to work on your dad's moves."

"Yeah, except I think I want to do that on my own."

"On your own?" he says, like it's never occurred to him such words might escape my lips.

"Yeah, sure. Maybe that's something I need to try to do, you know what I mean?"

"Work out alone? No, Beckett, that's doesn't make sense to me."

"Okay, well, maybe it's not about what makes sense to you or doesn't. Maybe it's about what makes sense to *me*."

Sam raises his eyebrows. "Okay, fine."

"Because I can do this by myself."

"I believe you. Do it up. You do you!" He says it but he doesn't mean it. He has that look he gets when he feels hurt.

This is not easy for me. There's a piece of me cracking inside, the piece that always wanted Sam and me to stay exactly the way we were, but that's not actually possible because nothing ever stays the same. Sometimes change comes on suddenly, one loud thump, a body hits the floor and everything is gone in an instant, but sometimes it's so slow you don't see it coming. It takes you so much by surprise you want to deny it but you can't because it is what it is and nothing will ever be the same again.

"Will wonders never cease?" Leah comes up behind me as I'm getting a tray of drinks ready for my newest table. "Look who Brenda just sat me."

The diner is inundated with people tonight and I'm brewing a serious sweat so I'm half-annoyed when I turn around, but instead I say, "Oh, shit."

"Mm-hmm."

Dax and a few of his friends are sitting there looking at menus. Dax is already trained on me and raises a hand in greeting. There's nothing overtly hostile in his gaze. Still the same cheerful look. I wrack my brain for a memory of telling him I worked here but come up empty. So this is yet another coincidence? He's back to reading his menu like I don't exist so . . .

"I'm so glad they're yours," I say, the jealousy rising. "I totally couldn't handle that tonight."

"Oh, well, I'm sorry to hear that because right after Brenda gave them to me, Dax requested you." She smirks as I lose focus. "Why don't I get their drink order for you?"

"Yeah, okay. Yeah."

A strange pulse starts up and I'm struggling to remember who got what of the drinks on my tray. I spend the next few minutes trying to gather myself and figure out why I'm so nervous and by the time I get to Dax's table I think I'm probably back to normal.

"Hey," I say. "Fancy meeting you here."

"You come to my work, I come to yours. We have to stop meeting like this," he says. His friends look on with interest.

"This is Jamie, Franco, and Josh." Jamie looks Latinx, and Franco and Josh are white. They're all some kind of scruffy and look like they just came from skating somewhere, which they probably did. They definitely don't look like the wrestlers I'm used to, but then again neither does Dax.

"What's up?" they say, each on their own but also in unison.

"Are you the wrestler chick?" Franco asks.

Dax has been talking about me.

"So what brings you over here?" I ask.

Leah walks by and winks at me and I try not to let my facial expression change.

"You, of course," Dax says. "Wanted to check on you after all that void-yelling the other day. How'd you recover?"

"Oh, you know. I've been battling my demons ever since, which is totally on you, but other than that, fine. Also, I started sleeping upside down during the day. Does that ever happen to you?"

"Right, right," Dax says. "I forgot to warn you that facing the infinite vastness of the universe could lead to everything feeling wrong way up."

Ralph dings the bell really hard and I look around to see a large quantity of my tables are giving me expectant stares.

"I'll be back. You want apps?" I say nervously. "I'll get you some apps."

While I'm at the counter I scribble an order for chili fries and mozzarella sticks and then run my food as fast as I can. Leah stops me on the way as we're both grabbing straws. "Something going on between the two of you? You're glowing."

"Shut up!"

"No, I'm glad. I think that would be sweet. And a relief too. I thought you had something going on with Sam there for a second and that would have been a total nightmare."

I slap some lemon slices on the sides of the iced tea glasses. "Sam. No. Never!"

"Uh-huh," she says.

I get the appetizers and the guys are all huddled together in conversation. When I drop off the food at their table and tell them it's on me, all of them make appreciative noises and Dax smiles widely.

"So how do you guys know each other?" I ask.

"We grew up together," Franco says, shoving a huge pile of fries in his mouth.

"Yeah, and Josh is Dax's cousin but he moved up here to live with his grandma so now we have to come this way to see him," Jamie says, leaning back in his chair and turning bright, playful brown eyes on me.

"So you're not wrestlers?" I say.

"Shit no," Franco says, wiping grease from his thin lips with the back of his hand. "He turned on us when he went jock. We used to skate on weekends and now we have to go to wrestling meets to be 'supportive.'" Franco makes bunny ears as he says this and shakes his head of curly hair in mock disappointment, but he speaks so warmly I can tell how much love there is between all of them, and now that I'm looking closer I remember these are the guys who were sitting next to the girl Dax was fist-bumping before his match. "We saw you though . . . at the last meet. That was you, right?"

"Yo, she got her ass *kicked*," Josh says, laughing.

Jamie whacks him on the shoulder.

"You were brave," Franco says. "It was kind of hot."

"Okay, that's good," Dax says, and they all dissolve into laughter. He mouths *I'm sorry*.

Leah passes by behind me. "Hey, I don't mean to interrupt but Mrs. Crawdad is about to lose her shit."

"Who's that?" Josh asks, watching Leah walk away. "She's gorgeous."

I leave Dax, who's giving Josh some sort of hard time while the rest of them go back to laughing.

A few minutes later the rush has calmed down and everyone has their food, so I'm chugging water behind the bar when I feel a hand on my shoulder. I turn around, wiping my mouth, expecting it to be Leah or Brenda telling me to get out of the way, but it turns out to be Dax. My stomach does another little leap.

"Sorry to come back into the employee zone."

"No, it's okay."

"I wanted to catch you before we get our check and everything. We have to go soon." If I'm not mistaken he seems a little stressed. "Something came up. I have to get home."

"Okay, sure." There was a car seat strapped into his back seat when we hung out. Maybe it has something to do with that. "Is everything okay?"

"Yeah, yeah." He says it but it's obviously not true. All the laughter has gone from his expression.

"Tell me something real?" I say, prodding him. Trauma comes quickly and I'm hoping he hasn't had that kind of news.

"Yeah, I would, but . . . it's nothing." His shoulders drop. "Just family stuff."

"Okay. Well, I'm glad you came in."

"Me too. But I didn't actually come in for you."

"Oh," I say.

"We just came to get some food and here you were."

"Oh."

This is so embarrassing.

"But it made me really happy to see you here. That's why I requested you."

"Oh!"

"Okay." He pulls me into a brief hug. "I'll see you the next time we bump into each other randomly in a weird place."

"Yeah." I think. "I mean, no."

"No?" Dax jingles his keys.

"No. I don't want it to be random."

"Okay . . ." He glances over to his friends, then back at me. He's in a hurry.

"Do you want to go out? Maybe tomorrow? I'm not working and I get out of practice at seven."

His cheeks do that pink thing I love, where he looks like he just got slapped. "But you said it's bad timing."

"It is. But I'm starting to think it's always going to be bad timing for everything. Life keeps happening."

"Tomorrow, huh?" he says.

"Yeah, why not? If you still want to. I mean, if there's nothing preventing you." For a second I'm not sure what he's going to say, unsure whether I'm going to find myself rejected.

"I do."

Relief washes over me.

He furrows his eyebrows. "But I might have something going on. I'm not sure yet."

I'm surprised by my level of disappointment. "Yeah, okay. I'll check with you in the morning, then."

"Okay," he says. "Yeah! Great."

"Okay!"

He squeezes me one more time.

I don't think I'm imagining things when I see a little more spring in his step as he heads back to the table.

I feel Dax's rays all over me, warming me everywhere.

CHAPTER EIGHTEEN

"Okay, here we are," Dax says. "What do you think?"

He got back to me while I was in math today and asked if I'd be willing to drive to Denver. He said he'd had this whole idea the last time he wanted to take me out and was hoping I'd be willing.

I was willing.

He's got on a button-down bowling shirt and a corduroy jacket and his hair's the right kind of mess, like he put in effort but not too much. I don't know if I'm striking the same kind of balance in my choice of outfit, a black turtleneck and jeans, my hair in two very short braids. My hair's still wet from the shower and a chaotic attempt to get ready for this date after practice went long, but I'm buoyed by the fact that I did pretty well, at least on the practice dummy. Soon I'm going to need an actual person to practice with. I even kept pace with Barney.

"OMG MINI?" I say, looking up at the sign. "What is this?"

"Ta-da! It's sushi plus mini-golfing with black lights," Dax says.

Of all the things I scrolled through as possibilities, this wasn't one of them. I didn't even know a place like this existed. I should leave Coyote Valley more often.

Dax is watching my face like he can't read my expression. "I didn't know if you'd be hungry or in the mood for being around a lot of people but if you'd rather go somewhere else . . . Do you hate sushi? I figured with it being mid-season and everything . . ."

"No," I laugh. "I love sushi, I'm starving, and my dad was a big golfer so I kind of know how this works."

"Oh, phew." He takes my hand. "Is this okay?"

"Yeah," I say.

Our hands warm each other in the cold outside and when we get inside Franco is by the door. "You're late," he says. Then he looks at me. "This hoser tell you how good you look tonight?"

"You look really good," Dax says, and I squeeze his hand.

"You're a waiter?" I ask Franco.

"Me? Shit no," Franco says. "I'm very bad at service. Golf ball retriever, wiper down of tables, runner of food. No being nice to people on demand. But for you, I make an exception." He says this last with an accent and strokes an invisible moustache. "Especially since you have my best friend so spun."

"Just take us to our table, jackass," Dax says.

We're guided through a maze of low-lit booths. A little ways off there are blue-and-orange black lights and people can be seen weaving through. There's the occasional shout and I'm so distracted by checking it out that I don't see right away that there's a pot of flowers on the table with my name on a card in front of it. They're the most beautiful orchids I've ever seen, white with mouths open.

"Oh, good. You like them," he says.

I nod, a little dumbstruck. "No one's ever gotten me flowers before."

"That tracks," he says. "I guess it's an outdated tradition."

"No way," I say. "It's sweet."

We scan the sushi menu and I get a couple rolls plus cucumber salad, which is always my favorite. He gets a Philly roll and sashimi.

"Did you say your dad *played* golf? Like in the past?" he says.

"Yeah, he died a few years ago."

He searches my face. I don't feel self-conscious talking about my dad but something about the way he's looking at me makes me want to go back to a few minutes ago when our foreheads were almost touching as we pored over the menu. That's safer than this. He's really watching me.

"Were you close?" Dax asks.

"Yeah. He was the high school history teacher and then wrestling coach. He always understood what it was like to be a kid." I think back. "Actually, probably better than what it meant to be an adult. And there was always wrestling."

"Right. Makes sense."

"Yeah, so I grew up around it and everything." I slurp on my water. "What about you? How did you start wrestling?"

He shifts around, shrugs. "Did I tell you about my anger management issues? Yeah, so when I was eight the school counselor thought I should do something about those, so she suggested I play a sport to get some negative energy out. I couldn't do a team sport and I really, really wanted to lay people out, so . . . there you go."

I can't read his mood but the air between us thickens with tension. I nod even though I'm sure there's more to the story. Like what was going on in his life to make him so mad all the time.

"Where are you going next year? For school?" I say, trying to change the topic.

"Where are you going?" he returns.

"I got into Boulder." I haven't told anyone yet and the words feel brave. It's decided. Boulder. Not Duke. Not with Sam. "I wanted to go

farther away, but they gave me some money and I'm actually kind of excited even though it's more of here."

"That's a great school," he agrees.

"But you? You didn't answer my question. You must have your pick
of places. You did the whole scout thing last year, right?"

"Yeah. But I'm going to try to stick around here."

"What?" I'm utterly shocked. "Why?"

The waitress places our Japanese sodas in front of us.

"You could have a scholarship to almost anywhere," I add. "You're
incredible, even with all the douchiness."

He grins. "Tell me more about my douchiness."

I feel myself redden. "You know."

"I do not."

"You make a joke out of wrestling when it's serious to people."

"You mean to tell me it's not fun when I do that? You aren't charmed?"

"Well—"

"I'm kidding, I get what you're saying. Sorry it feels like I'm making a
mockery. I don't totally get along with my team, I guess. I have other friends
and other stuff going on. I like to keep it in perspective, otherwise I get too
stressed out." He waggles his eyebrows. "Life's too short for stress."

We watch each other for a moment, and then he lets his eyes fall.
There's more to his story, I know there is, just like there's more to mine,
but I can't argue with the stress comment, considering that's exactly what
killed my dad. Also, a whole new world of possibility has unveiled itself.
Dax will be here. I will be here. The vision of us rolling around together
in a sea of violets while a picnic basket sits close by rears up like a sea
monster that's been lying in wait. I slap the image away. I bury it. Part of

me wants to run away right now and never come back, but I remind myself to have a good time on this *first date* and leave the rest alone. Begone, violets! Begone, picnic basket! Begone, imagined future!

Be here now instead.

Both of us absolutely decimate our food and then add on tempura and eat some more, and the conversation is easy. We skirt serious topics and stick with music and movies. When we're done with dinner, he gives the orchid pot and our jackets to Franco and we run around like we're five. We play golf until we can't stand up anymore, and at some point we rest under a mini troll bridge with Franco, who's hiding from his boss. By the time we're driving home, I'm a buzzing kind of exhausted. Exhilarated. I think that's the right word.

Happy?

Dax pulls into my driveway. The lights are all on but I don't see anyone in the living room.

"I had a really good time," he says.

"The *best* time," I say.

"Can I tell you something?" he asks.

"Sure."

"I was really nervous I would screw everything up."

"That we would go on a real date and not like each other?"

"No," he says. "I never thought that."

I clutch my orchid, not sure what to do with my hands. Normally I would get into it right here at the end of the first date. I'd be kissing and trying to find out when we'd be hanging out next, trying to keep it casual when I didn't feel that way at all. A month ago I would probably have gone down on him right here in the driveway, but I can't imagine that now. It's like I don't know how to initiate physical contact anymore and I don't know whether there should be any.

Thankfully, Dax makes the decision for me. He leans over, cupping my ear and cheek, stroking the line of my jaw, and his lips graze mine. I let myself sink into the kiss. His breath lingers with cinnamon from the candies we ate on the way out of the restaurant. He lets his hand dip down my neck and I open my mouth and we kiss deeper. My eyes closed, I'm in infinite space.

We pull apart and stare at each other. He doesn't make a single move to touch my boobs or undo the buttons on my jeans. He just looks at me.

I get out of the car, orchid in hand. "Bye," I say.

"Bye."

I turn around when I get to the door and Dax is still there. He hasn't disappeared or driven off and his expression hasn't changed. It's the same. It's . . . him.

CHAPTER NINETEEN

Coach appraises the room. It's time to grapple and he's about to pair us up. Santi and Buzz are doing my job now, holding the clipboards, the timer, picking up the dummies. No one's giving out water or towels though. The guys have had to make an adjustment. Not every need is being met exactly when they have it.

It's been two weeks since my first kiss with Dax and we've had two meets. Dax wasn't at either, which means so far I've dodged the bullet of having Dax and Sam in the same room, but tonight that's going to change. I had to take my car in for service and won't have it back until tomorrow because the one mechanic in town is so slow and Mom refuses to go anywhere else, so Dax is coming to pick me up.

Sam and I have barely been hanging out and I definitely don't care if the rest of the guys think I'm being traitorous. Things have gotten a little less boogery than they were because Sam and I have gotten into a routine of coming to practice, saying hi, doing our own thing, and moving on. It's not like we're giving each other the evil eye or something. We're just kind of getting used to not being the way we were.

"Beckett," Coach says, knocking me out of my daze.

"Sir?"

"You'll pair up with Barney tonight. You two can teach each other a couple things."

He's right. Barney's getting so good. He's won a few matches, although now his opponents are catching on to the fact that he's actually just fast as hell.

Me? I've gotten close to winning, actually, using a couple of the moves I found in Dad's notebook. The Frogger, in particular, has been really useful. So far no one sees that coming. Of course there have also been a bunch of forfeitures. Sometimes I don't get to wrestle at all.

Coach goes on, pairing Sam and Luke, Mase and Ty, until everyone has someone. Barney and I go into the corner by the bleachers.

"So tell me," I say, "how have you transformed yourself into the enviable athlete I see before me?"

Barney glances at me, trying to assess whether or not I'm making fun of him. He shrugs, assuming the start stance while I set up across from him. "Fear," he says.

"Yeah?" I think he's kidding at first, but he looks at me with sharp seriousness.

"Yeah, fear. Not mine, theirs."

Now he has my interest. "Tell me more."

He adjusts his headgear. "There's always a moment of hesitation where they're trying to figure out what I'm going to do. They take just a couple seconds to assess my move. I go in right then. I don't hesitate."

"No hesitation," I say.

He braces himself. "Now you show me something."

We approach each other and Barney goes in fast but I leapfrog him and get his leg and before he can do anything else he's down. I don't try to keep him there, let him sit right back up.

"That never gets old," he says, breathing hard.

"My secret weapon," I say.

"Got any others like that hidden away?"

"Maybe I do," I say.

Barney grins. We practice a few more times and then Coach calls break and we sit in the bleachers. Sam nods his head at me but doesn't come over.

Barney takes a sip from his Hulk water bottle. "At first I figured this was a joke for you," he says, "like it was for me at the beginning. A very, very bad joke."

"No," I say, eyeing Ty, "it's never been a joke. Revenge, maybe."

"Yeah, I can see that now."

Barney's not half bad looking and he's got this sweetness that radiates from inside.

"I had a couple . . . relationships . . . with the guys and they basically treated me like one of those dummies. No respect. No nothing." There's heat around the words.

"Yeah," Barney says, "I know. I heard them talking."

I don't know why I'm surprised.

"I am actually here in the flesh," he says. "I don't turn invisible as soon as we're in the locker room. I hear things."

I shake my head, take a sip of my water. "I don't know how I missed it. That's the part that really gets me. I don't know how I was around them so much and never knew that was what was going on."

I thought I was in love, I want to say. *I thought they loved me back.*

Only a couple weeks hanging out with Dax and I know what it feels like to have someone solid, someone who always chooses to sit with me, who holds my hand in public, who seems proud to be with me.

"Sometimes we see what we want to see, I guess," Barney says. "Especially when the alternative sucks."

"Say more, wise one."

"I didn't start wrestling because I was in love with getting smacked onto my back either, you know?" Barney looks at me searchingly, and it's like I'm seeing him as a real person for the first time. "Actually, I don't know if my reasons are so different from yours. I have four brothers."

"Yeah, I've seen them at meets." They're all huge and account for 70 percent of the spectator noise.

"I spent my whole life being told I was soft. They don't even call me Barney." He sniffles lightly. "They call me Sub." He glances up. "You know, like submissive?"

"I know what it means," I say.

"Yeah, well, I knew I didn't want to try playing football or anything, but I wanted to prove to them that just because I'm gay doesn't mean I can't play sports or something."

"You are?"

"Yeah," he says, "and vegan." He laughs. "I don't know what's worse in my household, the fact that I want a relationship with a guy, or the fact that I won't eat a steak."

"I'm sorry, Barney."

His eyes are a little wet but he smiles. "Don't be sorry for me. I don't think I came into this for the right reasons, even though my therapist thought exposure therapy would be a great way to face my fears. Really I was trying to be more like them or whatever. But I'm not sorry I did. I found out I'd rather be a sub than a shithead." He looks over at Ty and

Mase, who are high-fiving about something as we speak. "I also found out my brothers can be decent every once in a while. Everyone's got a story," he says. "Just some people are better at hiding it than others."

"You really are a wise one," I say.

"Watch this space," he says. "I'm just getting started."

I get my stuff without showering, wash up, and throw on my jacket. It's not like Dax hasn't already seen me sweaty and red-faced and I'm too tired to do more. This season is like a marathon. All evenings full, weekends claimed. I never realized how intense it is. As a manager, even though it takes up all the time, it definitely doesn't demand so much physically.

Sam is waiting for me outside the locker room.

"Hi," he says.

"Hi."

"I wanted to see if you want to give me a ride home. I thought maybe we could talk?"

My phone buzzes from inside my pocket. I know exactly who that is.

Dax.

On time.

Where he said he was going to be.

"My car's in the shop," I say. "I'm sorry. Can't Jen get you?"

"I didn't ask her." He sighs. "Actually I'm thinking it's time for me to get my own car."

We're walking outside now and the cold air is welcome. "Sounds like a good idea."

"My dad said I could have his truck. He and Mom are getting a new one or something and I—"

He cuts out midsentence when he catches sight of Dax, who's waiting leaned up against his car, watching the entrance to the building. I pause to take Dax in, relaxed in all the right ways, cord jacket over his hoodie, Dickies, lace-ups, one hand casually in a pocket. His skin is clear, face reddened from the cold, and a sweet grin comes over him at the sight of me.

I make Dax smile.

"What's he doing here?" Sam says, not smiling at all whatsoever.

"He's here for me," I say as lightly as possible and without more explanation.

Time stretches as Sam puts the pieces together, and I can feel the cloud of hurt settling over him, the years of our friendship and all its complications passing through both of us in slow instant after slow instant as we walk down the stairs. Obviously I've dated other people before, but not when things were so out of sync between the two of us, and besides, it was never out in the open so he didn't actually have to face it as anything meaningful. In fact, he knew it wasn't meaningful. At least not to the guys.

Sam, who looks incredibly uptight and tense next to Dax, bucks up and offers Dax his hand. "Hey, man." They shake.

I hug Dax and he holds me in close. "You need gloves!" He blows on my hands.

Sam almost convulses.

"You ready to go?" Dax says.

"Yeah," I say.

Dax looks over at Sam. "You need a ride?"

"No." Sam's voice echoes into the empty parking lot. "Buzz is still inside. He can take me. Or, uh . . ." He fumbles for his phone. "Jen can." He doubles back for the building. "See you later."

Dax still has his arm around me as Sam scrambles back up the stairs. Dax opens the door for me and I climb in.

Whatever Sam has to deal with next, I don't want to be there to watch.

CHAPTER TWENTY

When we get to my house we sit on the porch steps, side by side. Dax hasn't come inside yet but is getting incrementally closer, like he's inching his way toward my interior. I haven't asked him in because that would mean Mom-slash-Kevin-slash-Tiffany would be involved in what feels like something that's just mine for now. No outside influence or opinion needed.

"Thanks for coming to get me," I say. "Long way just to drive me a couple miles home."

"Of course."

The ball I have in my chest lately—not the one I'm used to that feels like a weight sitting between my ribs, but this new one that is warm and pulsing—it rolls and whirs.

"No sibling tonight?" I ask. The car seat that's usually in the back of his car is gone.

He lets out a small unidentifiable noise. "No." He doesn't offer anything further.

Mrs. Velarde walks by with her Bernese mountain dog, Sally. "Aren't you two cold?" she says.

"We'll only be out here a minute," I say.

"It must be nice to be young." She gives Sally a scratch behind the ear.

"It's okay sometimes," Dax says.

"You look cute." She smiles wistfully, eyes on my hands in Dax's, our legs rubbed against each other.

"Thanks, Mrs. V."

"Enjoy it." She makes a clicking noise and she and Sally continue down the block.

When she's gone, I give Dax a kiss on the cheek.

"I always want to tell people who say that being young is the best that they're only saying that because they're already through it," he says.

I look at him questioningly.

"They don't have to depend on adults for anything and whatever life they were going to have has already happened. They don't have the pressure of trying to figure it out. Whether they were victorious or failed, they're just finishing it out." He runs his fingers over mine. "We still have all of that ahead of us, you know?"

"So all we can do is make the best of it?"

Dax looks over at me and then down at our hands entwined between us. "I try to convince myself of that every day."

"Yeah."

A quiet settles like the air is hugging in to hear us.

"So, you have a sibling, too? What about the rest of your family?" I ask. We've been hanging out for a couple weeks now and Dax never talks about his family. I guess I don't talk about mine much either. Sometimes it's nice to exist without context, but I'm hungry for more of Dax, who he is, where he came from, what he means when he says he worries about the future.

"Oh, you know," he says. "The usual. They love me, they hate me. Lots of cousins, nice grandma. She isn't crafty though. She has a strict no-knitting policy. More of a sherry-while-watching-soaps kind of a lady."

"And your mom and dad?" I realize I don't even know who's in charge of him, where he comes from *really*, the bits and pieces that come to-gether to form Dax as a person.

"No," he says. "Mostly mom. Dad sometimes."

I wait for more, but he doesn't give it to me. Instead he hooks his index finger over mine and uses it to pull me toward him while also scooting my way. He kisses me and I love that I can anticipate the approach, the execution, how our lips will come together and feel as he brushes his lips against mine and his hands run over my spine.

It's been getting gradually more intense every time we hang out, but we haven't gone past this point. There are so many kinds of kisses: nibbling ones, ones that make your lips swell after, deep ones with tongue, little sweet ones, ones that make your insides burn and go all the way down your body, down your arms, your legs, below the belly button. I've never had the chance to feel that before, not when there was always a straight trajectory for the endgame. Kisses quickly turned to hands over the shirt, then under, then the search to undo the bra clasp, to get the jeans down, the panties off, the condom on, everything happening so fast I could barely take it in.

Now it seems like sex is eons away, like there's infinite time and it doesn't make any sense not to linger at each step.

The front door opens and Mom makes this little oops noise as Dax and I come apart.

"Hi," Mom says. "I didn't realize you were on the porch. I saw a car I didn't recognize in the driveway . . ." She squints. "Didn't we see you somewhere?"

Dax stands up and doesn't seem like he's dying on the inside even though my mom just totally busted us in a hard-core make-out session. He extends a hand. "Dax," he says. "We met at Petco."

"Right, right!" Mom teeters, trying to cover up how rattled she is. She does a bad job of it. "Well, it's nice to meet you." She glances at me. "I can't believe you two are sitting out here in the cold. Kevin's got a plate for you, Jo. You coming in?"

I'm about to invite Dax in too, but his phone buzzes and he pulls it out to check his texts. His expression only changes a little but there's enough of a flicker to make me wonder what's happening.

"I have to go." He shoves his phone back in his pocket. He lends me a hand to pull me to my feet.

"Bye, Mom," I say, because she's still standing there like she's confused about literally everything.

"Right," she says. "Nice to meet you, Dax." She disappears inside.

Dax gives me a quick peck on the lips. "I'll see you this weekend," he says. "We'll go out after the meet?"

"Yeah."

There's tension in him now, his movements quick instead of smooth. "Great," he says. "I'll text you."

My chest tightens. There's something he's not telling me.

When he gets to his car he looks back and for a moment the tension falls away from his shoulders and he's just looking at me on this cold winter night, with snow-covered trees all around us and holiday lights hanging from the houses, and everything about this and him feels perfect.

But then a shadow passes over him and he's eclipsed by whatever is happening. He gets in his car and drives away.

———————————

Kevin is fully upping his stepdad game. Instead of something I can't eat, he presents me with salmon, roasted broccoli, and a really decent-looking salad.

Mom and Tiffany are nowhere, probably doing all the bath time and bedtime things at the end of the house. Looks like it's just Kevin and me. I try to put my stress thoughts about Dax away and sit down at the table.

I start eating, then look up and say, "Thank you."

Kevin seems surprised. He takes the seat across from me with his own plate, which is more of the gloppy, family-friendly thing I'm used to seeing around here. Which means he made my dinner especially for me.

"You didn't eat?" I say. "Before?"

"Oh no," he says. "Figured I would wait for you."

For some reason, this makes my eyes fill and I have to look down at the plate to gather myself. "Thank you," I say again.

"Yeah, well, I realized you're always eating by yourself, you know?"

I swallow hard.

"The timing is funny for all of us sometimes," he says. "Everyone driving from here to there, me at the restaurant. Like your mom says, parenting is basically driving in circles." Kevin seems to catch my look. "Anyway, I know you're seventeen and everything, but you still shouldn't have to eat alone every night."

"Yeah."

We eat for several minutes in silence.

"It's good," I offer, instead of saying all the things that are suddenly at the edge of my lips.

"Thanks, Jojo," he says, trying my nickname like it doesn't quite fit in his mouth. He takes another bite, then pauses, fork in midair. "Uh, I wanted to talk to you about something."

"Yeah?"

"Yeah." He clears his throat and wipes his mouth with his napkin. "I heard there's a WWE thing happening in Denver in a couple weeks," he starts, checking my face for reaction. "I was thinking we could go."

"All of us?" I say, trying to imagine Tiffany sitting through a match without trying to leap into the ring, seeing Mom's disgust as she watches grown men throwing each other around, as she's reminded of Dad and his obsession with wrestling.

"Oh gosh, no," he says quickly. "The others would hate it. Just us."

I'm stunned, not sure what to say, frozen like a bird in a cat's mouth.

Kevin stands. "Shit, no, of course. That's your dad's thing, right?"

I don't think I've ever heard Kevin swear before.

"No, it's not that," I say, trying to recover. "There's just a lot going on right now."

"Yeah, of course." He sweeps his plate off the table and rinses it in the sink.

I want to stop him, to tell him of course I'll go, but he's already making a move for the stairs. "I'm going to check on Tiff."

He's gone so fast it's like he was never here and I'm left alone at the breakfast nook in the kitchen with a single light on over me. I watch the space where he was, tapping my fork against my plate, thinking.

CHAPTER TWENTY-ONE

I'm at Gutters with Leah, Jen, and Amber. I'm getting used to having friends who are girls and talking about stuff like dances. We also talk about Leah's horse, Mustard, Amber's trials as team captain of the cheer squad, and Jen's shitty home life.

Ah, yes. Jen's shitty home life.

Apparently they moved to Liberty to get away from one awful stepdad and immediately ran into another. Jen doesn't have siblings. It's just her and her mom so she feels guilty for wanting to leave.

"He's such a dick," she says now, grabbing hold of her pink bowling ball. "If literally anything is out of place in the house, he melts down. Like, towels have to be perfectly folded and all the cans lined up and in alphabetical order. He threw my UGGs in the trash because I left them by the door so I wouldn't get mud on the floor. I know there are way worse things but I can't wait to be in a dorm. I'm going to leave my stuff *everywhere*."

"But to be fair," Amber tells me. "It was probably time for those UGGs to go."

Jen lands a strike and Leah and Amber cheer. This is a weird way to bowl. No one seems to care at all about winning. No one is competing, not even Amber. We all just cheer wildly anytime it's not a gutter ball. I try to keep my eyes off the score but note that I am, in fact, the winner so far.

"What about you?" Jen asks. "You have a stepdad too, right?"

"Yeah," I say.

Across from us is a bowling league low-key dressed up like Elvis, slurping down beers. I wouldn't mind having one of those right now, actually.

"And he's not an ass?" Jen asks.

Amber stands for her turn. Her legs are six feet long all by themselves and all muscle. I've stopped thinking of them wrapped around Tyler for the most part, but I'm still in awe of their existence.

"I wouldn't go that far," I say, pulling myself back to the conversation. "He's a little bit of an ass but in an entirely nonthreatening way. I don't think I know him really even though I've been living with him for this long."

Jen takes a sip of her Coke. "You're lucky. He's not taking your phone when you're seventeen because you forgot to put a dish in the dishwasher. He doesn't make it so you're scared to speak at the dinner table."

"No, he doesn't do any of that," I agree.

A silence settles over us and the cries and shrieks of glory pick up in volume around us. The Elvises are winning and they're really pumped about it, rhinestones flying everywhere.

Jen munches on a mozzarella stick. "I think I had you wrong."

I prickle, sensing danger.

"I just always figured you wanted Sam, you know?" She fixes me with an intense gaze. "I thought you were a black hole and you were just sucking him dry, pulling him into all your drama."

I want to defend myself but I'm so stunned I can't.

"I mean, I see now it's not like that," she says. "I think I was just jealous."

"Jealous?" I think back to all the times Sam and Jen and I tolerated being around each other, spent time together, went to movies together, all the times I smiled an evil smile inside because Sam was paying more attention to me than Jen, laughing when I spoke, all our jokes, our fire promises, our easy physical way with each other.

"Yeah, that's not easy to live up to. You guys have been friends for so long. I know he helped you through your dad . . . He always says you saved him from middle school and then there's the whole wrestling thing. No matter what, I can't be part of that piece of his life and you can."

She's shaky. She must have been wanting to say this for so long.

"I thought you sucked," she says. "I thought you were doing it on purpose, leaving him dangling there so dependent on you, not letting him really be in a relationship with me." She sniffs. "I love him so much but I don't think I've ever really had him. He's always been mostly yours."

"You're up, Jennifer," Amber says, eyeing us with interest.

"Yeah," she says in a small voice, and goes to get her ball.

Amber and Leah talk about the dance playlist while I sit there so shocked it's like I'm drifting away from myself, the sounds of the people around me the only thing keeping me tethered to this bowling alley. I know I've always thought of Sam as mine. I've always thought that Jen would never measure up to what Sam and I had. But I didn't realize *Jen* felt that way, that she thought she didn't measure up either or couldn't compete or even was competing at all.

Holy shit.

This whole time I've thought Jen was the villain in my story, the one who swooped in and took my best friend away from me, but now I see it from her perspective and it makes me dizzy and turns my stomach.

Because *I'm* the villain.

When Sam and I took each other's virginities, I told him it would just be that one time. *I* told *him*. I told him I wanted us to practice on each other so we would know what to do when the time came for someone else. I used the word *practice*. I don't know how that's any different than what happened to me except that I told him outright instead of using him without his knowledge.

And Jen. I've been such an asshole to her. Making snide comments every chance I got, sending zingers her way or making her feel uncomfortable around her own boyfriend. When it's my turn I barely feel the ball in my hand or register my strike. I'm going over every minute I've spent with Jen, and I think what I'm feeling is . . . shame?

When we leave the bowling alley we all hug and say good night, then make sure we get in our cars safely. Amber is all about girl power and has given us all pepper spray with glitter in it for our key chains.

I never imagined a day would come when I wasn't sure I could be friends with Sam anymore and instead thought maybe Jen was the one I should have been friends with all along. I never thought I would think Amber was a kick-ass queen instead of Queen Bitch, and I never thought I'd be so excited about a school dance, but here we are. The world is an upside-down version of itself and I'm spinning, trying to find the ground.

CHAPTER TWENTY-TWO

Dax and I spill out onto the street with Franco and his girlfriend and Jamie and his boyfriend, both the alterna-sort.

We just finished watching a movie about a sea monster and lots of people running away from it and my ears are ringing from the noise and my eyes are trying to adjust to being outside in the light. It's worth noting that at no time did Dax try to turn our movie-watching time together into an opportunity for a hand job. It was just your average couple of hours in the dark. Except he held my hand the whole time and that did not feel average at all.

"You guys coming over to Jamie's?" Franco asks.

I've realized that Nina was the Asian girl I saw at the first meet where Sam beat Dax, which feels so long ago now. I've since learned she's Chinese American and so cool she makes my knees weak. Nina hooks her chin on Franco's shoulder. I'm told they've been together a long time and it shows in the way their bodies fit without them even noticing.

"Yeah, come!" Nina says. "Jo can tell us more about being the only girl wrestling with all these dudes."

"Yes!" Jamie's boyfriend, Nate, says. "Also you can tell us how you managed to hold Dax's interest for more than five minutes."

"Nate!" Jamie says.

Dax threads his arms around my waist. "Don't make me sound more interesting than I am."

"I wouldn't," Nate says. "All I'm saying is we haven't seen a girl with you more than once until now and I want answers."

"Not cool," Nina says.

"I think we're going to break off," Dax says. I notice he didn't address any of what Nate said.

"Fine," Jamie says. "Abandon us."

"Yeah, and take your fascinating girlfriend with you." Nina gives me a quick hug. "I hope we see more of you."

"I hope we see more of me too," I say.

Dax grins and we walk down the block, arms around each other. We pass the record store and the bagel shop, and finally he leads me into a restaurant that's brightly decorated fifties style. The waitresses wear poodle skirts and the waiters all have their hair slicked back. He hands me a menu.

"It's all cereal," I say after a quick scan of the options.

"Wrong. It's *every* cereal."

"Well, gals and guys, what'll it be?" the hostess says. "Booth or scounter?"

"Booth," Dax and I say in unison.

"Sure thing! Follow me." She swishes ahead of us, ponytail bobbing.

Ten minutes later we both have a bowl of sugar cereal in front of us. I remember the last time I was sitting across from a guy I liked with a bowl of cereal in front of me, in Ty's kitchen. This is nothing like that.

"So you have a little brother?" I say, crunching away.

"Yeah, Seth. He's three." His words are measured and effortful, like they cost him.

It does seem strange that Dax still hasn't invited me to his house, that he's never come into mine. At first it didn't, but it's been a month since we started hanging out. I know his friends, their friends, all the stories of how they met each other . . . but when it comes to his family Dax doesn't say anything at all, and he doesn't ask about mine either. Since this is the first time he's actually answered a question and offered more, I press.

"Tiff is four." I take another crunchy bite.

"You don't babysit her much?" he asks, and I can't tell the tone behind it or whether it's wistful or judgmental.

"No." I don't know exactly how to word it but I want to try, because I want Dax to try with me. "When Tiff was born, it was like she sealed the deal."

"What deal?"

"The one that made a new family for my mom. My dad died when she was pregnant. I just sort of never went home. I mean, I was there in physical form sometimes but . . ."

"But not your heart."

"Yeah."

He nods. "I get it."

"Who is Seth's dad? Do you have the same one or is it like me . . . with Kevin, I mean?"

Dax takes a big crunchy bite and waggles his eyebrows at me. "Want to go to the skate park after this?"

First of all, no. Second of all, he's doing the thing again where he isn't answering the question.

I shrug.

I hate the way my mind is suddenly swirling. Nate said no girl had been around for more than five minutes. That means multiple. *Girls.*

Everything I've heard about Dax being a player comes back in. He really hasn't pushed the physical but maybe that's because he's not into me that way. Maybe he doesn't want to introduce me to his family because he doesn't think I'm good enough to bring home. Maybe . . . *maybe* . . . his friends are in on it, used to going on mass dates with all the girls he seduces and casts aside.

Maybe it's happening again.

Dax puts a hand on my forearm. "Whoa," he says. "What just happened?"

I try to shake it off. "I don't know."

"Bullshit," he says. "Tell me. Did I do something wrong?"

"Yes. I mean no. Not really." I like spending time with Dax and I like kissing him, but I hate wading in shallow waters. I want him to know me like I want to know him and I don't want to have these doubtful thoughts anymore. If we're going to spend any more time together it has to be real. "That night at the party when we first met," I begin.

"Yeah?"

"You know how I said it was a really bad night?"

"Yeah."

"Well it was a *really* bad night."

Dax sits back, waiting.

"I had been seeing someone and I really liked him."

"You fall in love too easily."

"Right. I overheard him talking to this girl he was into right after he broke it off with me. He told her he was just using me for practice." I meet Dax's eyes. "Sex practice."

"Damn," he says under his breath.

"And he wasn't the only one. Turns out all three of the guys I thought I was in love with over two years were all doing the same thing. They said it to each other. They were all in on it."

"Practice girl," he says. "I've heard of it." He's holding my arm more steadily, all the cereal gone soggy in the bowls between us.

"You knew about me?"

"No. God no," he says. "But I've heard of that before. It's a thing. A super, super shitty thing."

"But boys will be boys," I say. "All you have to do is smile, right? Boys are always mean when they like you." I taste metal, like my hatred and anger have been born, elemental, in my mouth.

"Fuck no!" he says, then looks around and lowers his voice. "No. I am really sorry, on behalf of all piece-of-shit males, that that happened to you."

"Thank you," I say.

"What else you got?" he says.

"What?"

"Any other secrets you think are dirty but aren't at all?"

"I never wanted to be friends with girls until like a month ago and now I'm finding out . . ." I whisper, ". . . I kind of like them."

"OMG, no!"

We both laugh and sit back, things easy between us again.

"I'm planning a school dance," I say. "The Come as You Are Winter Ball."

"That's it." He cuts the air with his arm. "That's the deal breaker right there. Planning committees? You're out." He takes a drink of water. "No, seriously though. That's great. Sounds like fun."

The room seems to silence around us like we're the only ones there. "Earth Angel" starts playing on the loudspeakers as I make a neat pile of our dishes so it's easier for the waitress to grab as she hustles by.

"I have a reputation too," he says. "You know that, right?"

"I might have heard something. About you being a player? A fuckboy, one might say?"

"I was always up-front with the girls I was seeing," he says. "I didn't want a relationship. You say you get too into people too fast. Well, I can see what's attractive in a person but Nate wasn't wrong about the girls not coming around more than once. I wasn't trying to play them. I was waiting to feel attached to someone or for it to feel right and it never did."

My breath hitches.

"Until now, obviously. I never wanted to spend so much time with someone before. I've never been so fascinated and curious. I was up-front with them and I'll be up-front with you. I really like you, Jojo. I like you so much it makes me nervous and a little sick sometimes."

I'm pinned under his gaze and I pin him back.

The waitress comes by. "Can I have the check?" I ask.

We pay, not saying another word to each other. When we're back on the street, as soon as we're out of the restaurant doorway, I pull Dax to me and kiss him as hard as I can. I imagine him saying to other girls he dated that he wasn't feeling a full relationship. I imagine them getting hurt and angry, feeling played.

That's different than the way I was disrespected. That's forgivable.

He strokes the side of my ear, traces my jawline in the way I'm beginning to recognize as just for me.

"Dax," I say.

"Yeah?"

"Will you be my date to the Come as You Are Winter Ball?"

"I sure will," he says. "You know, my girlfriend planned it." He looks at me searchingly.

"Girlfriend." It's the first time anyone has ever used that word to describe me. It's every fantasy I've had about meaning something to someone, being special and wanted. I've been secretly calling Dax my boyfriend in my head for a couple weeks now, but this is different. This is out loud, clear, and spoken.

"Will you?" he says. "Be my girlfriend?"

I don't answer him with words, but instead with soft lips on a cold day on a city street, surrounded by people, feeling like I'm in a movie.

Feeling like I'm a star.

———

When I get home, Mom is waiting with condoms.

Literally.

She's sneaking around my room holding a box of double-fortified "you'll never get your sperm past this amount of rubber" rubbers, which makes me remember when Sam and I bought a box of condoms before we had sex and since we only used the one, we took the rest of them and stretched them over our feet and wore them that way, laughing so hard we landed in a heap in the middle of his bedroom.

Our coping mechanism, I guess.

"Mom, firstly what are you doing in my room, and secondly . . ." I indicate the large and clearly labeled box she's currently clutching.

"It's for sex," she says.

"I know it's for sex," I say. "I'm not having any and I can buy my own."

I want to tell her she should consider being less erratic about the ways in which she involves herself in my life. No need to jump directly into my vagina business.

She thrusts the box at me. There's a card on top.

"What's this?" I say.

"An appointment. I'll take you tomorrow. It's to get on birth control." She pushes past her obvious discomfort. "You can get an implant, an IUD, the shot . . . whatever you want, but I'd like you to discuss it with the doctor."

I don't know what to say so I look from the box and the appointment card in my hand to my mom and back.

"It seems like maybe you're spending a lot of time with Dax."

Ah, she remembered his name.

"You're a senior in high school and I have no idea if you're a virgin or not."

We quickly meet eyes and that's enough of an answer for her. She gives a slight nod. "I really haven't been here for you for any of it, have I?"

Again, I don't answer.

"Yeah," she murmurs. "That's something you should never have had to go through by yourself, unprotected."

"I've used protection, Mom. I'm not stupid."

"That's not the kind of protection I meant." She slumps into my chair, which means she's going to be here for a while, so I give up on my big "leave my room at once" energy and sit at the foot of my bed, saying a silent apology to Nanna for discussing sex while sitting upon the baby blanket she knitted for me.

"I should have talked to you about puberty—"

"Mom, please don't—"

"What it would be like to discover boys or girls or whoever else—"

I don't mention that I started having crushes on boys when I was eight, beginning with that kid Brian who did magic tricks in class and was *brilliant* at it. So charismatic.

"What it would be like to be rejected." She eyes me meaningfully. "Which happens to everyone and is so hard."

"Yeah," I say. "You know what they say. The first cut is the deepest."

"I didn't tell you even once that you have the right to keep yourself sacred."

"Purity rings went out in the 2000s, Mom."

"No." She picks up a picture of Sam and me, puts it back down. "Stop making jokes. Stop . . . kidding around about this." She puts her hands on her knees and leans forward. "You deserve to be valued, protected, cherished. I never told you any of that because my adult life has been a mess."

Sometimes when grownups are unexpectedly non-assholish there's something profoundly terrifying about it. If that can happen, perhaps the sun can also careen out of the sky, all the planets can lose gravity, and we can all float into oblivion.

"Mess might be overstating things—" I begin.

"No." She waves me off. "Mess is correct and I'm sorry because you bore the brunt of it."

I look at her, trying to assess just how open she is at this moment. Mom is usually a Peloton-fueled ambition machine whose blind attempts to create personal perfection make it impossible to carry on a meaningful conversation, but now I see a crack.

"Did you love Dad?" I blurt.

She moves like I whacked her and I want to retract my question.

"Yes and no," she says, after a long sigh and an even longer stare. At me. At her own hands. Back at me. "Of course I loved him when we met. He made me laugh so much. We brought you onto the planet and that's the best thing we ever did together. We weren't a good match and I let my dissatisfaction get the best of me. I should have left long before I did but I was determined not to have a failed marriage and not to mess things up for you."

I picture her trying to hold up the whole Earth on her own, trying to reverse its direction so everything happens the way she wants it.

"When I left your dad, I also left you. I didn't think you needed me." She lets out a pained exhale. "To be honest I thought you would choose to live with him, which you did, and that I'd have to fight you for a relationship—"

"Which you did." I remember weekends practically kicking and screaming, not wanting to come here to this house that seemed so neat and cold and boring, being so angry that Mom had made Dad sell our old place. Kevin seemed like a paper cutout of a person. Seriously, who is that nice? He looks like a stock photo of a dad you find in a Walmart picture frame. No wild brown curls like my dad, no mischievous eyes and unsymmetrical smile. Just white, straight teeth and a pleasant middle-of-the-road mouth. And when she got pregnant with Tiff? Forget about it. I actively wished she would burst into flames, or better yet, disappear altogether.

"I did," she says. "But when your dad died I got so tired I gave up. On you," she says. "I let you go through all these important years without any guidance. I accepted your rejection of me, which a parent should never do." She comes to sit next to me. I'm happy to find I feel less like shoving her onto the floor than I would have a few weeks ago. "And I just keep screwing up. I left you in Petco—"

"That's okay—"

"I left you by yourself," she insists. "I'm always leaving you by yourself."

This silences me.

"Your dad was like a really immature superhero," she says. "The last thing I expected was for his own heart to be his supervillain." She swallows hard. "And now you're having sex and I'm the worst at dealing with it."

"I told you I'm not having sex."

"But you have."

"Yeah."

"And you have had your heart broken? Recently, I mean?"

Not by a single person. I can't give Ty that much credit. By the world, maybe. By the way things work.

"Yeah," I say.

"And that's why you started wrestling."

"Yes."

"And that's when you met Dax."

"More or less."

"And you like him?"

"Yes." I love how my body relaxes when I say that, like every cell is exhaling at once.

"Good," she says. "We're keeping that appointment." She taps the card still clutched in my hands. "And use the condoms."

"Mom!" I say.

She ruins the moment of mirth by looking at me earnestly so I know this talk is not done yet. "I know I haven't been there for you in the way I should have been, so I've never told you this directly, but you deserve to be loved," she says. "You deserve to be loved for your whole self, your whole heart, all your flaws, wrestler or not, with or without sex. You deserve to be seen and appreciated for your essential being." She squeezes my shoulder. "You're extraordinary, Jo," she says. "And I am very lucky."

She gets up to leave.

"Hey, Mom," I say, and she stops. "Do you remember that time you bought me condoms and lectured me about my essence? That was cool."

"Ah, Jo," she says. "Sometimes you remind me so much of him it makes me want to weep."

CHAPTER TWENTY-THREE

Sam and I are standing a few feet apart in Leadership class. He's working the computer while I explain the slides. We did most of this project in school and have been going to the shelter at different times because I haven't wanted to be around him, but this morning feels different.

Everything has felt different since my movie and cereal date with Dax, and today is the first time I've seen Sam in weeks when I haven't felt an awkward pressure being around him.

"So as you can see, we've approached it three ways," I say to the class. "One, we gathered donations directly from the community and the school." The slide is showing Sam looking adorable, pulling supplies we collected out of the back of his dad's truck.

Sam switches the slide.

"We cleaned cages for a total of thirty hours each." Here there are pics of both of us playing with dogs, holding cats, and carrying piles of towels to the laundry room. Vicky, the animal-obsessed front desk lady, was more than happy to snap shots of us doing what she thinks every decent citizen should do with spare time.

"And finally Sam went over to the radio station and we advertised the annual spay-and-neuter-a-thon on air. Overall, their numbers for that event went up by 40 percent and we raised more than two thousand dollars in food and litter for them."

Sam steps up and the last slide, of Sam and me with ten cats, is on the screen behind him. "We feel we've exceeded the requirements for the assignment and that we've made a real impact in our community. We're proud of the work we did together and I hope you agree."

Miss Pike beams. We followed a campaign to change the sexist dress code, which will never happen, and a half-assed attempt to do Pennies for Patients that collected roughly 200 pennies in total. We definitely win for actually doing a good thing, although Sam did get a little squeamish over the neutering thing so I had to explain to him that he was not going to be forcibly neutered along with the dogs.

"Excellent job," she says. "This bodes well, not only for our community but whichever community you join when you begin to live your adult lives."

The class claps half-heartedly. Sam and I have always made a good team and it's nice to know we haven't totally lost it. He gives me a genuine smile and I smile back, all our years of friendship and knowing each other between us.

When class is dismissed we wander into the hall together.

"Glad that's over," he says. "Can't believe we're about to go on winter break. Everything is moving so damn fast."

"We still have the winter dance to get through and finals."

"I know," he says. "Still. Semester's almost over and then we just have one left and high school is done." He pauses. "Thanks for working on that project with me, even though we sort of did it separately."

"Yeah, we've both been so busy."

We linger and I want to tell him everything is okay, that we can put these very odd few months behind us now and move forward. I'm just about to say something when Jen emerges from the crowd.

"Hey, Jo," she says, looking between us.

"Hi," I say.

Sam leans over and kisses her. It's not a full-on make-out session like they used to do. It's sweet and private.

"I'll see you both later," I say. "You can go back to your cute love time now."

Jen nests herself into Sam.

"See you, Beckett," Sam says.

And it's not like things between Sam and me haven't changed but more like they have and it's okay. Everything's going to be just fine.

CHAPTER TWENTY-FOUR

We ended up getting Dax's friend Jamie to DJ, which is nepotism, I guess, except he was the only person who would do it for free and Dax wasn't being hyperbolic when he said Jamie is kind of a genius. The whole room is thumping, the snacks are carby and delicious, and I'm most satisfied to see that people took the nineties theme to heart. Chokers abound. Space buns are everywhere. Neon nail polish, black lipstick, everyone being as much of their fantasy selves as possible.

And I did it.

I was a part of it.

I helped fill the glitter bomb machine. I got the glow sticks. I helped Jamie figure out the playlist. People are dancing alone, in couples, in big groups, but the main, most important thing is that they're dancing.

Amber is surveying everything like she's the queen and we're all her minions, hands folded across her chest. "Okay, fine," she says. "You were right. This is better than the quasi-*Frozen*-themed thing I wanted to do."

"Thanks," I say.

Ty comes over to her. "Want to dance?"

"One," she says, "but then I need you to help me get more snacks."

"Okay." He doesn't hug me, but he looks like he wants to, like he would have before all of this happened and I put up a big invisible wall between us. "Hey, Beck," he says.

"Nope," I say, showing him my palm. "See you later, Amber."

"Sure will."

I go back to Dax and the little hub he's made with his friends. They're all here supporting Jamie. Technically it's illegal for kids from other schools to come unless they're a date but none of the teachers seem to be noticing at all. They're all dancing their faces off too since most of them are of the nineties.

Dax is a goofy dancer. He does not have smooth moves. He is not the kind to bump and grind, but he makes me smile the whole time we're dancing. He shimmies with me, he's temporarily my hype man, he jumps up and down periodically, and most of all he just does not care at all what people around him are doing. My stomach hurts from laughing by the time there's a break.

"We should have dances every weekend," he says.

"I see your future as a club kid."

"You know, I had no idea what I was going to do with my life until just now!" He wraps me in a sweaty hug. "Thank you for helping me see the light."

Franco and Nina come over to us. "Want to go outside for a few?" Franco says.

Nina threads her arm through mine. She's dyed her hair pink and has blunt bangs and the skin around her eyes is covered in body glitter. "Yes, come with us!"

"No, she's coming with me," Leah says, swooping in from the side. "There's going to be a riot if we don't get more cookies and soda out."

Nina releases me. "Oh, fine. But I have to go outside or I'm going to pass out."

"Come out when you're done," Dax says.

Leah and I tromp through the crowd that has mostly dispersed to the sides.

"Is he dreamy or what?" Leah says.

"He really is," I say. "I'm waiting for him to reveal his actual dickishness but it hasn't happened yet."

"And his friends are good too."

"Yeah."

"All I ask is you don't forget about us." She hugs into me. "I have you back and I don't want to lose you again."

"And you will not," I assure her. I really do like Dax's friends. They're so different and separate from everything I'm used to. But it's also been so good having Leah back in my life, and Jen and Amber have been a surprisingly pleasant addition to my world instead of the slow, arsenic-type poisoning I was anticipating.

I run into the kitchen and grab a few bags of chips while Leah fusses with what's left in the fridge. I get back to the table and empty a bag of pretzels into a bowl and Sam comes to stand next to me.

"Want some pretzels?" I say.

"I made weight by a hair last week," he says. "I'm holding it down with water and carrots."

I nod but I think I've found the thing that holds my weight where it needs to be, so I pop a pretzel in my mouth.

"Living dangerously," he says.

"You know me. A veritable adrenaline junkie."

"So," he says, "you've been spending a lot of time with Dax."

"Yep."

"Are you going out or what?" he asks, taking a sip of his water bottle.

"How is that your business?" I ask.

"Jesus, Beck, I'm just trying to look out for you. I don't want to see you get used."

"Yeah? Believe it or not, I'm not in any danger of that. Not with Dax," I add pointedly.

"Are you shitting me?" Sam says.

"You know, I was just beginning to think maybe things could go back to normal for me and you, but I'm not even sure what normal is anymore."

"I want things to go back to normal too. It's just we don't know this guy. His rep with girls is not good, and now he's dating you. You wanted me to look out for you before. You got mad that I didn't tell you what was going on. Well, I'm telling you that you should be careful of this guy using you like everyone else."

I wish for music. I wish for teleportation. I wish Sam would get sucked into a vortex and land on the moon.

"He's not using me," I say. "He is different than everyone else. *Everyone*."

Sam looks like he's been slapped.

"I'm sorry," he says. "I'm just being protective."

"Cool," I say. "Go protect someone else. I'm all good."

Sam puts his hands up, shakes his head, then turns and walks away.

After the final set when the lights come back on, Leah comes marching toward me. Amber is directing all the cheerleaders to pick up the room and everyone else is leaving in a stream. Silly String and streamers litter the ground. Glitter is everywhere.

"I need your help," Leah says urgently. "Jen got knocked off her saddle."

"What do you mean?" I say.

Dax wanders over, still a little sweaty. "I'm going to help Jamie load his truck, okay? I'll be back in a few."

"Okay." I have enough time to give him a quick peck before Leah drags me away. "What? What is going on?"

"Jen's wasted and Sam is AWOL."

"AWOL, like gone?"

"AWOL, like no one knows where he is and his girlfriend of several years needs friends right now."

She yanks on me and pulls me into the kitchen. Sure enough there's Jen, leaned in a crouch against the wall, blurry with drink.

"You okay?"

"Oh, yeah. I just had too many alcohols and my boyfriend is a dick."

Leah gives me a look. "She's coming to my house. She can't go home like this. Her parents would herniate."

"Agreed." And if she was driving Sam and he's disappeared . . . "I'll drive her car and have Dax follow."

I squat down so I'm at eye level with Jen. She reaches out and clumsily strokes my hair.

"Okay." Leah looks at me worriedly. "Let's get you up and out of here."

"Sam left me. He just *left* me at my own dance," she says as Leah and I try to steer her toward the door.

Amber and Ty appear and Amber gives Jen a sour look. "You're losing it, babe," she says.

"Sam said—" Jen begins.

"I don't want to hear what Sam said. You keep your wits about you and let no man have control," she says, then pats Ty's back. "Sorry but those are the rules."

"Understood," he says.

"Let me know when she's safe from herself," Amber says. "And someone take her phone. She can't be allowed to drunk-text tonight."

Jen starts gagging and Leah, Amber, and I get her to the sink just in time for all the contents of her stomach to slosh out of her. A smell that is both rancid and sweet rises toward us.

"Ugh, gross," Amber says, holding Jen's hair aloft. She pats Jen's head. "There, there."

Leah and I meet eyes behind Jen's back. Amber is so bad at being compassionate.

"Whoa." Dax is in the kitchen doorway. "Shit went awry, huh?"

"Sure did."

Jen's just rinsed her mouth with water and she points at Dax with a lopsided smile. "You're nice. I thought you were a smug asshole but you're not at all."

"Oh," Dax says, "she's truth-serum drunk."

"Oh, yeah," I say, dropping in for a kiss.

I tell him the plan and we caravan over to Leah's, leaving the last of the cleanup for the morning. The whole way I'm driving Jen's car to Leah's, weaving through the familiar hills, I'm thinking I'm grateful, grateful, grateful to have met Dax.

I haven't been to Leah's in four years. The last time I was here was for an awkward sleepover. I was already obsessing over boys and I wanted to talk about that, while Leah just wanted to hang out with her horse. We spent the whole night ignoring each other stonily.

Leah's parents are waiting at the end of the dirt road that leads into their ranch with the light on and already have the bed made up with the same comforter I used to use with the little pink roses on it. They both fuss and give me hugs when I cross the threshold into the house, both exclaiming how glad they are to see me, what a long time it's been, how much I've grown.

Her dad mutters something about how no one ever better be dragging Leah in like this in the middle of the night. The good thing is Jen is basically already asleep so it's just a matter of getting her between the sheets. Dax is outside waiting in the idling car and I cannot wait to be out of here and in it with him.

Leah's mom helps us get Jen into bed and then says, "I'm going to get a bowl in case."

"She already puked," Leah says.

Her mom pauses in the doorway. "Yeah? Still."

"Everything okay?" Leah's dad peers over her shoulder. He doesn't wait for an answer, just says, "Good, great," and then disappears down the hall.

Leah is in her room getting Jen a T-shirt to sleep in and I'm just about to tiptoe out when Jen's eyelids flutter and she moans. "Spinning."

"I'm sorry. That's the worst." I've only had the spins once and it was enough to make me extremely careful about how much alcohol I drink.

She grabs hold of my arm. "He always loved you the best. I know that. It's okay. It's not your fault." She smiles with her eyes closed. "It's just the way it is."

She's talking about Sam.

"Go to sleep, Jen," I say. "Have sweet dreams and don't worry about Sam and me. That's never going to happen."

"Mmmm," she says.

"He loves you," I coo. "Only you."

A few minutes later, she's snoring lightly.

Under normal circumstances I would try to find Sam, text and call until I could get answers, try to make him feel better because if I'm guessing right, he's somewhere in worse condition than Jen right now, probably in some emotional Sam hole. But I'm not doing that tonight.

When I go outside, Dax turns his music down and smiles, and that smile is enough to light up the night.

It's enough to illuminate everything.

CHAPTER TWENTY-FIVE

Dax's car is warm and totally devoid of puke, any trace of sick, or the smell of recent purge, which is an utter delight.

"How'd that go? I would have helped—" he says.

"No, no," I say, thinking of Jen's mumbling, fumbling words about Sam. "No. Absolutely zero need for that. Staying out here was perfect. *You* are perfect."

Even in the shadows I can see the pleasure moving over his features.

"Thank you for waiting out here for me."

"Literally nothing else to do."

This is patently untrue. Franco and Jamie and Nina and Nate were going somewhere to do something fun. Probably create a sculpture in some Denver park or paint a mural or something.

"So, I'll take you home now?" he says.

It's well past midnight. The lights go out one by one inside Leah's house. Her parents are probably settling down into their comfortable country brass bed right now falling asleep under their favorite family portrait.

"I don't want to go home. Not yet."

I'm nowhere near ready for sleep. My body's doing the thing where it's buzzing so hard if I tried to get in bed now I'd be in for several hours of staring at the ceiling.

Dax taps on the gearshift.

"What?" I say.

"My mom isn't here right now so my house is empty. My brother is with my grandma so . . ."

I have to admit the night has made me feel like I have a head full of polyester fluff so it takes me a second to figure out he's saying more than he's saying. If I'm not horribly mistaken right now, and there's an 85 percent chance I am, I *think* he's asking me to stay.

"Oh," I say, startling myself with the realization. Dax lives like thirty minutes away from here. If I go with him it would be to spend the night. Like, *allll* of the night.

A whole night with Dax. Alone.

"What am I thinking?" he says. "You probably have stuff to do in the morning."

He has confirmed it. I am not mistaken. He is asking me to spend the night.

"No," I say quickly. "Nothing."

"So, do you want to come?" he asks, then realizes the words he's spoken. "To my house, I mean? Oh my gosh, everything sounds wrong."

"Yes," I say. "I want to come to your house." Praise everything holy that I thought enough ahead to put my toothbrush and one of those dentist office toothpastes in my bag before I left for the dance. I have a hoodie in there too and fresh undies because you never know what could happen at a dance, plus life has taught me carrying around an extra pair of undies is never a bad thing.

I expect we're going to drop into that heavy expectant silence, but instead we chat the whole way to his house about music and skating and cartoons and school and before long we're twisting and turning through a Denver neighborhood I don't recognize at all. The houses are old, maybe even really old, with turrets and shingled exteriors. Dax pulls into a parking spot that's really just a portioned-off piece of sidewalk. It's a nice residential area except for the gas station I can see from here with a bunch of guys sitting in a cluster out front, one of them nodding out.

"This place used to be my grandma's," he explains, "before she moved to that condo in Liberty. My mom bought this place from her."

Even though I know there's no one here, I have the urge to creep around carefully until Dax flips on the lights. There's antique furniture everywhere and it smells musty but it's warm, with Persian rugs draped across the floor and lots of toys in baskets.

"Your brother likes Legos?" I say stupidly, since judging by the enormous Lego dragon before me, that is clearly the case.

"We both do." Dax is in the kitchen getting some water. "Want some?" He holds up his glass.

"Yes, please." I sound formal and now that we're here the nerves are making a comeback.

Dax comes over with the water and I take a few cool sips, pick up one of the framed photographs. Dax's mom is blond and petite, with glassy blue eyes and a pointy nose. She looks birdlike and bovine all at once, and even though Dax is standing behind her in the picture and his brother is tucked into her lap, her worry and discomfort sit lodged behind her smile.

"Want to watch TV or something?"

I put my water down and hug him, and within seconds we're back in that pool of feeling, or at least I am. Everything stills. Even the sound of the cars passing by outside is dulled.

"Where's your room?" I ask.

He raises his eyebrows for a second then takes my hand and leads me up the creaky stairs with small piles of books stacked in its corners.

"One more level," he says.

I catch enough of a glimpse of the second floor to see there are two rooms and a bathroom with a white sink and clutter all around it. The inside of what must be his mom's room is filled with muted pinks and lavenders and is otherwise dark.

Dax lives in the attic. I check to make sure the bed looks clean because it's a universal truth that boys don't actually wash their sheets. It's neatly made. In fact, the whole room is pretty together. A couple skateboards hang on the walls and his makeshift closet looks like a hanging rack in a store. Of course, there's the mandatory TV/PlayStation setup, the shelf of wrestling trophies, and old action figures, but I don't see anything super sloppy or creepy in here.

There is something about seeing where someone sleeps. It tells you a lot about them.

Dax gets a T-shirt from the drawers in the corner and throws it to me. "You can sleep in this."

"Okay." I take off my shirt, unclasp my bra, and throw on Dax's tee, a plain red one that's so worn and soft it's almost disintegrating.

Dax's mouth is ajar as I pull off my skirt, leaving my legs bare.

"I'm going to brush my teeth," I say.

"I—you're—" he says.

"Be right back." I take my backpack with me and traipse down the stairs pretending like my heart isn't beating out of my chest. Sometimes you just have to pop the cherry on something awkward, and showing your boyfriend your boobs when he isn't expecting it is one real way.

Dax slips into the bathroom next to me and gets his toothbrush out of the cup next to the sink. We brush together, catching each other's eyes in the mirror. This I've never done with a guy before, moved the brush up and down, spit into the sink, washed my face, put my hair in a short ponytail.

These small human rituals.

"We don't have to do anything," he says, toothpaste in the corner of his mouth.

I wipe it with my finger. "You're right. We don't." I've never considered the possibility that a guy might not be ready to be physical. It's been a little more than a month since the Petco thing and we haven't done more than kiss. Now that I'm armed with an IUD and the trusty condoms I've been carrying around with me, I think I'm ready for whatever comes next, but I don't know if the same is true for Dax. "But . . . do you want to?" I ask.

"So much," he says.

I kiss him and we walk up the stairs wordlessly. I have a reel I can't keep away playing through my head. All the times I've guided a guy to his own bed or mine. Every time I've been naked on top of one or under one or have reached for a condom or asked and answered questions about what feels good or what's working or what isn't. Looking back, it was all so technical. There is the physical reality of bodies meshing with bodies and how that feels, but there's also the other part, how much we like each other, and how great our bodies feel, and our kisses feel, and our hands feel. Yeah. That's there. The way his fingers feel tracing my skin, how our legs fit together, how our tender skin turns electric when it touches. All of it is happening.

But for once I allow myself to fold, to become a container for everything Dax is, to expand outward toward him. I feel like I can hold it all, like there's infinite space for him and for me. As my hair feathers across his chest and our mouths explore each other's bodies, even as the act is so physical, I'm taking in his laughter, his playful eyes, his kindness, his sadness, every wonder he's brought to me. I'm holding it and he's doing the same for me. He's making space for all of me and I'm so grateful for all the ways our bodies can meet, that I can press my ear against his chest and that it's delicate and sensitive enough to hear his heartbeat through his rib cage. I'm so grateful that the next time we kiss, I laugh. He laughs too, and it's like we're both saying, *hey, I'm here and you can see me and shit damn, isn't that a miracle?* And we both know what we're saying to each other and that *is* a miracle, and then there's an itchy feeling, one I've never felt before and it comes on like a wave I can't stop. It blows through me and it's like everything I ever kept held deep inside and away from everything, protected, is coming up and I want to stop it because it's scary as hell but I can't.

I cry.

I think he cries a little bit too.

We don't talk for a while, just lie there breathing, listening to each other, trying to get closer, closer, closer. We do some talking, doze off, wake up, but I get this feeling like we're both trying to cling to this, to pry our lids open, to live every second of this night, like we're afraid if we go to sleep we'll wake up and find out the whole thing was a dream.

Dax drives me home as the sun is coming up. We stop back at the Marshmallow Maven for hot chocolate and bagels and I marvel at how much has happened since the last time we were here. He never tells me we need to talk, that there's been a mistake, that this is awkward, and he holds my hand whenever it's free.

I doubt anyone will even notice I'm gone, and even if they did I could use Jen as an excuse, but I still want to get home before Tiff wanders out of her room for cereal and cartoons. I haven't slept and if anything were happening aside from the two weeks of holiday break that are stretched out before me, I would be upset.

Except for the fact that I feel totally calm, still even. It's amazing how the absence of busy, pointless thought can fill a space.

He pulls up in front of my house, goes around the car and guides me out of it, then hugs me close. "Here we are again," he says. "Except different."

"Yup. Different." The street is illuminated but hazy with pinks and oranges, like sherbet. I see the sunrise all the time now, but I can't say I usually notice it quite this much. I look deep into his eyes. "Dax, you make me feel like I could climb the highest mountain, like I could swim across the sea."

He smirks, but his eyes kaleidoscope furiously. "You kid."

"Sort of," I say. "You do actually make me feel like my internal organs have been replaced by fluff."

He kisses me and I flash on our careful toothbrushing this morning, somehow different from last night's.

I think about the guys I've thought I was in love with and I can see how it was just infatuation, overlooking things that weren't right or compatible, turning their flaws into cute little eccentricities, and meanwhile never even taking myself into consideration.

"I love you." He says it close in, so I feel the words against my still-tingling lips. It makes all my jokes seem like pitiful attempts at defense.

No boy has ever said this to me before in a romantic context. Only Sam, and he doesn't count. And definitely for sure no one has ever said it to me after sex, after all the nervous fumbling and weird noises and faces and the cleanup and the knowing this is as close as two people can ever physically get to each other on this earth.

"Too soon?" He cradles my head so my chin tilts toward him.

"No," I say. "I don't think so. But . . ."

He lets go of my chin and buries his face in his hands dramatically. "Oh, shit. There's a but. Ladies and gentlemen, she's going to leave me hanging. Or wait . . . is she going to leave me? Was my sexual prowess so subpar that she is fleeing?"

"No! Stop it. What I was going to say is that if you ever want to break up with me or you don't like me anymore—"

"Love you," he says. "I said I love you."

"Okay. If you don't love me anymore, promise me you'll tell me the truth. Promise we'll always be honest with each other, that I won't have to find out from someone else, that I'll always be the first to know. Not Franco, not Jamie. Me. You won't ghost me or treat me badly. You'll talk to me like I'm an actual person, lack of penis notwithstanding."

"Of course." He says it so simply, as if it's the most obvious thing in the world, and I believe him. He kisses me. "Also, I'm very glad for your lack of penis."

We press our foreheads together and the feeling drips like honey from head to toe. For the first time since I started having crushes on boys and definitely since I started sleeping with them, I don't feel like the bottom is going to drop out from under me any second. I feel like I'm standing on solid ground.

"I love you too, Dax."

He makes a triumphant fist. "Yessss," he says. "I knew it." He jumps and clicks his heels together.

Dax drives off into the sunrise trailed by soft, uncomplicated clouds.

I stand in my driveway waving at him.

For a second I can't identify how I'm feeling, this warmth even though the morning is cold enough for me to see my breath. My feet planted firmly. My breath even. No pit between my ribs. A pleasant soreness in my thighs.

But then I know.

After all of it, everything I've been through, every betrayal and anxious minute, I'm not afraid anymore.

CHAPTER TWENTY-SIX

We're kind of acting like a family tonight, making grilled steak fajitas with all the trimmings, plus a big salad. Kevin seems almost as nervous as me, moving in ellipticals as he gets everything ready while Tiff sets the table.

They want everything to be perfect. That's what Kevin said. Tomorrow is the district championship and even though they can't come they want to do something to celebrate with me. We're still a ways off from finals, but they're coming. Tiff and Mom made an apple crumble and it's nice how the house fills with the smell of brown sugar and butter.

But the other part of this and what's making me feel equal parts nauseated and excited is that Dax is coming over for the first time officially. We got through all of the holidays, all the celebrations and gatherings, sneaking off just the two of us. To the movies, to the park, to the tops of remote hills . . . anywhere we could be alone. But finally I decided I want him to meet my family because Dax and I say we love each other all the time now. Our hearts beat as one and stuff, and it doesn't seem right to have all that going on and not have my family even really know who he is.

I can't decide whether I'm more nervous to have him meet them or them meet him. Having been in his house that first night, I'm trying to see mine through his eyes. The butter and apple smell plus the candles Kevin lit all over the house do warm it up a little so it doesn't look so much like a catalog and I know he's going to like my room. Just the thought of being in a room with a bed with him sends me down a whole spiral of sex memories and I have to force myself back to where I am right now, chopping bell peppers into julienned slices the way Kevin taught me.

"That's great," he says. "Excellent chef cuts." He glances over to where Tiff is setting the table. "Remember the napkins go on the left of the plate."

"Which is left?" she says.

"The side that makes the L when you hold up your hands."

She does it, squinting as though to see better, then nods and re-arranges the napkins. She's been learning all her letters and is already almost reading. Tiffany might be smarter than anyone wants to believe.

"Can we put on some music or something?" I need some distraction.

This is a momentous occasion. I am bringing my actual, real boyfriend home. I am a senior in high school and this makes me feel like I'm doing a traditional thing I'm supposed to do in my high school career, a thing I thought I would never get to do maybe ever.

Mom fiddles around with the computer and in another second some old Beyoncé is playing, and my heart rate starts to slow. She comes up behind me, having pulled her brain out of real estate mode long enough to participate in the evening.

"You okay?" she says.

I'm on to onions and my eyes are starting to tear. "Yeah," I say. "Hand me that rag."

She gets the red towel from the oven handle and I use it to blot my eyes. She checks the dining room where Kevin is going over Tiffany's tablescape and setting job like he's preparing for the queen.

"He wants you to know he cares," she says.

"It's sweet," I admit. "He's like a really domestic Ken doll."

"He's more than that," she says. "I hope you're so lucky as to have someone you can really count on."

I know she's talking about Dad and all the ways in which he failed her, and my blood pressure spikes. She seems to sense it, lets a hand linger over my back.

My phone buzzes on the counter next to me and she releases me and gets the heavy cream, pours it into the mixer's bowl.

I wipe my hands and look at the screen. There's a message from Dax.

So sorry i can't make it. I'll call you later.

I suck in my breath like I've been punched. I *feel* like I've been punched.

What's wrong? Are you okay?

I watch the screen for a while, but after there's no response I put the phone back on the counter and try to gather myself.

Mom had started the mixer but now she flips it off.

"Something happen?" she says.

"Dax isn't going to make it." I try to keep my voice light, get another onion for the pile.

We have little bowls of salsa, sour cream, avocado . . . everything's almost ready for this pointless event.

"Well why not?" Mom says.

In the dining room, Kevin perks up like a gazelle sensing a lion.

"He didn't say. Just that he couldn't come and he would get in touch."

Mom furrows her brows. "Okay, more apple crisp for us!"

"Yeah."

Mom sticks a finger in the whipped cream and licks it. "Perfect," she says.

Kevin hovers and Mom gives him a look I don't miss. It says, *Don't talk to Jo right now.*

I try to focus on the task in front of me, on cutting the onions. I'm doing an awful job and Kevin doesn't even correct me.

Mom starts wiping down the counter. "You know, the first time your dad introduced me to Nanna it was a total disaster."

"Yeah?"

"Yeah," Mom says.

Mom's dad died a few years ago and she never got along with her mom, who's English and so critical of everything Mom does they tacitly agreed never to speak except on holidays. Dad's mom, Nanna, moved to Florida after Dad died. She had friends there and didn't have anyone here except me and Mom, and with Kevin the new husband it didn't make much sense for her to be hanging around.

I feel the void where my grandparents should be. Nanna is on social media and looks like she's having the best time ever. I'm waiting for her to invite me to visit her but I'm not sure she ever will. Nanna and I should have grieved for my dad together, but some things are too painful for people to get past.

I resume chopping onions and now am even happier onions make me cry.

"Your dad had the great idea that he was going to bring me to his family's Thanksgiving, but it turned out to be a mess. I walked in and Nanna was in a fight with her mother-in-law."

I love the stories of Dad's family and their arguments and debacles. Mom was from this buttoned-up conservative family. Dad must have been a total hurricane in her reality. Or maybe it was like she had been buried alive and he dug her out. Depending on the day, she could give you either version and both are probably true.

"Uncle Bob was drunk in the corner playing with the corgi and Aunt Marie was standing over him yelling because he had too much whiskey, and Julian was eating all the pie even though it wasn't even dinnertime yet." Mom opens the oven to check on the apples. "And Nanna was screaming at Granny Q because she brought a boiled chicken to Thanksgiving."

I laugh. Granny Q was a tiny woman, but she had survived World War II and some pieces of her had never gone back to right. Plus, she could be so salty no one would stand up to her except Nanna.

"Nanna towered over her saying, 'What kind of a person brings a boiled chicken to someone else's Thanksgiving?' and Granny Q screamed up at her, 'I wanted a backup in case you burned the turkey.' And then Nanna got so upset she threw her apron down and left. It was so different from anything I'd ever seen before. I knew your dad was embarrassed, but I sort of loved it. It was so wild. And I was in love. I don't think I knew it yet, but I was smitten. Your dad had been wooing me, doing a great job of it too."

"Wooing? No one says wooing."

"Okay, courting then."

"Sigh, Mom."

"Whatever you want to call it. He serenaded me after my French class one day; he left flowers on my dashboard. He wrote me passionate love letters. He told me that he knew he was in deep water when he met me, and he saw no reason to pretend it was anything else."

"So he did make you feel like you could count on him?"

"In that way. I never doubted he loved me." She puts the dessert on the cooling platter. "Do you? Have doubts about Dax?"

"I haven't until now."

"Then trust that. Starts are always a little rocky. Meanwhile, we've got all this good food. Let's not have it go to waste."

We eat, everyone quiet at first, but pretty soon we're all talking to each other about Tiff's ballet, the house Mom just sold, the sous-chef at Berlin Kevin might want to fire for dipping into the wine supply. I don't forget about Dax or stop wanting to ask him a hundred questions about what could possibly be so important that he had to miss this after all the effort everyone put in. But then I remember his open face, his trusting eyes, and I think I owe him that same trust. I have no reason to think he would ever betray me or blow me off without talking to me. If he wanted to break up with me, he would just tell me.

He promised.

I stare at his message again. It's strange for sure with its lack of details and the way it came at the last minute. But Mom is right. I have to trust Dax. I have to get over myself and my fears and give myself over to him completely.

> I'll see you tomorrow
>
> I love you

I try not to be bothered by the fact that my words hang there and that the next time my phone buzzes it's a message from Leah asking me how the night went.

I try not to tell myself that I will never learn.

CHAPTER TWENTY-SEVEN

Sometimes when little dogs get excited about seeing someone, they pee. They also do this when they're afraid. This is exactly how I feel the morning of regional semifinals. It's the first time I'll have the chance to try out my dad's moves in a competition and it's also pretty likely (due to a combination of upper-body strength issues and terror) that I'll wind up on my back. It's also true that I've been working a lot with Barney and he's taught me his tricks too, namely the speed part, the no-hesitation part, and the part where you pretend your life depends on it.

"Feeling okay?" Sam says.

"I'm feeling great!" I say, partially trying to avoid a conversation with any depth and partially trying to make it true. Maybe if I smile hard enough and do enough positive visualizations, I'll be okay.

"Did you see the lineup?" he asks.

"No, why? Do I have to fight Chad again?" I picture him, unibrow and taut muscles, breathing his foulness into my face. Nay, please, anything but that.

"No," Sam says, light, clear eyes filling with hope because I haven't shut down the conversation immediately. "Shiloh Velazquez."

"Oh, great. Does he have special skills I need to know about? Some kind of lockjaw issue?"

"Nope. Shiloh's a girl. She's just your size, Beckett."

I scan the room rabidly looking for this girl and I find her stretching. It has to be her. There aren't any other girls on the docket. She's petite, Latinx, smaller than me but built so wiry she looks like she could be cast as a superhero. She's *that* in shape.

Curse my laziness. If I had worked harder, I could be as ripped as her. I should have kept on with the extra workouts instead of focusing on dances and boys. I should have made more of an effort. Now that this Shiloh girl is in front of me and I know she's going to be my opponent, it's clear that I've been lying, telling myself I probably won't win against a boy so it's okay if I keep losing. I haven't had any real skin in the game except a persistent desire to make the boys on my team see me.

Now though.

Now Shiloh the girl wrestler is bringing a whole other dimension into it. Slow and calculated as an alligator, she raises her head and meets my eyes, observing me coolly from her section of the floor like I am but a mite, but a microbe in her world. Her hair is in two French braids that are so tight they pull at her eyes so it's hard to tell whether she's actually giving me a death stare or that's just what's happening to her face.

Oh. Nope. That's a death stare.

"She's hot," Mason says. "Controversial opinion: There should be more chicks in wrestling. Why stay divided? Let's put some mixers in the blender, get on that Twister board, and see what happens."

"Ew, Mason," I snap.

"Sorry!" He bends over into a hamstring stretch. "I didn't realize your Aunt Flo was in town."

I really want to smack him. Really, really badly.

Instead I turn my focus back to Shiloh, hoping I'll get some hint about her tactics. She gives me a small tilt of the chin and her eyes flash. Why I am suddenly in an eighties movie, I do not know.

I wave to her and smile. She does not smile back.

Okay, fine. I go back to my corner and stretch, trying to make the entire place disappear, suddenly so grateful neither Leah nor my family could make it today. Or Dax.

I push that aside, expunge his name from my brain sphere. Just thinking about him still makes my eyes fill. I waited a day before I blocked him on my social media, two before I blocked his number on my phone. Two days of sending unanswered messages, of checking Snapchat and Instagram for signs of his existence and there was nothing.

Nothing. He didn't even open any of them. I would have reached out to Jamie or even Nina but I kept thinking about how they talked about the rotating door of girls. I won't be the butt of another joke, and is that what I am? Can it really be that I was so totally duped again? I blush all the way to my internal organs every time I think about all the feelings, how Dax promised me he'd be on the level. I try to keep all those thoughts away, but they crash like birds against a window, causing cracks, cracking me.

There's nothing for it but to put one foot in front of the other (again) and try to hold my head up high (again).

The Dax nightmare has actually fueled my resolve to put all my focus on the team for the remainder of the season, to be a single-minded automaton so I at least know that even if it was only for a couple of months, I gave this my all.

But now here is Shiloh Velazquez looking for all the world like she's planning to eat me for lunch. How are her muscles so sinewy?

"Jo, you look a little peaked," Barney says.

I feel a little peaked.

"She has a demonic aura," he says. "Good defense strategy." He grins, pulling his glasses down. "But she's no match for everything you've got in your pocket. The Donkey Kong, the Frogger, the PAC-MAN? The AC/DC? Come *on*! She doesn't stand a chance."

"Thanks, Barney. I appreciate that."

"Yeah, and think of it this way. It's a short reprieve from the circle jerk that is sports." Reading my shocked expression he says, "Oh, I kid. Mostly. I keep coming back, don't I?"

"There is a mysterious gravitational pull to all of it," I say.

"Indeed. Good luck, my friend," he says, "and may the odds be ever in your favor."

"Oh, ha. You are hilarious, Barn."

"That's what they tell me." He snaps his arm straps and saunters away.

I can't say I totally understand Barney, but I do really like him.

"Beckett vs. Velazquez meet at mat #3. Repeat, Beckett vs. Velazquez meet at mat #3."

Somehow, I'm walking to the mat.

Somehow, I'm getting into position.

Somehow, I'm shaking her hand and trying not to notice how hard she squeezes.

And then it starts. I don't hesitate but I'm not thinking either. My body is on automatic as I go for her legs to try to pull her down, but she's just as quick and it doesn't work. Someone must have given her the same advice, to be faster than everyone else. She's so strong.

All I have to do is keep moving, keep her from pinning me. She almost does it but then I picture Tyler. I picture him saying I'm just a practice girl. I picture him saying other things too, things he never said but I'm pretty sure he thought. That I am worthless. That I'm too easy to be given any respect when he and his boy band of a team are screwing anything they can get their hands on. They're the ones who are worthless, cheap, lazy, rude little assholes.

Shiloh Velazquez squeals as I spin around on her.

"Thirty seconds," the ref says.

I don't want to feel uncertain. Uncertain makes me mad. Mad like PAC-MAN.

Mad like Donkey Kong.

I get out of her grasp, rise above her, and pin her with the Q*bert in a single flash. The look on her face tells me everything I need to know. Sheer panic has smoothed her features, widened her eyes, and tensed every muscle under me. She can't get free.

"One, two. That's the match." The ref slaps the mat and I stand up, legs shaking.

"Good job," Shiloh says.

"You too."

What I'm not expecting, other than how nice Shiloh was once the match was over, is how much love I get from the guys and from Coach. It's like I've performed a miracle, like they now believe anything can happen. Actual wings can sprout from my back and they won't even do a double take. They cheer. They yell. They sing. And the whole time I'm feeling like I almost wish they knew it's my conflicted loathing of them and everything they stand for that got me through it and helped me put Shiloh on her back. I'd like to set up a lunch date with her, find out exactly how much we have in common.

Either way, because of our performance today, the Sentinels are going to finals, March 7th at 9 a.m. at the Denver Convention Center. We will be there and because of this win today I get to compete.

Sam is the last to hug me. He's been hanging back, watching, but now he approaches. He won his match too (of course) and now we can relax. "That was incredible," he says. "You looked furious. And wasn't that last move something your dad used to do? I forgot about it and then all of a sudden it came back to me."

"Yeah," I say. "Me too."

Sam hugs me for the first time in what seems like forever. "I'm proud of you," he says.

I have to fight all the snarky comments that want to spill forth, about me not needing his approval or his pride in me either. I did this myself. I can feel him wanting to sink into one of those long hugs, wanting to go limp against me and let me hold him up. Obviously, I can see there's something going on with him. He has that look. Despite his strength and his extremely developed chest, Sam is basically a marshmallow, and I know that even though he's telling me he's proud of me, what he really wants is someone to absorb his stress. My resistance to that is visceral as I push him away.

"Thanks, Sam. I appreciate the support you've given me," I say woodenly.

He lets a pained breath slip. "You are quite welcome," he says in a dramatically robotic voice. "Nice to meet you, ma'am." He slips his bag over his shoulder and gives me a long look. "What happened to us, Beckett?"

"Happened? Nothing."

"Yeah." He looks like he wants to say something, but instead pushes the words down. "Okay."

He walks away to join the other guys and they troll off to wherever they're going.

I head to my car. I have no interest in joining them.

That night at 66, I am executing all my orders like a machine. Leah is having a more complicated night so I'm trying to help her out when Amber and Jen blast through the door. Amber seems to be chasing after Jen who is careening right toward me.

I can tell she's been crying. Her face is streaky and red and blotchy.

"Whoa, Jen, are you okay?" I say.

"For the record," Amber drawls, "I told her dumb ass not to come over here. She needs to stop getting yanked around by that POS and draw a line. This is about him and his behavior, not about you. Also, it's boring. I thought we were getting our nails done tonight, not having emotional breakdowns."

"Shut up, Amber," Jen says. "Just because your heart is a vampire zombie mash-up doesn't mean the rest of us got so lucky."

Amber shrugs and looks away disinterestedly.

"And to answer your question, I'm not okay!" Jen says, turning back to me. "I'm really super far from okay!"

I think about her drunken words to me at the dance, but that was weeks ago, before Christmas, before Dax and I crossed over, and I haven't seen any sign of things being awry since. I guess I never did find out what happened with Sam that night.

"Okay, I'm sorry to hear that," I tell her, grateful we happen to be in a lull and all my tables are happily eating.

"What's going on, Jen?" Leah says, shuffling us all into a corner.

"Oh, Sam's acting weird again," Amber says. "What's new these days? Dude's been turding it up for months."

"Yeah, for about as long as you've been on the team actually. And it's gotten so much worse since you started seeing Dax." Jen's face crumples and Amber pats her like she might have cooties. Jen shakes her off. "I noticed you and Sam haven't hung out in a while. I thought maybe it was just for my benefit, that you were pretending . . . I thought maybe there was something else going on."

"No!" I say. "Nothing."

"Trust me," Leah offers dryly, "all she does is talk about Dax. There's nothing going on with Sam."

"But why?" Jen presses. "Why haven't you been hanging out? There's a missing piece somewhere."

"No. No missing piece. I think we were hanging out so much we needed a break from each other. We were practicing and going to meets and hanging out outside of school."

"A break, huh?"

"Yes, I swear." I'm pleased to find that everything I'm saying feels true. "As far as I know, he loves you, Jen."

Jen's expression trips from upset to questioning and finally to resolute acceptance.

"He loves me?" she says quietly. I see in her the same wish I have. To be loved and not to have to be afraid, to feel like no matter what happens as we move through life, we know we'll have this one person by our side. We won't be humiliated, or abandoned, or rejected. We'll be partnered and cherished and cared for in spite of our shortcomings. And I know we're supposed to be strong and independent and do it all on our own, but sometimes we just want to let our guard down and be loved. Right now, she is me and I am her.

"Yes," I say. "He loves you."

"Really?" she says.

Amber looks up from her phone, suddenly alert as though sensing drama worthy of her attention.

But I don't say anything.

I can't bring myself to reassure her.

CHAPTER TWENTY-EIGHT

As soon as I got home from work and showered the smell of fries and BBQ out of my hair, I got myself into some comfy pj's and came out onto my back deck. Now I'm wrapped in a blanket in a lounge chair trying to let the vastness of the universe pull me out of my selfish little problems. But even though there's this huge sky above me, peppered with stars, and that should make everything else irrelevant, I keep trying to understand what the hell happened with Dax. If Dax is doing what Ty and Luke did, then he's not the person I thought he was at all. I really thought he was different, but more than that, I thought *I* was different, that I had changed enough I wouldn't have to go through the same thing again.

Really.

I hear the back door slide open and fully expect it to be Mom or Kevin telling me it's too cold to be out here (even though it's downright balmy for January). I even, for half a second, dare to hope it's Dax. But it's not.

"Holy shit," I say.

It's Sam, quilty vest on, in jeans and a button-down shirt, looking almost formal.

"Yeah," he says. "Surprise!"

He sits at my feet and I scoot up to make room. We're silent for a few minutes and then he turns to face me.

"I decided this bullshit that's been going on between us has to end," he says. "We've been friends for too long and the guys are way too stupid for me to rely on them for anything other than the occasional wedgie."

"They *are* stupid," I agree.

"So, what's wrong?" he says.

"What do you mean?"

"Well, you're in your pj's, in a blanket, and you have bunny slippers on and are staring at the sky. That means you're trying to make yourself small to give yourself perspective and that means something is wrong."

Warmth rises like a tidal wave. It's so nice to be known when I'm starting to feel like I don't exist. "Yeah." I consider him. "Can I talk to you about Dax?"

He groans a little then makes a come-hither motion. "Hit me. I can take it."

"We slept together. A lot."

He nods for me to go on. This, he had assumed.

"He told me he loved me." I check Sam's face for sign of a reaction. "I said it back. We said it so much I started to believe in it. It seemed really real. But then he was supposed to come here for dinner a couple nights ago and he didn't show. He sent me some text about not being able to make it and I haven't heard anything from him since. He wasn't at the meet or anything, and now I'm getting this feeling that the exact same thing that's always happened to me is happening again. He was just practicing on me and now that he's done with me, he's . . . done. So maybe I made a huge mistake. Maybe we weren't meant to be together at all. Maybe it was all another joke—"

"I broke up with Jen," Sam says suddenly.

The silly little words I was going to speak die on the vine and I snap my mouth shut, though I can still feel the echo of everything I just said, and all the while Sam was sitting here with this bomb.

"They call that burying the lede, Sam. Why didn't you start with that? Why did you let me talk?"

I'm about to tell him about Jen's outburst at 66 but he's gone quiet and is staring at me, pleading for me to understand.

"I think I've known for a while," he says.

I have the urge to cover his mouth, to stop what he's going to say next, because once he says it there'll be no undoing it and at the same time I want him to admit what I've been suspecting but haven't had the guts to articulate.

"I think I was always supposed to be with someone else," he says.

He scoots toward me, never taking his eyes off mine, and then it's happening. Sam has leaned in for a kiss, mouth open against my own, softly and searchingly. I don't fight it or push him away. I let it happen, let him slide closer to me, pressing at the base of my back and as he leans in farther, a slew of thoughts tumble forth.

I've been lying to myself for years.

I've loved Sam since we were both kids.

I lost my virginity to him.

He knows me better than anyone else.

But I don't love him anymore and I don't want this.

I pull back, look into Sam and his knowing eyes, understanding and defeat already passing over his features. We're still only millimeters apart, our lips almost touching, my hand on his knee, his fingers still digging into my back.

And then I hear Dax's voice.

"Jo?" he says. "What are you doing?"

CHAPTER TWENTY-NINE

Someone presses the fast-forward button on reality and Sam looks at Dax, who is in my backyard holding a bag with red tissue paper poking out the top. In the same instant I see the crumbling hurt on Dax, but more than that, the shadows playing over his face and a new flintiness to his eyes. When he locks on Sam it's like he has supernatural powers. Sam launches himself out of the chair before I can make a single sound of protest and a second later the two of them are wrestling on Kevin's prized exotic grasses.

They both grunt but it's mostly a quiet event. I don't want to freak my mom or Tiffany out. "Stop it!" I stage-whisper, yanking them apart. "Stop!"

They fall onto their butts, heaving. All they've done is flip each other around a couple times and neither of them looks seriously hurt. Not physically, anyway. Dax gets to his feet and without another word, storms out. I follow him through the side gate. He's almost to his car when I call for him to stop.

When he does, I almost wish he hadn't.

"I can't believe you," he says, gesturing to the backyard. "I completely trusted that you and Sam had a legit friendship."

"*Me?*" I say, all the stress of the last couple days roiling. "What about you? You bailed the night you were supposed to meet my family. You completely blew me off. You didn't call or text or post anything on social media. You could have been dead for all I knew. You did what every other guy has ever done to me. You left me without any warning!"

Dax looks stricken. "You blocked me! On social, on the phone . . . everywhere! I had so much shit going on and you blocked me so I thought I would come over here and explain."

"Why haven't you introduced me to your family? Why would you abandon me when I'm trying to let you into mine? After you said you loved me? Why?" I yell, reaching for some other flaw in him egregious enough to justify what he just witnessed. "Because I'm not good enough? You only took me over to your house *to have sex* when your mom and brother weren't around. We've been dating for a while and you haven't come over, and then the night my family goes to so much trouble to cook for you, you don't show and you don't give me any explanation. You just disappear!"

I clutch my own shoulders, suddenly feeling ridiculous in my fleece pajamas, especially as I see the pained expression on Dax's face. His eyes flash with uncertainty, but then his shoulders slump and he says, "My mom's an alcoholic."

"What?"

It's a stupid thing to say but it's all I can manage. My lips are still tingling with Sam's kiss and now all my righteous anger is replaced with the cold realization that whatever Dax says next is going to prove what a giant asshole I am.

"Yeah," he says. "She's been in and out of rehab for the last four years. Usually when she drinks if she's out she calls me to get her from the bar and bring her home. Most of the time she nods out in front of the TV, sometimes she goes to stay with my grandma for a few days when it gets bad."

"Like the night of the dance . . ."

"Yeah. But the night of your dinner, she didn't call me. I was home with my brother, waiting for her so I could come over here. She said she was going to run some errands and I don't know what happened but she wrecked."

"Wrecked? Like, her car?"

He nods.

"Oh my God, is she okay?"

He shakes his head and then shrugs. "She's at the hospital and she's seriously banged up. I've been taking care of my brother. Today she stabilized and my cousin and grandma are there so I told them I needed to check in with you. I'm sorry I didn't answer your texts. I couldn't have my phone on in that part of the hospital and by the time I got out you had already blocked me. I should have done more. I should have called you, but I was panicking, not thinking straight. I did what I always do when there's trouble: disconnected and tried to deal."

I take a step toward him and he steps back like I'm wielding fire.

"No," he says.

I imagine Tiff trying to deal with something like Mom getting into an accident and I can't even picture it. And I may not fully understand what Dax is going through, but I do know the numbing shock of the unexpected, how it makes you feel like everything you thought was solid in your life was actually molten.

"Dax, what you saw? It wasn't what you think, I swear to you."

Dax swipes a hand through his hair and looks at me, face contorted with pain and reproach. "I probably should have told you about my family," he says. "My dad left a few years ago. My mom almost drank herself to death." He laughs bitterly. "Even a city can get pretty small when your family is legendary for getting into trouble, for being worthless. I caught my own reputation too. I thought if I could have a good attitude, do better, be better, I could change the way things are. I have always believed that. But maybe you're right after all, Jo. People see what they want to see no matter what you do."

"Dax—"

"What? What could you possibly have to say?"

I struggle searching for the right words, about how that kiss wasn't a hello, but a goodbye.

Sam has come out of the side gate, and is not moving, frozen and trained on Dax with a new expression of understanding.

Dax looks from me to Sam and back again, and thrusts the bag he's been holding into my hands. "I heard you won today," he says. "Congratulations."

He starts his car, giving Sam one last dirty look, and then he's gone.

I can't hold back the tears anymore.

"Beckett—"

"Don't, Sam," I manage, before I run inside.

Mom is already at the door. I'm prepared for her to start lecturing me but she doesn't. She follows me to my room, and when I collapse onto the bed sobbing, she rubs my back.

A memory comes heaving in, of her doing this when I was upset when

I was little. Dad was the person I spent the most time with, but Mom was who I went to and who I needed when things were really, really bad.

They're really, really bad now and she does what she did then. Rubs in slow circles so I have a distraction from my aching heart. No, it's not just aching, I think, as I calm enough to begin drifting into sleep.

My heart is broken.

CHAPTER THIRTY

It's not easy waking up to the full, clear comprehension of your own shortcomings, but that's what happens. Dax's haunted and disappointed expression is basically superimposed on whatever I'm looking at and my eyes are so swollen I have to apply ice to them and lie flat on my back for fifteen minutes before I can slither into clothes and head to work. I could probably call in, but then what? I would just be feeling like a jerk at home in front of my family instead of in the restaurant where at least I'll be distracted enough for moments of reprieve.

I keep thinking if I actually made choices and executed them instead of reacting to the endless wounds inside myself, my whole life would be different. I would have thought through my own feelings about Sam instead of trying to pick up hints about his. I would have clearly stated what I wanted from Ty before I made myself vulnerable to him. I would have been more certain of Dax as a person I could trust. There are always risks that have to be taken in relationships, ways in which we put our hearts out there to potentially get kicked around. But coming from a strong foundation is completely different than floundering all the time. Seems like my whole life has been watching my heartbreak and that of others and I know I can't stop it from happening. But I can stop it from happening without my full and honest consent, without a choice to put myself there and a decision that whoever or whatever is involved is worthy of my leap.

Dax and his hurt and crumpled face, carrying all the pain of what his mother is going through, needing to care for his brother, walking in on me doing a thing he thought I wasn't even capable of. That's what I can't let go of. I can feel in my own skin and all my oversensitive nerves exactly what that's like and it's not good. I can also feel the hard truth of exactly who I am settling over me, and a new determination to change from this moment forward, to be the kind of person my dad would want me to be.

I don't do my hair or makeup, just throw on jeans and my 66 T-shirt and drive over there, a cup of hot black coffee nestled in my cup holder. I slump through the door and Leah looks up from where she's setting a table. She narrows her eyes.

Dread settles over me. I know I have a lot to face, but I hadn't totally thought through this particular reckoning.

The silver she's holding clatters onto the table. "How could you?"

"Leah . . ."

"You kissed Sam!" She stomps past me to get the tray of honeys and begins depositing them angrily on the tables. "Did you even think about Jen? No. Did you think about anyone but yourself? No. As. Per. Usual." She punctuates each word with another thump on a table.

"It was a complicated moment that got away from me." I don't see any point in denying anything now. I think of all the searching looks and direct questions Jen asked, how I lied to her with so much certainty, covering over what was underneath and was actually there all along.

That was the wrong thing to say because Leah only doubles down on her frantic hostility.

"Oh, I see. You're a victim again." She slaps the empty tray on the table nearest me so we're very close. "And let's talk about this best friend of yours, shall we? Isn't he the same person who completely screwed you over, probably laughed with all those guys while they talked shit about you? He let you be demeaned and didn't say anything, and you know why? Because Sam is a coward. He has always been a coward. Maybe that's why you've always clung to each other. Neither of you can make decisions off the mat. You both just let things happen until you've fucked over everyone around you. And you can't read the writing on the wall for shit. He's not good for you and you are not good for him." She throws up her hands. "I don't know why you keep choosing him over us. I really don't. But you always do."

She's not saying anything I haven't already thought about in the last twenty or so hours but this last gets to me, cuts into a festering wound. "What are you talking about?"

"You did it in seventh grade and you're doing it again!"

"You're bringing up seventh grade right now? Please, Leah. You are the one who picked shitty girls over me then and you're doing it again, not even giving me the chance to explain!"

"Oh, you mean because I have allegiance to the girl who *didn't* kiss someone else's boyfriend five minutes after they broke up? You mean because I'm choosing girls who choose me back and understand what it means to be a good friend? When was the last time you asked me about me, Jo?"

I'm stumped. What does Leah say every time we see each other? *Tell me everything.* And then I do. I know some things about Leah. I know she loves her parents and horses and not boys and that she's well put together and a giving, loving person. But . . . okay. There's no way that's *it*. That's not *it* for anyone.

EVERYONE IS FIGHTING A BATTLE YOU MAY NOT KNOW ABOUT it says on the magnet on my fridge. I hate that magnet, always think it's stupid and cheesy. But now I wonder what Leah's battle is. I didn't investigate her any more than I investigated Dax. Again I realize how selfish my own pain has made me.

"I've been a good friend to you," Leah says. "Amber is a good friend to you. She hasn't let Ty anywhere near her heart, but you? She tried to protect you when Jen wanted to attack you. She's been protecting you every step of the way. And don't even get me started on Jen. She's been friendly with you even though she's suspected there was something going on between you and Sam, which, *by the way*, I promised her there was not. She opened up to you, trusted you would tell her the truth if there was a truth to be told, and all that in spite of the fact that you've been sabotaging her relationship and treating her like crap from day one!" Leah makes a disgusted noise. "You know, maybe you like being friends with those guys because they don't call you on your shit, but they *also* don't actually see you at all. They lie to your face. They disrespect you. I won't lie to you. I never have and I never will. You fucked up, Jo. Now own it."

As I watch Leah walk away and Brenda poke her head around the corner of the back worriedly, I wonder at my capacity to stay standing even though I'm completely empty of everything except sorrow.

Leah's right.

Obviously, she's right.

I've always prided myself on being a guy's girl, on not being vapid or shallow enough to care about makeup or to cluster in groups and giggle in the hallway. I've always thought I was different.

No, not different.

Better.

Even though I felt like I never measured up and no one took me seriously and I have genuinely been used so much, I still wanted to be that
girl, sleek and independent and strong. The girl all the guys would hang
out with when their girlfriends gravitated to each other. So maybe those
friendships were easier, less demanding, requiring a lot less introspection.
But I'm not sure anymore what they're made of.

Nausea strikes so hard I double over a little.

"You okay, hon?" Brenda says.

"Fine," I muster.

My wrongness is a physical thing. All my mistakes are monsters.

And now the question is, how do I do things differently? Because I do
have choices and the one in front of me is either to keep going like I have
or to start digging myself out, one way or another.

I search inside myself, letting the warm smells of fried food and the
sounds of old country music soothe me and quiet the flush of adrenaline. I have to figure out how to dig myself out of this mess and calm the
hungry, hurt beast in me.

CHAPTER THIRTY-ONE

"Come on in." The woman who meets me at Jen's door is compact but curvaceous, draped in harem pants and a flowing silk shirt, both black, with horn-rimmed glasses perched on her nose. She's at once stylish and laid-back, like she might have a joint in her purse, but like her purse is probably designer.

Also, this woman is clearly Jen's mom, because she's like an older twin. She has a pen in her hands like I interrupted her writing something. "You're Jo." This is not a question. "I've seen you at meets and Sam has told me all about you," she explains. "And of course now I've heard all about you for different reasons." She gives me a knowing look. "I'll go and get Jennifer."

She disappears up the carpeted staircase.

She is neither hostile nor friendly and her whole demeanor sets me off-balance, mostly because she herself is so calmly certain of herself. Jen's house is an extension of that certainty. Plants and vases are carefully placed, books are staged in visually pleasing small piles throughout the house, and a small stack of *New Yorker*s sits atop the credenza in the hallway. There's no sign of dogs or cats or toddlers or any kind of disturbance. It looks like the kitchen is never used. Its counters are pristine and there are no appliances in sight except for a bullet blender in the corner.

There are also, I note as I slip farther into the house past the entryway, pictures of Jen and Sam in silver and wood frames between the prized items throughout the living room. I'd forgotten they went to Mexico last year, but there they are with Jen's mom and a handsome man, all laughing, sun-bronzed, looking like something out of a magazine. I think about everything Jen told me about him and the way he treats her, and I remind myself not all wounds are visible. And then there's junior prom. Jen's buttercup-yellow dress I thought made her look like a fairy back when she wore it, her hair done in a Dutch Crown, the beautiful necklace Sam gave her hanging from her neck.

I want to run, especially when I hear the sound of Jen's voice in obvious protest coming from upstairs. I want to shout, *Hey, Jen, I'm sorry I barged into your perfect house uninvited and I know I'm an utterly heinous person, but I totes had an epiphany so can we forget about all that?*

I've had almost twenty-four hours of cycling through everything I've ever done to Jen, Leah's voice ringing in my ear like a severe and angry conscience. I've come to the place where I can only hope all the damage I did to Sam and Jen's relationship might eventually be forgiven.

This is one small step I can take.

Jen comes down the stairs in pajamas that are unexpectedly girlish, white with roses on them. She looks like she hasn't slept or eaten. I've always thought of her as a flower, but now she looks wilted and in need of water, the freckles that are usually a subtle enhancement to her features looking splotchy and pissed off.

"Did you come over here to gloat?" she says, sweeping past me into the kitchen and swinging a cabinet door open. She gives me a bitter smile. "Or no, let me guess. You came to lie to my face again." She pulls out a glass and goes to the sink, flips the switch on the filter, lets the glass fill, then leans back against the counter, waiting.

"No," I say, trying not to let the stress take over. I need to be able to talk. This is like a match. Same pressure only there's no one holding a timer and I can't tap out. "I came to apologize, to try to explain."

"I asked you if there was something going on with you and Sam. I got shit-faced and couldn't even come home to my own bed. I begged you to tell me the truth. And you know why? Because nothing was making sense. All of a sudden the Sam I knew disappeared. Just *poof*, like he never even existed in the first place. I felt him slipping away and there was nothing I could do about it."

How many times I scoffed at Sam when he talked about her. How I called their potential offspring spawn. I said terrible things about her every single chance I got. I played the cool, slightly masculine girl to her delicate flower and took every opportunity to stomp on her petals.

"I'm so sorry, Jen, really."

Her anger gives way to shock for a second but then the fury is back.

"Are you really?" she says.

"Yes. I don't know what that was . . . with Sam. But whatever it was it's over, okay? It didn't mean anything. Sam and I are done—"

Her eyes darken.

"It never was," I try to correct, but it's too late. "There was never anything going on between us. Not like you think."

I've lost her. Her face goes blank.

"Fuck you, Jo," she says, devoid of emotion.

"Jen—"

"Get out of my house. I'm done talking to you." She doesn't move, but everything soft about her is gone and I realize she's seconds away from a physical attack. I leave, sorry I'm the person causing her pain instead of the person I should have been: her friend.

CHAPTER THIRTY-TWO

It's early in the morning again. The sun's not up yet and it's a cold February morning. Valentine's Day, to be exact. In an alternate universe where I haven't trashed my life, I'd be somewhere with Dax today, maybe going on some weird date tonight that he invented. I'd be wading through the day, exchanging texts with him until I could see him again.

Instead I'm here in Coach's office, looking outside at a world newly blanketed in snow. Buzz and Santi are getting ready for the boys to come in for their workout.

"I don't understand it," Coach says. "I keep having this feeling like I don't understand anything at all these days."

"I know," I say. "I'm sorry." I've been saying sorry so much these days my mouth is saying it automatically now.

"First you quit, then you came back, then you *win*, and now you want to quit again."

"That's right," I say.

"And you're not going to tell me why."

I want to. Genuinely I do. But I also understand that to talk about this and tell him everything that's been going on would reduce it to some petty drama and that's not what it is. Lives are being made, shaped by my actions and how we're all orbiting around each other. I can feel it.

"No," I say. "I can't."

He leans back in his rolling chair and crosses his arms, looking at the ceiling. "You know, sometimes I'm annoyed your dad talked me into this line of work. 'The kids are great,' he told me. 'They're so worth all the rest of the trouble.' But I don't know. Sometimes I just don't know."

"Sorry, Coach," I say again.

He fixes me with a look. "I was going to use you for finals, you know that?"

"I know."

I can hear the sound of the crowd, smell the tension, feel my stomach curling in on itself with anticipation. This is the last time I'll ever have the chance to wrestle in a competition. I'm going to graduate in a few months and I won't be wrestling in college like some of the guys.

So this is it. But this is also the new Jo. The one who makes good decisions.

"I have my reasons," I tell him, standing. "I'm very sorry it's so late in the season, sir."

He waves me off. "I don't have anyone else in that weight category. Guess we'll have to let it go."

"Guess so," I say. "Again, I'm sorry."

By the time I'm leaving Coach's office the guys are here. I don't stop to talk to them, I just make my way out the door. I'm almost to my car when Sam catches up to me, the exact thing I didn't want to happen.

"I really just don't want to talk about it," I say, as he reaches my car at the same time as me.

"So you're just going to ignore me after that kiss?"

Sam is so beautiful, such a familiar sight. But I think of Jen and Leah, everything they've said to me over the last few days. I think about the person I want to be, the kinds of friendships and relationships I want to be worthy of.

"Why now?" I say.

Sam looks taken aback.

"No, seriously. Why did you kiss me now? We've been friends for so long. You've watched me get dragged through the mud without saying anything. If you ever had feelings for me before, you never told me. I thought you were going to marry Jen. So what happened?"

Something flickers over Sam. I know him so well I recognize it as him absorbing something then deciding to ignore it. "Are you going to tell me you don't feel the same way, Jojo?"

He softens me with that nickname. He knows exactly what will get to me. He can't call me that without drawing on all the years we've been friends and everything we've ever done together. But I'm not letting him off the hook that easily. He chased me out here and now he's going to have this conversation. I decide to do something different today.

I'm going to be completely honest with him.

"I did," I say. "Even though I didn't know it for a long time, I've had feelings for you ever since we started being friends."

He keeps his eyes trained on me, breathless for whatever I say next.

"And even though memory is faulty, I'm pretty sure now that when I told you I wanted to practice having sex with you I wanted you to fight me. I wanted you to tell me that I was so special I was more than that to you, that we were perfect for each other."

He isn't moving a muscle. I don't even think he's breathing.

I sigh. "I buried it so deep even I couldn't find it. I couldn't say it. I was too scared of you leaving me, not wanting to be friends with me, not letting me snuggle up to you anymore, so finally I made it so not even I could access the truth. Jen made us both safe in a way. With her there we couldn't be together in the way I really wanted. It's my fault, I think. I dug myself a hole being in denial like that." I reach for his sleeve, then let my hand drop away. "I went to Jen's. I saw all those pictures of the two of you. It wasn't what I thought all this time. I know she wasn't just arm candy for you. I know you really loved her and I know hearts can be split and sometimes it's hard to understand what's happening inside."

"So—"

"I'm not finished," I say. "I think the reason you let me get dragged around without ever defending me or standing up for me is that you didn't want me to have a real relationship. You didn't want me to be with someone else the way I was with you. It worked out really well for you that people thought of me as disposable."

He sighs loudly, like he's letting go of something he's been keeping in tight for a long time but can finally exhale.

"But I found someone. Finally. *Actually.* I met someone who treated me right from the beginning. He never messed with me or put me down or made me feel like I was less than because I didn't fit into the exact prescribed box we're all supposed to go in. I was happy. So why now, Sam? Answer me honestly. Why did you pick this exact moment to reach for me?"

"I don't know. Sometimes you can't choose when you realize something . . ."

"No. That's a cop-out."

"Beck—"

"I'll tell you why. Because I finally moved on. I finally got with someone who gives in a real way and you couldn't stand that because you've always been empty and needing whoever you're with to fill you up and tell you who you are. Everywhere except on the mat."

Now he looks shaken, but I have to tell him the rest.

"You do what everyone else expects, what will make you look the best. You dress how people think you should. You wrestle because it gives you status. You were at least partially with Jen because she helped define you. And you were best friends with me because I was constantly telling you how amazing you are. You needed my light to shine on you. You don't know who you are."

The air vibrates around us like it knows the sound of the truth too, like it loves to be around when a knife cuts to the quick.

"I love you." There's something desperate about the words, a last, clinging effort.

My heart twists. All this time, this is what I was really waiting for. Someone who really knows me telling me I'm worthy of love. But it doesn't do what I thought it would anymore. It only strengthens my resolve. I may have lost Dax, but I'm not getting sucked into something that isn't 100 percent what I want. There's too much between Sam and me now for us ever to have that, too much that's sticky and complicated. I want to be a person who can walk down the halls with pride, who fights for the right thing, and who never ever lets anyone near my body or my heart who isn't completely worthy. And I want to be smart enough to be able to tell the difference.

Sam has been there for me when no one else has.

He's also hurt me worse than anyone.

And I know, even though he doesn't, that he's just looking for something to cling to now. Because I can finally care for myself now and because I am not acting from weakness, Sam wants what I have.

"That's not love, Sam," I say, and I get into my car.

I don't look in the rearview mirror as I pull away, even though I know Sam is still standing there, hands in his pockets, that same old navy-blue vest over his Sentinels hoodie.

Our friendship can never go back to what it was.

I'm done with wrestling.

I'm done with everything that came before this moment.

This is ground zero and the only way is up.

CHAPTER THIRTY-THREE

As part of my whole new self, I decide to participate in the family ritual of breakfast on Saturday. I would normally be at the meet that's happening in Fort Collins today, but instead I let myself sleep in until the sun beats on my face aggressively enough for me to get up. It may be winter, but we get three hundred days of sun in Colorado, so it doesn't matter. The sun only gets sharper in the cold season.

I considered hanging out and watching Netflix in bed all day, but then decided that's what old Jo would do and I'm now working on my relationships, beginning with the one I have with myself. Since I pretty much don't have any left except with my own little family, I head into the dining room. There's normally bacon and coffee and eggs and I don't partake, favoring smoothies or oatmeal, especially lately.

But today only Kevin is there, watching a basketball game he probably recorded last night. At the sight of me, he sits up straighter. "Hey, kiddo."

"Hi."

"Your mom and Tiff went to Michael's to get some supplies for something. Your mom wanted to beat the crowd."

"Oh." I want to run back into my room like I always do.

"You hungry?" he asks hopefully.

"Yes." I try the word on for size.

Kevin's face brightens with the light of a thousand suns. "Yeah? What can I make you?"

"Something carby," I say.

"Got it." He pops up and goes into the kitchen.

I sit at the island instead of going to the couch with my phone. "Why are you nice to me when I'm such a jerk to you?"

He looks up, waves of surprise crashing on each other. Then the left side of his mouth quirks up. "You're a teenager. That's part of it. And you were so close with your dad. I get it." He washes his hands. "But I didn't just marry your mom. I got you as part of the deal too, even before your dad died. I knew we would all do a great job of raising you, the three of us, plus whoever partnered with your dad at some point. He was such a charming guy there was no way that wasn't going to happen when he was ready."

One thing that always surprises me is how odd it is that people exist in so many ways. I can only think of my dad as my dad, but Kevin thinks of him as a man and Mom thinks of him as her ex-husband. He was so many things I'll probably never know about now.

"So, how've you been?" Kevin asks.

"I've been very bad," I say. "But also good. Better than in a long time, I think. Maybe better than ever."

"Do you want to talk about it?"

"Okay." Mark this date down in the calendar as among the stranger, more vortex-feeling ones.

Kevin gets a mixing bowl and some eggs and milk from the fridge. "Yeah?" he says. "That's a pleasant surprise. Okay. Shoot."

"I think I ruined everything with Dax."

Kevin nods, cracking an egg. "I heard there was a kerfuffle the other night."

Kerfuffle.

"Yes. So I really like him and he's not speaking to me. And the thing is I'm super confused because on the one hand it's like I get the message over and over again that girls are supposed to be strong and not want a boyfriend or a girlfriend or whatever . . . we're supposed to be okay alone is what I mean."

"Mm-hmm," Kevin says.

"But it's like my insides are made of strolls along the beach and sunsets and cheesy bike rides or something." Or indoor mini-golf and sushi. "Life hasn't been a happily ever after or a bunch of meet-cutes, but that's what I still expect, even after everything."

"I can tell you happily ever afters are real," Kevin says. "They're just different than I imagined. It doesn't end the day you decide to be together. That's just the beginning of a heck of a journey."

"You found Mom."

"I did. And more than that, I chose her and I keep choosing her every day."

"It can happen and it's important, right? So why are people always talking about how you don't need to have a partner?"

Kevin pauses his mixing. "I think it's more about being okay either way. We all need people to some degree, but it doesn't have to be romantic and you *definitely* don't need another person to make you happy or fulfilled. Life is complicated and it throws you surprises and you learn as you get older that no matter what, when you get into relationships it's not going to be easy. Every person has something they're working on. Getting over insecurities, developing a talent, learning to be brave or aware . . ."

"Learning not to take everyone in life for granted and treat them like garbage . . ."

"Right," he says. "That too. So it's not about actively trying to stay away from romance, it's about knowing when it's the right one. You should be able to have conversations with someone you're dating. You should be able to be yourself and talk about the things you want or need from them. You should be able to laugh and have morning breath—"

"Ew—"

"We're human! We're flawed. That's part of the deal." He pauses. "Some people don't want to be in relationships or ever partner. Maybe they like being alone or just want to hang out with friends. That's a perfectly fine choice. It's a great choice even! But if you're going to enter the fray of being with another person, you should be treated well is what I'm saying. You should be choosy about who you let into your heart. You should know the other person is thinking of you and taking care of you and not always just worried about themselves. And I think what people mean when they say you don't need another person is that you don't need the *wrong* person. You are way better off alone than dealing with someone who isn't on the same page as you."

Dax was always thinking about me, about his brother, about his mom. He wanted to know how I felt about things, asked questions, paid attention. Even with sex, he made sure I wanted to do it, every step of the way.

But me? I was only thinking about my own fears, about whether he liked me or not.

And what about Leah and Jen? Shouldn't the same level of caring be applied to friends?

"What do you do when you've completely screwed up?" I say. "I mean, supposing you screw up like that."

Kevin looks up from the griddle, looking surprised that we're still talking. "You fill up the hole you made. At least that's what my dad taught me." Kevin's dad. He died when Kevin was young like me. I have literally never thought about that for a second until now. "You try to repair what you've broken, and most important, you don't have expectations. If the person can't forgive what you've done, you let it go knowing you did your best to make amends." He smiles ruefully as he pulls a plate from the cupboard. "Your mom and I owe you some of that."

An unexpected jolt of sadness zaps me in the solar plexus.

"Don't think we don't know you've come out on the shit end of this whole thing. We've tried to make a stable home for you, but that's it, right? We try to be together for meals and go do things together, but the meals are at the wrong time and the things we do are right for Tiff, not you. The whole time we've been telling ourselves you wouldn't want us around and we would just be in your way and pushing away your family is part of being a teenager, but that's been an excuse. We haven't tried hard enough."

"You've been busy—"

"Yes, and so what?"

He puts the plate in front of me. It's a pancake in the shape of a J.

"So, see? Don't be too hard on yourself. People keep screwing up, keep learning. That's life."

Life. Life that stretches out long before me. Or I hope it's long. Everything up to now has felt like a fight, but things are looking better even though they probably won't be easier. Or maybe they're just clearer. I think I get it. Life will keep peeling off layers of ignorance and I'll see more and more as I go. It's worth it.

It will be worth it.

"So why are you suddenly asking my advice?" Kevin says as he wipes down the griddle.

"I don't know." I take a maple-syrupy bite. It's perfect, crisp and soft on the inside and buttery. "I think maybe it's time to fix what I've broken."

CHAPTER THIRTY-FOUR

Sometimes (and I never thought I would ever be saying this) the only answer to a conundrum is glitter glue. No phone call or text or dramatic social media post will do. You have to go old school, cut things out, use paste and sequins.

Or at least that's my hope.

Because I don't know how else to do what Kevin said, to fill up the hole I've made, to repair.

After a run and a workout it turns out I *want* to do, and after Mom and Tiff get home from Michael's, I drag out the refrigerator box from Kevin's recycle pile in the back and lay it out flat, dividing it into two pieces and then I go to town. I pilfer what I need from Mom's craft zone, convince Tiff to help me, and we make hearts and stars and every goofy, gooey thing the girls were talking about doing for the Winter Ball. I put on music while we cut out snowflakes and sprinkle glitter over the whole thing and thank all the powers that be that it's a nice day out.

Tiff and I also indulge in some light dancing before standing back to survey our handiwork.

"I think it's very good," Tiff says, patting me on the back.

"Thanks, Tiff. Think they'll forgive me?" I didn't tell her much on account of her being four, but I did tell her I was trying to make up with my friends and that I had done something that wasn't very nice.

"Maybe or maybe not," she says. "But I love you."

I look at this little creature my mom and Kevin brought into this world. She's a cream puff of taffeta and blond hair. She's always been a crying, screaming ball of demands having the world served up to her like an ice-cream sundae with special sprinkles. But actually, she's pretty cool.

"I love you too, Tiff." I get to my feet. "Now help me tie this art project to the roof of my car."

———————————

For a second I hesitate to defile the pristine yard at Jen's house, imagine her small but fierce mother coming for me, or worse, her neat-freak stepdad. But nothing happens. It feels ceremonial as I lay my giant apology cards across her porch.

I'M SORRY, they say.

GIRLS ROCK

YOU WERE RIGHT

FORGIVE ME

I'LL LEARN TO HAVE SCHOOL SPIRIT

(BUT SERIOUSLY I MEAN IT)

I have banners too, strung with silver ribbon. By the time I'm done her porch looks like it's been filled with holiday decorations. I don't know if this is the perfect thing to do or if Jen's going to hate me more for my feeble attempt at reconciliation, and I realize her parents will probably never want me around again, but Kevin was right. It feels good to do something intentional to try to fix this. Whether or not Jen and Leah and Amber can ever forgive me is out of my control, but at least I'm doing something.

———————

When I get home, Tiffany follows me into my room. I get the little bag Dax gave me (thrust at me angrily) and plop onto the floor. Tiff drapes herself over my leg and peers at the bag with interest.

"It's a present?"

"Yes."

"From who?"

"Dax."

"Are you going to open it? Presents are the best!"

I want to, but I don't think I can. "You do it." I hand Tiffany the bag.

"Does this mean I get to keep it?"

"Just open it!" I can't handle any more waiting.

"Okay." She reaches into the red paper and pulls out a small white box. I had a feeling it would be something like this. I snatch it out of her hand and tear it open.

It's a little megaphone necklace made of silver. There's a small card attached. "I will be the void. Use this whenever you feel like screaming."

"What's the matter?" Tiffany says. "Do you need a tissue?"

"No." I scrape myself off the carpet. "Come on, Tiff. We have a care package to put together."

She jumps to her feet. "I will get the glitter."

I pull down the box of Dad's precious things, all his words of wisdom, and I get to work with a fresh pad of Post-its. I write things like DAX RULES and BELIEVE IN YOURSELF and I LOVE YOU. Turns out I'm not much of a writer either. I find a soft blanket I don't think Mom will miss, some bubble bath, a couple chocolate bars I had stashed, and a loofah. And then I give him my very favorite thing, a Finn the Human action figure. I know this is probably not what he needs, and definitely doesn't even come close to making up for the way I acted, but I hope it tells him something about the way I feel about him. All I want is for him to know that I may have kissed Sam, and I may have been insecure and overreacted when he didn't show up for dinner; I may even have been infatuated with a bunch of idiots over the last few years, but I was not in love with them.

I'm in love with Dax. Hard-core, amazingly, totally in love with him.

I understand I may have blown it beyond redemption, but I need him to know.

CHAPTER THIRTY-FIVE

I'm caught in a vacuum of my own thoughts and I try to stay there and not escape it, not watch TV or stare at my phone. Just be. It's uncomfortable but I also realize it's something I've never done before. I'm always trying to achieve something or run away or throw myself into something. I don't go completely limp though, not like before. My workouts are habitual now and I love the early-morning runs, the tiniest hints of spring and all the newness it brings with it. It's still cold but cold with the possibility of flowers and that's something to cling to. It's almost enough.

I try not to think about the fact that in spite of my efforts I haven't heard from anyone in the last week except Amber, and her text was something like When are you bitches going to get your shit together? I'm bored and want coffee dates and gossip! It blows my mind to think that I might be relevant enough that when there's a rupture with me, the whole group falls apart, that I mean something and that what I do has a ripple effect. I think about that for *several* days.

Right now though, all the guys are on the bus heading to finals. I know Coach has that determined, near-grumpy stare and will not be talking to anyone the whole ride there. Santi and Buzz will both be chugging coffee and gossiping worse than Amber, and all the guys will be asleep because they stayed up too late last night because they have the memory and foresight of French bulldogs.

Tell the truth to yourself, Jo. You are sad.

I am sad. So sad not to be there.

There's the gentle knock on my door that is neither Tiff's aggressive barging nor Kevin's tap-tap (pause) tap and can only signal the approach of my mother, who has been circling me like I am a land mine for the last few days.

"Cmmffin," I say into my pillow.

Along with Mom comes the minty smell of recently brushed teeth and face cream, which wafts up as she sits down and strokes my hair.

"Sweetheart," she says. "I left some breakfast for you. I have to go stage the Wickman house and Kevin got called into the restaurant."

"Clive again?" Clive is the sous-chef Kevin's been having problems with.

"Yeah," Mom says. "Apparently he's having anxiety."

"And when you say breakfast?" I sniff the air, detecting a whiff of butter and an undertone of sugar.

"Chocolate chip cookies," she admits. "I had to make them for the open house."

"Perfect," I say. I plan to spend the day in bed and the addition of a plate of cookies is ideal.

"I just wanted to say I know you've been hurt . . . a lot. I want you to know I'm sorry about that. It's just a bowl of shit."

"Mom!"

"It is. And when that happens it's hard to keep your heart open. But I hope you will. Your dad always said 'Heart wins' for a reason. He didn't just make those Post-its for others. He made them for himself too. They were as much to remind himself not to give up as for anyone else."

She sighs and I remember how she used to do that all the time, sigh like that, just in the middle of a room, in the middle of the day, for no reason. She'd be lost inside herself and Dad would say, "What is it, Lou?"

"Nothing," she would say, looking like she'd been caught doing something she hadn't meant anyone to see, and then she'd be shrinkwrapped in plastic, and it would be like she was disappearing right in front of me.

I peel my face from my pillow and sit up, my eyes adjusting to the light; I blink hard. "What is it, Mom?" I say.

She looks like she's about to do it again, deny what she's feeling, but instead she rests her hand on my leg. "It's hard for me to talk about your dad honestly. I don't want to hurt you but sometimes I wonder if I'm hurting myself too by not telling you the truth of how it was."

"You can tell me," I say. "I'm almost eighteen."

"From my perspective, your dad was this brilliant but extremely unstable person, like he was fine but could go radioactive. He had one thing he could always really focus on."

"Wrestling."

"Yeah. Wrestling didn't send him into an existential crisis. But I did." Her fingers worry the cotton by my calf. "When we met we were both teenagers, both kind of wild, both obsessed with grunge music and raging against the man and staying up all night watching the stars and functioning on three hours of sleep."

"Sounds fun."

"That's truly shocking coming from someone who is currently spending twenty hours a day in bed."

"Thanks."

"Anyway, when I had you everything changed. I wanted a real life and marriage and home. I wanted to have a little ground under me. He hated that." She sniffs. "The first time I made Thanksgiving dinner and I was so proud of it, he looked from the table to me and said, 'Who *are* you?' Well, I had taken this vow and I had you, but I knew right then we were in trouble. You were so precious I just wanted to protect you and give you everything. Your dad fell into teaching because of wrestling and got an alternative teaching license after college. I had a degree in English so I took any job I could get that had some sort of practical application for my skill set."

I remember vaguely. Mom up at all hours with her computer.

"When he was home, he watched TV and messed around on his phone. He never even looked at me. He was obsessed with wrestling, sure, but he never once changed a diaper for you, made you a meal, packed your backpack, helped with your homework, bought you clothes. When you were really little, before you could wrestle, he never once said, 'Hey, I know you have three jobs and never sleep because of the baby. Why don't you take a nap, a break, anything?'"

"Why didn't you say something?"

"Oh, honey, anything I said would have sounded petty. Besides, your dad was great in so many ways."

"Just not as a husband."

"Not as a grown-up, really. He was selfish, slept in on weekends, never planned anything for us as a family that didn't involve sports . . . it just wasn't for me."

"Then you met Kevin."

"I did. You know, I started to have flashbacks after Tiff was born and Kevin was at Berlin all the time. I started to worry I had just found a different version of the same thing. But you know what Kevin did when I started to stress?"

Yeah, I do. "He hired someone at Berlin so he could be home with the baby some of the time."

"That's right," Mom says. "He made a commitment to be here. I know not everyone can do that and there's some privilege involved, but even if he hadn't been able to do that specific thing, he would have found a way to be there for me so I didn't feel alone. And you know what? That's romance. That's love. And about Kevin and this idea you have that he's totally vanilla?" Mom says, bristling a little. "He's a chef, Jo. You don't get to be a chef in a major Denver restaurant without having some edge. But no matter how passionate he is about what he does he will never put it before any of us. And that includes you. You and Tiff will always be first and I will always be right after that."

I give her a look.

"Yes," she insists. "After Tiff and you, and that's great. His work comes last. So, he'll bust his ass and remodel the kitchen in his spare time and keep everything extra clean and cook all the meals because frankly I am *done*, and he'll do it all with love, because he is a man, not a boy. A man is able to cherish a partner in a giving, balanced way. I get to be the wild one!" She laughs like she can't believe it.

"All right, let's not go overboard. Also, did you just say ass and shit in the same conversation?"

"Don't push it," she says, but she's smiling. "He holds the center for all of us, whether you realize it or not."

I think about all that, everything I never knew, how I was just in my dad's bubble with him and thought of my mom as this uptight person trying to bring both of us down. I get why she likes neutral colors and I get why she likes Kevin.

I guess I like him okay too.

Mom takes my hand.

"About a month before your dad died, when he'd finally moved out of that motel into his own place above Bailey's, I went over there to get you and you were napping hard. Your dad told me you guys had been up all night watching movies. We hadn't talked in a long time. It hurt to be around each other because we went from being kids to adults together and we did it really badly. I know it seemed like I left with no explanation, but it was really because I couldn't deal with telling him the whole truth. It was too much of an attack on who he was as a person and things he couldn't change about himself. It didn't seem fair. So anyway, we had the chance to talk and we did. I was heavily pregnant with Tiff and he wished me well, told me he understood my reasons and he would never have wanted to break up but in a way it was good. He told me he was finally doing his own dishes."

"He was!" I remember going with him to pick a dish rack.

"And I'm grateful to him because in the end he got a cheaper place so he could still give me child support for you, and he also had enough awareness to buy an insurance policy, which is now in a trust for you. He pulled it together in ways I thought he never would, but he only did it once I was gone. Understand?"

"But," I say, "did you want him to quit teaching? Because I'm pretty sure that's what he thought. That you wanted someone with more money."

"No!" she says. "I mean, don't get me wrong, I love money. Money can mean freedom in a lot of ways and that's why I'm always trying to get a leg up, but I knew your dad was never going to be that guy. I just wanted him to make a little room for me. He was so good at showing up for others, but not at home. People are complicated. I don't know.

"That day, before your dad and I woke you up so I could bring you home, we hugged and for a few minutes it was like we were teenagers again. Not like I felt all the wiggly, intense love feelings, but we both acknowledged that we had traveled our whole lives together, gone from being little kids to adults together, that we had made an entirely new human being and she was perfect. We thanked each other for that. No matter what flaws your dad had or I had, in the end we made peace. I hope that can help you in some ways, because things can get hard and they do and they will, but they can also be moved through."

"Really?"

"Really," she says. "The real secret is that it's about the quality of the love you give, much more than what you get in return. Real love, that is."

I think about the way I decorated Jen's porch, the effort and energy I put into it, how it made me feel so good to do that, to let her know how much I care. And the box I made for Dax, wrapping each gift, putting in the Post-its . . . it doesn't matter what I get back. It only matters what I give and how I give it, not from a gross, needy place but from a place that knows they're worthy of it, a place that wants to make amends and create joy for others.

"You okay?" Mom asks. "Was that too much sharing?"

"No!" I say, snapping out of my thoughts. "Please do that all the time."

She stands up. "Oh, and I should mention there's someone waiting for you downstairs." At first, I think she's kidding, but then she throws me a pair of sweats. "I recommend pants."

"Someone has been waiting this entire time? We've been in here talking for like ten minutes!"

"I believe in inconveniencing people when it's deserved."

I want to ask her more questions, but she's out the door. "I'm late!" she calls backward down the hall.

I tear out of bed thinking maybe it's Dax or Leah or even Sam. I practically fling myself down the stairs and then stop cold. It's the last person I was ever expecting to see, pacing at the foot of my stairs.

CHAPTER THIRTY-SIX

"Ty?"

"Hey, Beckett," he says.

"What are you doing here?" My hair is disheveled and I'm looking wild and a little loopy in my nightshirt and sweats, but I'm more aware that even with my new friendship with Amber, Ty and I have barely said a word to each other since his vile, awful party, since he threw my life onto a completely different trajectory.

"I'm here to get you," he says matter-of-factly.

"For what?"

"Uh, for finals. You're part of the team and you have to come with us."

I don't say anything.

"I'll wait." He seems smaller than before and nervous. I think the last few months have been interesting for him too. Amber has probably corrected a lot of his ideas about himself.

I force myself not to answer immediately. I ask myself what I want and an answer comes quickly. My feelings about this have changed in the last week since I talked to Coach. I want to go. I'm really good. I have trained my ass off and I have kept myself at weight. I've checked every morning and every night.

"We were dicks," Ty says, taking my silence as rejection. "I was a serious asshole. But you should be there. You're good, and you can win."

He says it with such simple conviction I know he's not bullshitting.

"I never really said I was sorry." He can't meet my eyes. "After we hooked up and after what I said to Amber. That was shit. I knew I was hurting you. But I am. Sorry, I mean. I don't expect you to ever forgive me. But don't let what I did or what anyone else did keep you from what you were meant to do. You're a wrestler. And we need you."

I remember the heat between us, him unsteady over me in his bed, just like I remember the laugh in his voice as he called me a practice girl. All of that will always be between us. I think I can live with it.

"Okay," I say uncertainly. Then, "Yes, I'll go."

"Yeah?" He brightens. "Awesome!"

We stand there looking at each other.

"But, Beck . . ." he ventures.

"Yeah?"

"Can you hurry the fuck up?"

CHAPTER THIRTY-SEVEN

It's total chaos in the gymnasium. I've been to probably ten finals meets in my lifetime, but it's completely different coming in as a competitor. On the way here I told Ty I didn't think Coach would let me wrestle and he said the whole team wanted Ty to get me, but Coach most of all.

The stands are peppered with families and it's so big the whole place echoes with hoots and whistles and dings. I might puke everywhere. That would be a hell of a story. *I don't know what happened but that chick from Liberty Township just spewed everywhere. They had to cancel the meet! There were riots!*

I think about my dad, what he would say right now.

You already won.

You make me so proud.

As soon as this is over, we'll get pizza. We'll watch movies all night. We'll howl at the moon and listen to Iron Maiden and it will be badass!

And mostly, *This doesn't get to define you. Who you are on the inside defines you.*

Sigh.

I walk over to the team side by side with Ty and they all stop their stretching and talking and look at me. Coach is huddled with Buzz and Santi, but looks up at me. "Great," he says. "I already added you in. You're against Chad Collier again. Up for it?"

I nod, but inside I'm remembering his smarmy face, the way he smelled like hormones and infected pores up close, the way he grunted with satisfaction when he got me pinned. I want to fuck him up so badly, which I realize is not necessarily the spirit of the sport, but I'm trying to be more honest with myself, right? That's honest.

"Yes, Coach," I say.

"Well, what are you waiting for? Go weigh in!"

Sam is waiting outside the door when I come out from the scales. I knew I was going to see him, of course I did, but I don't want to focus on boys right now, not unless I'm completely dominating them.

"Hey, can I talk to you?" Sam says.

I checked the roster and Sam and Dax are about to go up against each other. That means Dax is somewhere in this building, which also means even though I can't see him he might be able to see me. The last thing I need is for Dax to witness me talking to Sam in some corner.

"Later," I say to Sam, and breeze by him.

Maybe he thinks I'm being horrible, but I can't care about that right now. I turn back into the main stadium and it's like Dax is a magnet for my whole body, which locates him right away. He's sitting with Franco and Nina, with Jamie behind them and a little boy by his side. It takes me no time to figure out it's Dax's little brother, Seth. He's like a mini version of Dax. Same dark eyes, same red cheeks, and the same look Dax had before this went down . . . all mirth and good-natured mischief. They're all chatting except for Dax. He's looking right at me, no smile, no change of expression. Just his fiery eyes trained on me, practically jumping with emotion. All my limbs and organs are instantly pulled in his direction. His messy hair and his hoodie are reminders of everything else about him that's comfortable and familiar and authentic in every way. We lock eyes and everything else stops. I wonder if he got the box, if any of it helped. I wonder if his mom is okay, how his little brother's doing. I want to go sit with my back between his legs, have him play with my hair, feel like we're two bodies sharing one vision of the world. Mostly though, I want to be there for him.

My eyes flicker to Nina. I expect her to give me a nasty look and flip me off or something, because she seems like the kind of person who flips people off when they hurt her friend. She does make a hand gesture, but not the one I thought. Instead she gives me a thumbs-up where no one can see it, then the slightest wink before she goes back to canoodling with Franco.

Dax stands and for one hopeful second I think he's going to come over to me, all my thoughts about boys and not wanting to deal with them totally thrust to the side, but instead of coming my way he unzips his hoodie and walks over to the mat to face Sam.

The Dax I'm used to has a sense of humor about everything. Last year at finals he was acting the fool the entire match, which just pissed Sam off even more since Dax almost beat him. This year is the polar opposite. Dax looks like he could blast Sam out of the building with the force of his ire. He looks like he's about to settle a score.

And Sam, when faced with Dax's silent ferocity, looks shrunken and afraid.

I don't know who to root for—my own team, or the boy who probably maybe hates me with semi-good reason.

Until they step on the mat.

Then I know.

I want Dax to win. A lot.

Sam and Dax circle each other for a few seconds before Dax goes in. It's like a cobra strike and I know by Sam's look of surprise that it isn't what he was expecting. I see the determination take hold of Sam's features and he turns on Dax. This isn't the messy, emotional yanking and swearing that happened in my yard. This is the clean, steely matching of two wrestlers who are equally skilled.

Sam exposes Dax's back to the mat twice and both times he wriggles free, silent and serpentine.

"Thirty seconds!" the ref announces, stopwatch in hand.

They have thirty seconds left and equal points. Sam needs this final glory. Although his scholarship deal is sealed, it would be way stronger for him to go to Duke as a champion than the guy who lost his last high school match.

And Dax? For him, this is personal.

My heart jumps as Sam gets him pinned again. It looks like he's going to hold him the two seconds. I want to yell, "*No!*" but I would instantly be mobbed as Mason and Ty are both jumping and yelling for Sam to finish it.

But I know he won't, because I see Dax's muscles tense. I see the slight tilt in his jaw. Dax is never going to let Sam win this one.

The next instant Sam is on his back and Dax has his arm laid across Sam's chest in a way that renders him powerless. Sam strains with his neck, does everything he can, but the two seconds pass and *ding! ding!*

"That's the match! Dax Furlong is the winner!"

Franco and Nina hold Dax's brother up high and they are all jumping and yelling. Dax goes over to them, picks up his brother and hugs him, shakes with everyone, and then pulls his sweats and hoodie on again. It's almost like the match never happened. Almost.

"Shit!" Mason says. "We're fucked now."

"We could still do it," Ty says, looking my way.

Mason rolls his eyes. "Yeah, okay."

I leave them there to debate my worthiness, not even stopping to say anything to Sam, who's drinking water on the bleachers, trying not to look devastated. I go into the hallway. This pressure is all nothing. I may be our last chance at a championship but it's really not about that. It's about me, doing my best, knowing I tried.

The door squeaks open and I'm half expecting Sam to be there wanting a shoulder to cry on, but it's Barney.

"Um, hey," he says.

"Hi, Barn." I really don't want to talk to anyone, not even Barney, but he's so adorable and his glasses are slipping down his nose because he's sweating. He may still get a sweaty nose when he's nervous, but he's also changed a lot this season. He just has a different energy now, more confident or something.

I can't send him away, no matter how swirly everything is right now.

"I got you something before we left this morning." He shifts around uncomfortably. "I kind of stole it so don't get mad, okay?"

I'm imagining he somehow got hold of a bra of mine or some other nightmarish scenario, like someone took a picture of me naked and posted it on the internet or something.

"I won't get mad. Just lay it on me." I put my hands out, and Barney gently places the picture of my dad from the gym in my hands. "Barney," I say.

"Oh, good. Cool. You're not mad. I wasn't totally sure you were coming but I was *pretty* sure."

I look up, tears pooling at my lids. "Mad? I'm not mad. This is so *nice*. It's so thoughtful."

"Aw-shucks," he says. "I just thought you might want to touch it before the match. You know, for good luck."

"I want to be you when I grow up," I say. "Okay?"

"Yeah, well, kiss it or do whatever you have to. You need to win." And he leaves.

I don't answer. I'm looking deep into the picture of my dad and I'm seeing things I've never seen before. A whole man. I can see the crow's feet at his eyes and the parentheses starting to form around his mouth. I also see the scraggly almost-beard he always had, his sharp incisors, and the way his eyes have so much depth. They seem to be laughing and crying at the same time. I guess that's what life is. I guess we don't get to be just happy or sad or winners or losers or in love or not. We have to be people and that means always being mysteries, even to ourselves. I know one thing though: my dad believed in my capacity to do anything I wanted to do in this life. I lost sight of that after he died. Without him to tell me all the great things about me, I faded. I hug his picture and say, "Dad, please be with me today. Please help me know the right thing to do. Please help me be the person you always wanted me to be."

I wrap the picture carefully and put it in my bag, feeling like maybe he heard me, and then I walk out into the gym.

Screaming fills the air and I hear, *"Jojo is my sister!"* in that shrill little voice.

I look up into the stands, which I swore I wasn't going to, and there is my mother, Kevin and Tiff beside her. And on the other side of her is Leah, holding up a sign that reads: I LOVE YOU NO MATTER WHAT! JO ROCKS! BFFS FOR ETERNITY! Amber examines her nails, looking up briefly to give me a sly smile, and I wonder if maybe she had something to do with Ty's apology this morning. I can just see her letting him know what will happen if all this bullshit isn't resolved. I can also see Ty understanding exactly what he did with the help of Amber's explanation.

"Josephine Beckett vs. Chad Collier. To your mat."

I always thought maybe I wanted people here for me, to watch meets, to see what I can do, but now I'm not so sure. Right now, I think it might be better for everyone to go home and leave Chad to kick my ass. Except that's not what's going to happen. I remember the look on Shiloh Velazquez's face when she was about to wrestle me, but more than that I think about Dax, how calm and certain he was as he approached the mat with Sam. It's like I feel him flowing into me as I take every step. I'm not going down easy.

And there's Chad. Good old Chaddy boy, just smiling his face off. He's not forfeiting. He wants to lay me out. We shake, the bell dings, and this time he knows my move. He doesn't hesitate and he's not being careful because I'm a girl. He lunges at me and gets me down, grabbing at my shins.

A hush falls over the gym. All the chattering stops. I wonder if Dax is watching. I wonder if everyone can see that I am going to lose in the first five seconds of the match. But then I see Chad. He's already gloating.

Two seconds can take forever in a match. It does now. I have time to see the glint in his eye, the curl of his lip. I can see him showing everyone his biceps later, saying this is how it's done.

I can't have that.

I fight to my stomach and quickly escape to my feet. Without giving Chad a second to think, we lock up and I execute a flawless fireman's carry.

"What?" he says.

That's right, asshole. He scrambles away from me trying to get his bearings and we both have time to get to our feet again. My body is running on muscle memory now and my mind is sharp. He'll have studied me. He'll have watched all the YouTube videos and seen the Frogger, the Donkey Kong, the PAC-MAN. He'll know everything. Well, almost everything.

Heart wins. I can hear my dad like he's right next to me. My skin gooses up. It all slows down again and suddenly I hit a switch. Chad is now on all fours, my chest is against his back, and I am on my toes to keep the pressure on him. I quickly create some space then slip in a leg between his to prevent him from escaping. Simultaneously I wind up my other leg and swing it around him like a windmill, combined with the hardest legal cross-face possible. This drives Chad straight to his back. I quickly release the leg and sink in a head-and-arm lock and squeeze with everything I have. The ref blows the whistle.

The match is over.

And I have won.

The crowd erupts. The gym is a din of yells and cries and protests and congratulations. My team is there and they're picking me up and Coach is tearing up and I can see my family and the girls bobbing up and down as they jump. Even Amber is on her feet now.

I am somewhere far away, floating on a pool of bodies. I have achieved something I wanted so badly, and it has sent me heavenward. I have always been so mad at my heart, for being soft and pliable, and easily fooled, but now I'm grateful for it. It's big and beautiful and smart, and it got me here, which is exactly where I wanted to be.

And I can hear my father, his voice rising up above the crowd. He is saying, "*Yes, Jojo! Yes. Yes. Yes.*"

CHAPTER THIRTY-EIGHT

"Can I have everyone's attention?" Coach says.

We're all piled into the locker room they gave us to use and I've been invited in like in the old days when I was manager. We all have our bags slung over our shoulders and Sam and I are next to each other, Mason on the other side. Mason, who has told me he's sorry too.

We all get quiet and look at Coach. "This was the final meet for many of you. You'll be moving on and going to college or whatever it is you do from here. I won't be there to yell at you—"

There are some quiet titters.

"And I won't be there to make sure you eat right and take care of yourselves either. This season wasn't what we expected. I know I've been surprised, concerned, terrified."

Again, there's laughter.

"But I think we can all agree our biggest victory came from being a team, overcoming our dramas and differences and looking out for each other. And none of that would have been possible without our very own Jo Beckett, the heart of our team."

Sam starts clapping and for a horrible second I don't think anyone else will, but then they all do, hoots and all.

"Let's go get pizza and sundaes!" Mason yells. Then slings an arm around me. "You're coming, right?"

"Actually," I say, slipping from under him, "I'm going to 66 with my family. But I'll see you around, Mase."

"Oh." He furrows his brow. "Yeah, okay."

I start walking out, looking forward to the cool air, to being away from them and done with all of this, but I hear a voice behind me. "Beck."

It's Sam. I can't avoid him forever. I'd like to, but it wouldn't solve anything. So, I turn to him, and shivers of recognition go through me. I see him at ten, at twelve, awkward at thirteen. My shadow. My champion. My best friend for seven years.

"I'm really sorry," he says. "I seriously messed up. I don't know what happened to me, but I'm sorry."

I can see he means it. We lost our virginities to each other. We lost other things too. Pride, trust, the purity of the friendship we had for so long. He's always going to be important to me, but right now I have to figure out who I am in this world without Samuel Sloane by my side. We'll always have parents who are neighbors. I'm not going to lose him for good anytime soon.

"I know you are, Sam," I say. I don't offer anything else.

He reads my face. "So that's it?"

"For now," I say. I squeeze his shoulder. "Everything's going to be okay."

"Fire-promise?" he says.

"Oh, yeah."

We both grin as we make fire motions with our fingers.

It *will* be okay. A promise is a promise.

CHAPTER THIRTY-NINE

I can see my parents in the minivan, waiting for me to come out. They're going to have to wait a few more minutes, because I also see a familiar car and a familiar face.

"Dax!" I call.

His door is open and he's leaned in like he's talking to someone in his back seat, but he pops up at the sound of my voice. The sour look is gone, replaced by something else. Uncertainty? Hope?

As I get closer, the necklace he got me dangling near my throat, I can see his brother strapped into the car seat, playing with something. It's the Finn the Human action figure I sent in the box. Dax did get it!

"Good job out there," he says.

He is so delicious I am a literal furnace when I get near him. I don't know what I'm going to do if we ever hang out in summer. Just die, probably.

"You're still speaking to me?" I say.

"Maybe." And he looks like that's what it is. A maybe, like he's on the precipice of a decision. I wish I could read his mind. Or maybe I don't.

"I know this probably isn't what you want to hear, and you probably don't even like me anymore, but I love you. I need you to know how much I love you and how sorry I am. I've never felt this way about anyone before. I don't know if I ever will again. I said I fall in love easily, but

I was wrong. I have never been in love before now. Ever. I just need you to know that."

He doesn't move, and I think, okay, this is when you slink away into your minivan and then go power-eat as much of Brenda's food as you can and put this entire nightmare behind you.

But then Dax lights up. He reaches for the necklace, lets the silver slip, and rests his fingers against my skin before they fall back to his side.

Then Dax smiles.

ACKNOWLEDGMENTS

I am not a wrestler. At Jo's age I could be found skulking around school parking lots listening to music with friends or reading in a corner. This is why I'm grateful for YouTube, which made research a little more doable in COVID times, and am also massively indebted to wrestling coach and expert Josh Bennett, who helped me block and write every wrestling sequence on the page. I'm also grateful to hockey star Kendall Coyne for helping me understand the challenges girls face in traditionally male-dominated sports, what it's like to be on a boys' team, and what it takes physically and emotionally to make it through.

As I said, I am not a wrestler. But I am a person who has had a lifetime of trying to understand relationships and the roles my body and heart play in my soul's evolution. Questions about trust and love have been at the center of my journey for as long as I can remember, and I don't think we talk enough about sex and desire and what it can cost. Being a high school teacher has given me the opportunity to witness that although there are infinite sexual and emotional experiences to be had, some aspects of the quest for the fullest self are universal and worthy of exploration. Thanks one million to my editor, Jenny Bak, for giving me a place to tell a story that's important to me and for nurturing these pages into fruition. I have absolutely loved working with you.

Of course, books don't happen exclusively in the inspired cocoon, and I'm grateful Jo has been in Viking's extraordinary hands. Many thanks to

Ken Wright, publisher; Gaby Corzo, managing editorial; Abigail Powers, production editorial; Patricia Brown, copyeditor; Jessica Jenkins, cover designer; Janelle Barone, cover artist; Opal Roengchai, interior designer; Lyana Salcedo, marketing; Felicity Vallence, digital marketing; Anna Elling, publicist; Vanessa Robles, production; and Sola Akinlana and Madeline Newquist, proofreading. You've made this book lovely and creatively complete.

Sara Shandler, Josh Bank, and Viana Siniscalchi! My most excellent collaborators and makers of dreams! I love all of you so much it's ridiculous, and I consider it my great luck to have come upon you. I hope we make many more.

My agent, Emily van Beek. What a year. What a life. What a journey. I mean . . . are you kidding me? I hope for countless joyful, triumphant adventures with you, but I'm also humbled and forever indebted to you for your unwavering presence when things fall to pieces. You're right there, all the time, a beautiful, glorious blessing.

Laura Ruby, Noelle Fiore, and Jerelyn Elkins, thank you for your generosity of time, attention, and love, for checking up on me, and for sharing your experiences so openly. You're all my heroes.

Jeff Zentner, Kerry Kletter, Kathleen Glasgow, David Arnold, and Jasmine Warga, aside from being some of the best authors writing for children and young adults, thank you for being there extra.

In the last year, I've been literally and figuratively held by the following women: Laine Overley, Linda Cannon, Kristin Moore, Mindy Laks, Johanna Debiase, Cobey Senscu, Elisa Romero, Robin Shawver, Joy Romero, Yvette Montoya, Rachel Bell, Shandra vom Dorp, Samantha Samoiel, Breanna Messerole, Elizabeth LeBlanc, Sonya Feher, Sarah Jane

Drummey, Sarah McKee, Dr. Lilly Marie, Stephanie Gutz, and Amani Caraccio. Thank you.

To my students and colleagues at Taos Academy. You know how much I adore you and how hard it was to step away. I'm always inspired by you.

Thanks to my wild, free-spirited, giant family, and to my other-mother brothers, Eliam Kraiem, Sasha vom Dorp, and Alexander Eagleton. You all make rough seas more bearable.

My brother, Christophe Eagleton, thank you for dropping everything to be with me when I needed you most. I will always do the same for you.

My mother, Dhyana Eagleton, I'm so glad we've found real gratitude for each other. I've loved the time we've spent together.

My daughter, Lilu Marchasin, my son, Bodhi Marchasin, and my husband, Christopher Painter, my greatest gifts. I take every step for each of you, every day, all along, forever, always.

To all the readers, librarians, teachers, bloggers, and especially the young people who have come to this story: thank you for knowing everyone deserves to be seen and loved for who they are, and no one should ever be practice.